After graduating with degrees in history and political science, **Eva Shepherd** worked in journalism and as an advertising copywriter. She began writing historical romances because it combined her love of a happy ending with her passion for history. She lives in Christchurch, New Zealand, but spends her days immersed in the world of late Victorian England. Eva loves hearing from readers and can be reached via her website, evashepherd.com, and her Facebook page at Facebook.com/evashepherdromancewriter.

Also by Eva Shepherd

Wayward Wallflowers miniseries

A Mistletoe Match for the Earl

Rakes, Rebels and Rogues miniseries

A Wager to Win the Debutante
A Widow to Defy the Duke
A Marriage to Scandalise the Earl

Rebellious Young Ladies miniseries

Lady Amelia's Scandalous Secret
Miss Fairfax's Notorious Duke
Miss Georgina's Marriage Dilemma
Lady Beaumont's Daring Proposition

Those Roguish Rosemonts miniseries

A Dance to Save the Debutante
Tempting the Sensible Lady Violet
Falling for the Forbidden Duke

Discover more at millsandboon.co.uk.

A FAKE BETROTHAL FOR THE DUKE

Eva Shepherd

MILLS & BOON

All rights reserved including the right of reproduction in whole or in part in any form. This edition is published by arrangement with Harlequin Enterprises ULC.

This is a work of fiction. Names, characters, places, locations and incidents are purely fictional and bear no relationship to any real life individuals, living or dead, or to any actual places, business establishments, locations, events or incidents. Any resemblance is entirely coincidental.

Without limiting the exclusive rights of any author, contributor or the publisher of this publication, any unauthorised use of this publication to train generative artificial intelligence (AI) technologies is expressly prohibited. HarperCollins also exercise their rights under Article 4(3) of the Digital Single Market Directive 2019/790 and expressly reserve this publication from the text and data mining exception.

® and TM are trademarks owned and used by the trademark owner and/or its licensee. Trademarks marked with ® are registered with the United Kingdom Patent Office and/or the Office for Harmonisation in the Internal Market and in other countries.

First published in Great Britain 2026
by Mills & Boon, an imprint of HarperCollins*Publishers* Ltd,
1 London Bridge Street, London, SE1 9GF

www.harpercollins.co.uk

HarperCollins*Publishers*, Macken House, 39/40 Mayor Street Upper, Dublin 1, D01 C9W8, Ireland

A Fake Betrothal for the Duke © 2026 Eva Shepherd

ISBN: 978-0-263-41879-8

04/26

Printed and Bound in the UK using 100% Renewable Electricity
at CPI Group (UK) Ltd, Croydon, CR0 4YY

To the friendly staff at Spreydon Library who welcomed in the homeless Word x Word writing group.

Chapter One

Kent 1891

Jacob Ashford, the Duke of Rosedale, was not a man easily irritated, but his patience was beginning to wear thin.

This uncharacteristic ill humour wasn't due to being forced to hide out in the Kent countryside, far from the pleasures of London. Nor was it the result of his friend Henry, the Earl of Northwood, hosting a weekend party at his estate and inviting a coterie of debutantes, all determined to bag themselves a husband before the Season had hardly begun. It wasn't even the thought of the scandal waiting for him back in London that was undermining his even temper.

All those things were irritants, but the final straw was an annoying piece of cardboard that had lodged itself between two cushions and was jabbing him in the back of the neck.

It had taken him a long time to find this hiding

place. In the late afternoon, the morning room was ideal for his purpose, even if it was not at its finest at this time of day. The large sash windows which overlooked the grounds no longer had sunlight streaming into the expansive room, and the traces of the debutantes' morning activities were yet to be tidied away by the busy servants. Piles of embroidery and coloured threads littered a nearby table, and an easel set up in the corner displayed some young lady's unfortunate artistic endeavour. All of which reminded him of the need to hide.

But, despite hints of their previous occupation, the room was empty now. There was not a twittering young lady or determined mother in sight and there was a settee on which he could stretch out. In other words, it was perfect. Or it would be if he wasn't being attacked by a vengeful piece of stationery.

Disturbing himself as little as possible, he reached over his head and grabbed the offending card. Just as he was about to toss it onto a nearby table, something drew his eye. His legs swung off the settee and onto the floor. He sat up straight and looked down at the cardboard square. Then he laughed. Louder and with more pleasure than he had since he'd escaped London.

Still laughing, he perused the cartoon some cheeky individual had drawn of the guests attending the weekend party. The artist had caught them all to perfection. The debutantes were drawn as a herd of shy fawns, with large doe eyes and long fluttering eyelashes. Their mamas were depicted as ferocious sheepdogs, trying to corral a group of roosters around the fawns, the roosters obviously being the unmarried gentlemen.

In the centre was a peacock, his ostentatious train taking up more space than all the roosters combined. That person was undeniably him. The artist had even put a coronet on his head at a jaunty angle, in case anyone failed to realise it was a duke.

The only jarring note in an otherwise amusing cartoon was the depiction of the flower in the far corner, winding its way up a pillar like clinging ivy towards an open window. That young lady's expression was not comic but one of desperation. The bottom of her stem was being held by the feathered wing of a honking goose, whose other wing was flapping vigorously in the air in a futile attempt to draw the attention of the roosters strutting in front of the fawns.

He hadn't noticed any wallflowers among the herd of pretty young things Henry had invited for the weekend, but then he'd been paying the debutantes as little attention as politeness would allow. But one thing he did know; it would be best to dispose of this drawing. The poor girl did not need to know she had been the subject of a cruel jest.

The door opened and Jacob quickly put the cartoon behind his back. A young lady entered quietly, stopped and stared at him, as surprised to find anyone in the morning room at this hour as he was.

He bowed his head in greeting. He'd probably been introduced to her at some stage but could not for the life of him recall her name. One thing was however certain; she was the wallflower in the picture.

The artist had accurately caught her pained expression, the way her dark eyebrows knitted together, and the manner in which her full lips pressed tightly in disapproval. That was exactly how she was looking at him now.

She walked across the room towards him and as she drew close it became apparent the artist had failed to capture her large hazel eyes, which would probably be quite pretty if she was not scowling, the lushness of her thick chestnut hair, the curve of her high cheekbones, nor the delicacy of her soft creamy skin.

'Your Grace,' she said with a perfunctory curtsey.

'Miss... Whitmore,' he said with a bow, pleased that her name had jumped into his head. 'I believe most of the party have gone down to the lake for a picnic.' He pointed to the window, hoping she would take the hint that he wished to be alone. 'Those who haven't chosen to take advantage of this delightful spring day can be found in one or more of the drawing rooms.'

He smiled and waited for her to depart. She did not.

'Yes, I am well aware of that, but you've got something of mine and I'd like you to return it.'

His polite smile died and he looked at her in disbelief. Not just because of her accusation, which was entirely unfair—he had taken nothing from this young lady—but the way in which it was said. He was a duke. When people spoke to him, especially for the first time, and especially if they were a young unmarried woman, they never forgot that for a moment. Their eyes would be lowered, their tone deferential, and they would never, ever accuse him of anything as untoward as theft.

'Miss Whitmore, I can assure you, you are mistaken.'

She sighed lightly and came very close to rolling her eyes, another behaviour which a debutante would never exhibit. If this was indicative of her usual manner, was it any wonder she had ended up a wallflower stuck in the corner?

'You are hiding my drawing behind your back.' Her hand stretched out towards him, palm upwards, in the manner of a schoolmarm demanding a slingshot off a naughty schoolboy.

'Your what?' he responded, doing his best to act like a dignified peer of the realm and not a recalcitrant child being reprimanded by Nanny. She surely could not be the artist, not when the drawing depicted her in such an unflattering, insulting and, well, downright cruel manner.

'You are hiding my sketch behind your back and I wish you to hand it over,' she repeated, still sounding like a disapproving schoolteacher. 'I was drawing in here earlier today and I left it behind.'

'You did this?' He removed the drawing from behind his back and looked down at it.

She said nothing and remained standing in front of him, her hand outstretched.

'I found it wedged between two cushions.' He pointed over his shoulder at the site of his discovery.

'Yes, that is where I left it.'

'Am I to assume you did not want anyone to see it?' The sketch amused him, but he knew what outrage it would cause if any of the other guests were to see it, especially those strutting roosters. He doubted the barking mamas would see much humour in it either.

'You can assume whatever you like, but may I please have my sketch?'

'It's rather good.'

'Thank you,' she said, not sounding the slightest bit pleased with the compliment and not lowering her hand.

'In a few strokes of the pen you've captured everyone perfectly.' He continued to stare in admiration at the drawing, then looked up at her. 'I assume the peacock is me.'

She said nothing, just continued to stand there, her demanding hand not moving.

'It's better than many of the political cartoons in the newspapers. Perhaps *Punch* should employ you as a satirist.'

'In case you haven't noticed, I am a woman. Women are not employed in such jobs.'

He had indeed noticed she was a woman, a rather intriguing one, but thought it wisest not to mention that.

'But why did you depict yourself as a wallflower?' he said instead.

Her eyes grew wide, as if to say, *Is that not obvious?*

Perhaps it was. She quite clearly did not understand the behaviour expected of a debutante. But she was not unattractive and would be rather pretty if she stopped frowning. As discreetly as possible he flicked a quick glance up and down. There was nothing about her feminine curves that would put a man off, all in the right places and in perfectly acceptable proportions.

If this young lady was a wallflower, it was due to her appalling attitude and as it was her own fault he would not feel sorry for her.

'My sketch,' she repeated in that stern voice.

'So, this is how you see the weekend party, is it?' He looked back down at the picture he was reluctant to surrender. 'I take it such social events are not something you enjoy.'

She huffed out an exasperated sigh, either at the question or his refusal to do as he was told, but at least she lowered her hand.

'Presumably, that's why you've drawn yourself heading for that open window.' He gave a snort of laughter. 'And I assume the goose is your mama, who is trying to stop your escape.'

He looked at her and waited for an answer. She said nothing.

'I know exactly how you feel,' he said.

'I very much doubt that.'

'Believe me, it's not much fun being a peacock and having all those fawns, well, fawning over you, or being corralled by those determined sheepdogs.'

This weekend party was certainly not what he'd expected when he'd fled the brewing scandal in London. He'd hoped for a few quiet weeks, alone in the countryside with his old schoolfriend, a visit to the local village being the most sociable activity in which they would be likely to partake.

He'd forgotten that Henry had decided the age of thirty was time to settle down, and this Season he would begin his search for a wife. Hence the weekend party, and hence Jacob having to flee to this morning room, away from the relentless pursuit of debutantes.

'My heart goes out to you,' she said, her words

dripping with sarcasm. He'd never encountered such audacity in any woman he'd ever met. Whether that was a good or bad thing he couldn't say, but she was certainly entertaining. 'And if you'll excuse me for saying so, Your Grace, you can leave any time you please. Whereas I...' She pointed one finger towards the desperate wallflower trying to escape through an open window that was out of her reach.

While he noted her deference in asking him to excuse her, he suspected that, no matter how he had reacted, she would have spoken her mind anyway.

'Well, under normal circumstances I might be able to escape whenever I chose, but for the time being I'm rather stuck out here in the countryside.'

Those dark, knitted eyebrows rose slightly and she nodded slowly. 'Yes, I heard a rumour about your reason for being here. Something about a married woman and an irate husband.'

Jacob's mouth actually fell open at the extent of the woman's candour. Such things were never discussed openly in polite society, especially not by women, and absolutely never by a debutante wanting to make a good impression. Young women were expected to appear completely innocent of the ways of the world and, in particular, ignorant of anything that men might get up to.

He closed his mouth and made a quick attempt to

regain his equilibrium. 'Yes, it was something like that, and I take it that you do not approve.'

'It is hardly my concern,' she said in a decidedly disapproving voice.

'Well, just so that you don't think me completely beneath contempt, yes, that is the reason I am stuck here, but it's all for the sake of the woman in question, so her husband has time to calm down and life can carry on its merry way.'

'As I said, it's no concern of mine.'

She was completely correct, it wasn't her concern, but for some reason he wanted her to know that he did have some redeeming features.

'It is the lady's marriage I am trying to protect.'

She continued to stare at him as if nothing he said or did would change her opinion of him, that he was a vain, self-important peacock.

Once again, she extended her hand, and with reluctance he placed the drawing in her palm, but before she could take it, a footman entered carrying a silver tray and bowed in front of Jacob.

'A letter for you, Your Grace.'

Jacob quickly tucked the cartoon inside his jacket pocket, thanked the footman and opened the letter as the man departed. He could have allowed Miss Whitmore to take the drawing, and the outraged expression on her face made it abundantly clear she was not happy that it was now in his pocket, but this had been the most enjoyable conversation he'd had during this dull weekend party, and he was rather pleased to have been able to further delay her escape from him.

He quickly scanned the contents, eager to continue the teasing of Miss Whitmore, then emitted a low groan.

'What's wrong?' she said, stepping towards him.

He looked up to find her staring at him with what appeared to be compassion. It was rather nice to be looked at like that, but he doubted she would have much compassion for him if he revealed the contents of the letter.

'I've had some rather unfortunate news,' he said with a woeful expression that was hopefully worthy of her pity.

'I'm so sorry. Is there anything I can do?'

Jacob shook his head slowly, then a decidedly wicked idea occurred to him. 'Yes, there *is* something you could do.'

She tilted her head and waited.

'You could marry me.'

Margaret huffed out her exasperation. The man was either completely deranged or playing a stupid, childish game. Either way, she had no intention of remaining in this room a moment longer than necessary, but she did need to retrieve her incriminating sketch.

'My drawing, please,' she said, giving his absurd statement the attention it deserved.

His lips continued to quirk with amusement as if there was nothing outrageous in his behaviour and she continued to glare back at him, letting him know she was not impressed by his attempt at humour in the slightest.

He really was a superficial, frivolous peacock, just as she had depicted him. And thank goodness that was how she had drawn him, and not as a Greek god, as she had initially intended.

She would hate him to think she saw him in that manner, but his height and masculine physique, combined with his dark blond, slightly curly hair, his blue eyes and sculpted lips did remind her of the statues of Greek gods she had seen in the British Museum. But she had depicted his personality rather than his appearance: overly confident, self-entitled and far too glib for her liking.

Whether a peacock or a Greek god, he seemed to think every woman should fall instantly under his spell, including her, and she would not be doing or saying anything to further inflate his puffed-up opinion of himself.

'I'll return your drawing once you've heard me out,' he said, smiling at her in a manner she assumed was meant to charm.

It was tempting to grab it off him, just as she would

do with her younger brother when he played such silly games, but the thought of getting close to this man was disconcerting to say the least, and she certainly was not about to put her hand inside his jacket. The mere thought of it did strange things to her she'd rather not think about, so she frowned at him in an even more severe manner.

'There's nothing to listen to and I don't appreciate being the butt of your jokes,' she said, her tone as full of reproach as she could make it.

'There are no butts, no jokes, just a sensible proposition. And what have you got to lose by just listening? And I promise once I've said my piece you will get your drawing back.'

Margaret drew in a long, slow breath and released it just as slowly, hoping she could exhale her irritation and several other emotions she chose not to name. She couldn't. His continued refusal to return her sketch made it obvious she had no choice but to listen, so she gave a small nod to inform him he could continue.

'As you already know, I have got myself into a bit of bother in London. Things were getting rather messy so I thought it prudent to retreat to the countryside while tempers cooled.' He looked down at the letter in his hand. 'Tempers, it seems, have not cooled but have become more inflamed, and it is time to take some drastic action.'

Margaret said nothing. She had agreed to listen to what he had to say and that was all she intended to do.

'It would be in everyone's interest if I presented myself to the world as a reformed man, a respectable man, a man who has met the woman who changed everything—the woman he is to marry. Then the aggrieved party would be appeased and everyone will be happy.'

'Have you finished?' she asked.

'Yes.' He smiled again, those blue eyes crinkling at the corners. She suspected it was a smile that had won over countless women, but she would not let it affect her, so she kept her expression impassive and ignored the fluttering in the middle of her chest.

'Look,' he continued, making a lie of the statement that he had finished talking. 'I know it's a bit unconventional, but it is obvious you hate all this marriage mart business, and you're about to face another Season. What will it be—your second? Third?'

'Fourth,' Margaret said, forgetting her intention to say nothing.

'And if you don't find a husband at the end of your fourth, will there be a fifth? A sixth?'

Margaret's jaw tightened. That was a prospect she was trying not to think about.

'We wouldn't have to actually marry, but becoming engaged would save you from having to go through another Season, which you clearly abhor.' He continued to smile at her in that unsettling manner. 'So, what do you think? Our engagement could be the window you are seeking. It could provide you with a means to escape from all those weekend parties, balls, soirees and so on, which you obviously do not enjoy, and you'll never again be paraded in front of the strutting roosters.'

'I can see you only have my wellbeing at heart,' she said, packing as much derision into those words as she could, and once again holding out her hand for the drawing. 'But I would never—'

'My dear, this is where you are hiding!' A shrill voice cut through the air, causing Margaret's body to tense. 'Look who I've found.'

She turned to see her mother clasping the arm of Baron Edgeware with an iron grip lest he attempt to make a run for it. And, judging by the stricken expression on the Baron's face, she was certain the moment she released him, that was exactly what he would do.

'I told him he simply must meet my daughter, but it has taken us an age to find where you are hiding yourself.'

Her mother looked at Baron Edgeware as if expecting him to agree, but the poor man was staring at the door, no doubt formulating his own escape plan.

'Oh, you're here with the Duke of Rosedale,' her mother added unnecessarily, making a low curtsey and pulling on Baron Edgeware's arm as she did so, causing the man to almost tumble.

'My daughter has attracted the attention of the most eligible man available,' she said to the Baron as he attempted to stand up straight. 'As I said, she is a young woman whom any man would be happy to take as a wife, which I'm sure the Duke can see as well.'

Margaret's teeth clenched so tightly she suspected she was in danger of chipping a tooth.

'The Baron is also looking for a bride,' her mother continued. 'And I told him you won't find a better wife than my daughter. While she is not considered to be the prettiest debutante available, and she is now facing her fourth Season, these are advantages, not disadvantages, when seeking a bride.' She looked back at the struggling Baron. 'It means she will be eternally grateful to any man who finally offers for her hand, and will make a good, obedient wife.'

Her mother beamed at the two men, oblivious to the fact that she was humiliating her daughter.

Neither man responded, and Margaret took a quick look in the Duke's direction, certain that his reaction would cause her to feel an even greater level of mortification. As expected, he was staring at her mother with a mixture of shock and disbelief.

It was a look she had become accustomed to seeing on men's faces over the last three years, and would no doubt be seeing again in the coming Season. As she watched the Duke watching her mother, a wicked thought occurred to her. She turned back to her mother and the imprisoned Baron.

'Baron Edgeware, I wish you well in your search for the perfect bride but I'm afraid it won't be me.'

Relief crossed the man's face.

'That is because, before you entered, the Duke of Rosedale asked for my hand.'

She turned to face the Duke and smiled at him, a gleeful smile full of delicious revenge, letting him know he was not the only one who could play games and in future he had best think twice before he toyed with her.

'And I accepted.'

Chapter Two

A loud shriek cut the air, almost knocking Jacob off his feet. Mrs Whitmore released her hold on Baron Edgeware and pushed the man away, sending him flying across the room and into the arms of a waiting chair. She then stepped towards Jacob, her arms outstretched as if to embrace him.

Jacob suspected that his face now bore the same look of terror he'd seen on Baron Edgeware a moment ago.

'My darling, darling girl!' Mrs Whitmore cried, and thankfully it was her daughter who was on the receiving end of the hug, along with much vigorous rocking from side to side. 'I hoped and prayed you would find a husband this weekend, but never imagined it would be the Duke! And to think I was prepared to settle for a baron.' She sent an accusatory look towards the door through which Edgeware had quietly slunk.

She released her daughter, who stepped backwards, looking as if the life had almost been squeezed out of her.

'Mr Whitmore is going to have to eat his words,' the woman said to Jacob. 'He told me to leave well enough alone. That if Margaret didn't wish to marry, I shouldn't try to force matters. I can now tell him I managed to secure a marriage to a duke, no less.'

'Yes, that was very enterprising of you, Mrs Whitmore,' Jacob said, and sent Miss Whitmore a quick wink to let her know she had his complete sympathy.

He thought he'd at least get a smile in return. Instead, those lips once again pursed and the brows drew together. It was evident she would tolerate no insults from him towards her mother, no matter how frightful the woman was.

He shrugged that off. If she was loyal to her mother, that presumably was an admirable trait. He wouldn't know about such things. He could barely remember his own mother, but from what he'd been told she'd been a cold woman who had never wanted her only child and had no attributes that would illicit loyalty from anyone.

'Mr Whitmore even tried to talk me out of accepting the Earl's kind invitation to this weekend party, saying he was only doing so to appease my brother, the Earl of Ledbury,' the mother twittered on. 'He said that Margaret would have to suffer enough during the Season so I should refrain from inflicting further suffering on her with this party.' She laughed loudly, a sound unfortunately reminiscent of a honking goose.

But her statement did explain their presence at this party. Henry had only invited young women he was considering as a future bride, and Miss Whitmore did not fit any of his friend's criteria for an ideal wife. She was far too headstrong, intelligent and candid. But Ledbury and Henry were both notorious gamblers. No doubt Henry was in debt to Ledbury, and was indeed trying to appease him by helping his niece find a husband.

'Suffer?' I said to Mr Whitmore,' the mother continued. 'How could anyone describe the Social Season as suffering?'

If it had been possible to get a word in edgeways, Jacob could say that both he and Miss Whitmore would describe it thus, and the drawing in his pocket was proof of that.

'I told him he was talking nonsense,' she went on, oblivious to the fact that this was a one-sided conversation. 'And I was right. Now my little girl is to become a duchess.'

She once again took her daughter in her arms and squeezed her tight. Despite this rather embarrassing display, it was apparent the mother did love her daughter and wished the best for her. A small part of him envied such affection from a parent. A *very* small part.

'So, when do you intend to marry?' the mother asked, turning to Jacob and this time waiting for him to reply.

'We haven't discussed—'

'As a duke you can get a special licence,' she interrupted. 'There's no need for a long, drawn-out engagement. You could be married by the end of the month. Even by the end of the week.'

'Mother,' Miss Whitmore said in a commanding tone, 'for propriety's sake I believe a long engagement would be more suitable, otherwise people might wonder at the rush. Tongues might wag.'

'Nonsense,' the mother shot back, her panicked gaze moving swiftly from her daughter to Jacob and back again. 'Tongues won't wag, and if they do it will probably be because they're all envious. You may have had three disastrous Seasons but once you are a duchess you will be the toast of London.'

She leant towards her frowning daughter. 'I really do advise you to marry the Duke as soon as possible, my dear.' Her tone lowered a little, as if hoping Jacob would not hear, despite standing a few feet away. 'You don't want this one to slip through your fingers.'

Miss Whitmore's posture stiffened and Jacob suspected there was a story behind that statement.

'Mother, we either have a long engagement or we

do not marry at all,' Miss Whitmore stated slowly through clenched teeth.

Jacob looked at the mother, curious to see what the comeback would be.

There wasn't one. The daughter's insistence had seemingly taken the wind out of Mrs Whitmore's sails and for once she was lost for words.

Miss Whitmore continued to glare at her mother, who quickly gathered herself and stared back at her daughter with narrowed eyes, in a silent battle of wills. If Jacob had been a betting man he knew which one he would back. Mrs Whitmore might be the one who made the most noise, but the daughter had such a defiant look in her eye he could not see her backing down.

'Yes, perhaps a long engagement might be for the best,' Mrs Whitmore finally said, albeit with an uncertain note in her voice.

'Good, that's settled,' Jacob said, clapping his hands once with finality. 'A long engagement so we have lots of time to really get to know each other,' he added, threading his arm through Miss Whitmore's, and drawing another reproachful look from the young lady.

'Ye-es,' the mother conceded reluctantly. 'I believe three months would be long enough.'

'Or three years,' Miss Whitmore responded, removing her arm from his.

'No,' the mother gasped.

'Yes,' the defiant daughter insisted.

'Ladies, shall we compromise?' Jacob suggested, rather enjoying this sparring. 'We'll announce the engagement immediately, with the intention of marrying at the beginning of next Season. So, an engagement of one year.'

The two women held each other's gaze as if waiting to see who would flinch first, then both nodded at the same time, accepting the compromise.

'Oh, I must go and tell Lady Chedmore,' Mrs Whitmore said, almost singing the words. 'She will be green with envy. She was so smug when she told me her daughter was to marry a viscount. Hmph, a viscount is nothing compared to a duke.'

With that, the beaming Mrs Whitmore bustled off, leaving Jacob behind with his future bride.

The moment her mother left, Margaret turned to the Duke. 'I assume you realise we will not actually be marrying. But a year's engagement will get me out of the Season. Hopefully, by then I'll have come up with a way to free myself from this charade.'

'Your enthusiasm for this match is so flattering,' he said with a wry smile.

'As you said, it is a convenient arrangement that gets us both out of an unwanted situation. There is no point pretending it is anything else,' she shot back with more sharpness than intended.

'Yes, ma'am.' That was followed by a facetious salute as if she was some sort of sergeant major. 'And I am more than happy to save you from the tedium of the Season, but in exchange it would be advantageous to me if we are seen in public together on occasion.' He gave a small laugh, as if this was all a jolly jest. 'And it would help if you looked at me with a modicum of affection, rather than as if I were the devil incarnate.'

Margaret was unaware that she had been looking at him like that, but it was not an entirely inapt description of how she felt about him. He certainly had a devilish reputation, and she was undoubtedly not the first woman to see him as devilishly handsome.

'You know the reason why I agreed to this arrangement,' she said, hoping her words contained no affection, not even the modicum he had requested. 'So, are you going to tell me the full story of why you suddenly decided it essential to be engaged to marry?'

He pulled the letter out of his pocket and looked down at it. 'It's a bit, shall we say…' He sent her a sheepish look.

'Sordid? Scandalous? Not fit for a young lady's ears?'

'Mmm,' he added, rubbing his hand around the back of his neck.

'Gossip is bound to reach me eventually, so I might as well hear it from you. And please, do not spare my blushes.'

'Well, how can I phrase this? Baroness Winterborne and I have been involved in a certain dalliance.'

'She is your lover?'

His eyebrows shot up his forehead at her frankness. That was, she hoped it was her frankness he was reacting to and not the slight quiver in her voice when she said the word 'lover'. But it was hard not to quiver when thinking of the Duke in that way.

'Yes, well, she was. It had all rather run its course when her husband, for some unfathomable reason, took umbrage about his wife straying.'

Margaret tried to keep her expression blank but found it hard not to frown at such a flippant attitude to the sanctity of marriage. 'You find the husband's objection difficult to understand?'

'Mmm.'

She waited for him to continue. He did not.

'There must be more to it than that. As I said, please do not try and spare my blushes. I wish to know exactly what I am getting myself into.'

And please do not blush, she said to herself. She had to focus on her abhorrence of this immorality, not on the ridiculous heat rising within her every time she thought of him being some woman's lover.

'If you insist.'

'I do.'

'Well, yes, Helena Winterborne was my lover, but I was certainly not her first and I doubt if I'll be her last, which makes Baron Winterborne's behaviour all the more difficult to understand. He has not objected to his wife's behaviour in the past, especially as he has been seeing the same mistress since before he married, continues to see her, and they have several children, all of whom he supports rather lavishly.'

Margaret tried hard not to show what she thought regarding this appalling behaviour, but suspected it was written all over her face.

'And what?' she said, her voice carefully modulated. 'You're worried about your reputation if it gets out that the two of you were lovers?' She smiled inwardly, pleased that this time she'd got the dreaded word out without any telltale signs.

'I wish that was all it was. No, Baron Winterborne has threatened divorce proceedings. I'm sure you know what being dragged through the divorce courts is like for a woman, particularly a member of the aristocracy.'

Margaret nodded, knowing exactly what Baroness Winterborne would face. The press loved nothing better than to report on every salacious detail of such goings-on among the aristocracy. While the men got off relatively lightly, the women were depicted as wanton, immoral and debased. If she had children, which Margaret believed the Baroness did, they would be taken away from her and it was unlikely she would ever see them again. Even other members of her family, particularly the females, would be tainted by the scandal and they'd all be shunned by Society.

He passed her the letter so she could read the Baron's threats for herself. His hand lightly touched hers as she took it from him. It was the merest brush, hardly any contact, but the annoying tingling that rippled from Margaret's fingers, up her arm and to her chest was impossible to ignore.

'I don't know what Winterborne is thinking,' the Duke continued, while Margaret tried to concentrate on reading the letter. 'This is so unlike him. But hopefully, when he realises it is all over between me and his wife, and that I am a reformed man, he will drop all talk of dragging this through the courts and destroying his wife's reputation.'

Margaret nodded again, conceding that this was a valid reason for their engagement, although it would have been better if the Duke had not become involved with a married woman in the first place. She owed Baroness Winterborne nothing, but no woman should have to go through the ordeal of the divorce court, particularly when men could behave in the same manner and never be held accountable.

Holding the letter by the edge, she handed it back to him, careful to ensure their hands did not touch.

'All right,' she said slowly. 'This arrangement will be mutually beneficial, and hopefully, as you said, by the start of next Season Baron Winterborne will have settled down and forgotten all about this and our engagement can be terminated.'

And if Baron Winterborne went through with his threat, once it reached the divorce courts, Margaret would have the perfect excuse for ending the engagement. Either way, she could not lose.

She smiled to herself. What had started out as a bit of wilful mischief had turned out rather well, and she had to admit she had played this game rather skilfully.

Her smile faded. The only drawback to an otherwise ideal plan was that she would have to spend time with the Duke of Rosedale, a man who disconcerted her in ways she barely understood.

Chapter Three

The Duke wished to announce the engagement at the ball planned for that evening, and Margaret agreed. Knowing her mother as she did, it was certain that by the time of the ball, word would have spread far and wide and everyone present at the weekend party would be aware that the couple were to wed.

While it was customary to wait for the father's consent, that too could be overlooked in this instance. Few men, even Margaret's steadfast father, would have the fortitude to stand in the way of something both Margaret and her mother wanted.

Once the minor detail of the announcement had been discussed, Margaret departed the morning room. It wasn't until she was back in her bedchamber that she realised she had forgotten to retrieve her drawing, the whole reason she had got herself into this peculiar predicament in the first place.

But there was nothing to be done about that now, so

she settled herself in the chair beside the window and pulled her sketchbook and pencils out of her leather bag. Hopefully, some quiet time, lost in her drawing, would give her a chance to gather her thoughts and still her jangling nerves before the evening's ordeal.

She looked out of the window at the garden below, her pencil poised above the paper. She knew she was being foolish. There was no reason for such agitation. She should be feeling relieved. Tonight, everyone would know she was to marry the Duke of Rosedale. Or at least, tonight everyone would *think* she was to marry the Duke of Rosedale. Only she and the Duke would know the truth.

She had every reason to feel free at last. Yet her nerves didn't seem to understand. One would almost think she was under the illusion that a real courtship with the Duke of Rosedale was about to begin. Perhaps her turmoil was simply due to the sudden change in circumstances. Whatever it was, Margaret wished the churning in her stomach and the skittering of her heart would settle down.

With as much determination as she could summon, she attempted to focus on sketching the sweeping gardens outside her window. Nothing was better at taking her away from her troubles or stilling her jumbled thoughts than focusing on her art. All she had to do was concentrate on capturing the look and feel of this spring afternoon, with the delicate green leaves of the beech trees fluttering in the soft breeze and the first blossoms of the lime trees about to burst into life.

She pressed harder on the page than she should, the pencil biting into the paper, the hard lines nothing like the tranquil scene before her. Dissatisfied, she ripped the page from her sketchbook, crumpled it up into a tight ball and tossed it to the floor.

Taking a slow, steady breath to still her thoughts, she tried again, but had hardly settled into her work when her mother burst in, already dressed in a ballgown, followed by Margaret's lady's maid.

'Put that away!' her mother cried out, flicking her hand at the sketchbook. 'You have to get dressed for this evening.'

'What? There is still plenty of time.'

'No, there is not. Tonight, you have to make a grand statement with your appearance and demeanour and be the undeniable belle of the ball.'

Margaret sighed and placed her sketchbook and pencil on a nearby table.

'Tonight, the world will know my daughter is to become a duchess,' her mother said with her hand over her heart and her eyes closed, before turning to the maid. 'You must ensure she looks the part.'

'A duchess?' Molly sent Margaret a questioning look.

She gave her maid a quick nod to tell her it was

true, even if neither of her mother's claims were completely correct. They were about to announce her betrothal to the guests of the Earl of Northwood, not the world, and she was not about to become a duchess, merely the temporary fiancée of a duke.

'Would you like your hair styled more ornately than usual?' Molly asked. 'Something more fashionable?'

'Yes, she would,' her mother answered for her. 'As ornate as possible and the very height of fashion, as becomes a duchess.'

With resignation, Margaret crossed the room and sat on the embroidered stool in front of the dressing table. In the looking glass, she could see Molly's expression of delight as she got to work with her combs, brushes and heated tongs, every action monitored by her attentive mother.

While the style Margaret usually wore required a minimum of work, this creation involved much backcombing, plaiting and curling as if creating an intricate sculpture, and it seemed to take an age.

Finally, Molly declared her work finished and stepped back, looking towards her mother, rather than Margaret, for approval.

Her mother observed the hairstyle from every angle, then finally declared it a success.

Margaret had to admit, it *was* a work of art. Her hair was piled high on her head, seemingly defying gravity, and somehow Molly had given it more volume than any head of hair could ever naturally have. Twists and braids were interwoven into the high chignon, and soft curls cascaded delicately down her neck and onto her shoulders.

'So, what is she to wear tonight?' her mother asked Molly.

Her lady's maid removed the gown carefully from the wardrobe. 'We brought the pink one with the silver embroidery for the ball,' she said, which her mother surely knew as she had been the one to select it.

When packing for the weekend party her mother had insisted on that dress, saying it made Margaret look young and innocent, like an eighteen-year-old about to face her first Season, rather than, as implied, a twenty-four-year-old who was close to taking up residence on the shelf.

'No, no, that will never do,' her mother said, frowning at the gown being held up for her inspection. 'That might be suitable for a debutante but not for a future duchess. It's all wrong. You'll have to do something about it.'

'Something, ma'am?' Molly said, turning the gown towards her.

'Yes, something. It needs to make a statement. It needs to say "I am the young lady who captured the most eligible man available this Season. I am to be a duchess".'

Margaret cringed, knowing that neither statement was true and never would be, and a gown certainly would not make them so.

'I suppose I could remove some of the lace around the neckline so it has a deeper décolletage?' Molly said with some uncertainty.

'That would be perfect,' her mother declared, flicking her hand at the maid in dismissal.

'Molly can hardly start making alterations now,' Margaret said, hoping to put an end to her mother's interference. 'Even starting this early—' she looked over at the clock ticking in the corner '—we'll be late for the ball.'

'You're about to become a duchess, my dear. People are going to have to get used to waiting for you.'

'I will be as quick as I can, miss,' Molly said, draping the gown over her arm.

'And tell my lady's maid to join us,' her mother instructed as Molly left the room.

'Why on earth do I need two ladies' maids?'

'Gertrude has much stronger hands than that little slip of a thing,' came her mother's peculiar reply. Then she frowned at Margaret. 'I wonder if you should wear rouge tonight. Your cheeks are rather pale.'

'No, Mother. I will not be painting my face,' Margaret said, turning to look at her reflection, which was no paler than usual.

'No, perhaps not. But let's just give those cheeks a good pinch.'

Her mother leant over Margaret's shoulder, her fingers taking on the appearance of lobster claws.

Margaret flinched away from the nipping fingers. 'The Duke proposed to me when I was wearing a plain grey skirt and white high-necked blouse with my cheeks as colourless as they always are. I don't believe we need all this artifice.'

'Perhaps,' her mother conceded, lowering her hand. 'Oh, my dear, you don't know how happy this has made me.' She placed her hand over her heart, closed her eyes and gave a small sigh, causing a twinge of guilt to twist inside Margaret. She did not like deceiving her mother, but then, if her mother hadn't all but thrown Baron Edgeware at her this would never have happened. She had no reason for guilt. But that realisation did not make her feel any better.

'I believe Lady Chedmore turned green when I told her. Then she had the audacity to imply that I was making it up, or had been mistaken, or was even starting to become a deluded old woman. But I suppose that's jealousy for you. It makes people behave in such an unfortunate manner.' Her mother shook her head and sighed, as if in pity for Lady Chedmore, but her beaming smile returned as bright as ever, suggesting delight at the other lady's envy.

'No doubt everyone is already talking about your forthcoming marriage,' she continued, fluffing out the skirt of her gown and taking a seat in a nearby armchair. 'You know what gossips women can be. But it's still going to be good to see their faces tonight when you are on the arm of the Duke of Rosedale.'

Her mother sighed again with pleasure, her hand back on her heart. Then her expression turned serious. 'I've sent a telegram to your father telling him about your forthcoming marriage. That Percival is going to have to eat his words and admit that for once his wife was completely correct and right to insist you attend this weekend party.'

'Hmm,' Margaret said non-committedly. She hated deceiving her father even more than her mother, as he had never been anything less than supportive of her.

While her mother had been unable to concede defeat and accept that Margaret was all but on the shelf, her father had always said he would support her whether she married or not, for which she was eternally grateful. Most young ladies did not have that luxury and had no choice but to find a husband, any husband, if they were to avoid the ignominy of becoming a governess or an elderly lady's paid companion. Fortunately, her father had assured her that would never be her fate.

She knew that both parents cared about her happiness; it was just unfortunate that her mother thought the only way a woman could be happy was to marry, to whom was an irrelevance, although a man with a title would of course be the preference.

Hence her reason for this subterfuge. But she doubted her honourable father would understand or accept the duplicitous scheme she had concocted with the Duke. So on this one occasion she would leave him in the dark as to her true intentions.

A decisive rap on the door interrupted her thoughts and announced the arrival of Gertrude. Her mother rushed across the room to open the door and whispered something to her lady's maid.

'Gertrude is going to help you with your undergarments while we wait for Molly,' her mother announced, once again taking her seat. 'As you said, you don't want to be late for the ball.'

Margaret suspected that a concern about punctuality was not the reason for Gertrude's presence but consented to her helping her out of her dress and stays. When she turned her back so Gertrude could do up her corset, her mother's plan became obvious. Gertrude's strong fingers pulled in the laces so tightly the air burst out of Margaret's lungs.

'I can't breathe,' she gasped out, as Gertrude's fingers worked methodically up the crossed laces, pulling the corset even tighter, the whalebones digging into Margaret's ribs. 'Please, not so tight.'

Her plea fell on deaf ears. Gertrude gave the laces one last decisive tug, tied them at the top and turned her around to face her mother.

'Perfect!' her mother declared. 'You're quite the hourglass now.'

'Mother, I will not…' she panted out. 'I can't…' But her cries were ignored as attention turned to Molly, arriving with the altered dress.

Before she had time to demand they release the constricting corset, the gown had been lowered over her head and the buttons up the back secured. Then all three women stood back to survey their work.

'You have such a lovely figure, my dear,' her mother declared. 'Now that your days as a debutante are coming to an end you should show it off more.'

Margaret walked across the room to inspect herself in the full-length looking glass and could hardly recognise the woman who was staring back at her.

'No, I can't go out looking like this,' she said, pulling at the top of her dress, only to have her hands swatted away by her mother.

'If you must cover up that ample bosom, do it with your fluttering fan, so you can give the Duke sly hints of what will soon be his.'

Colour exploded onto Margaret's cheeks and a strange tingling rushed through her body, while her heart hammered in her chest as if trying to escape. The Duke was going to see her dressed like this. He was going to think she was making all this effort for his benefit. He was going to think she was taking this make-believe engagement seriously.

'Oh, good, you don't need rouge after all,' her mother said. 'Make sure you blush like that when in the company of the Duke and try to look suitably coy when you do so. And be a bit more flirtatious tonight than you usually are. Until you've got the Duke up the aisle there's always a danger he'll slip through your fingers. And no one wants that.'

Margeret drew in a deep settling breath, or at least she drew in a breath as deep as her restricting corset would allow. The last thing she intended to do was be coy and flirtatious in front of a notorious rake. When it came to women he hardly needed the encouragement, and she certainly did not want him thinking she would soon be his, or that her plunging neckline was some sort of enticement.

This was all starting to feel like a very big mistake. The impulse to confess all was growing increasingly stronger. She should admit the truth. Then she could hide away in her bedchamber and never see the Duke again, and certainly not dressed as if she was trying hard to keep his interest and not let him slip through her fingers, as her mother kept saying.

But there was no going back now. She'd got herself

into this situation. Now she would just have to face this evening with as much composure and dignity as she could muster.

'Right, let's get this over and done with, shall we?' Margaret picked up her gloves and fan while doing her best to ignore her still pounding heart, knotted stomach and burning skin.

'Oh, don't be so sour-faced, Margaret. This is the happiest day of your life. Well, your second happiest. The happiest will be your wedding day.' Her mother sent her a coquettish look. 'Not to mention your wedding night.'

No, do not mention the wedding night, Margaret wanted to entreat her mother. Even though that event would never take place, she did not need to imagine what it would be like to be in the Duke's bed. If she was to have any hope of keeping her jittery nerves under control, she could not think about him in that manner.

Desperately trying to collect herself, she stood in the middle of the room, her feet seemingly incapable of moving, but just as Margaret was needing more time, her mother seemed to finally see the need to make haste.

'Come on, my dear,' she said, linking arms with her daughter. 'I think we've kept your future husband waiting long enough.' With that, she all but pulled Margaret out of the door, down the stairs and towards the ballroom, where they were announced by the footman.

All chatter fell silent, with only the sound of the chamber orchestra filling the air, and every head turned in their direction.

This was a new experience. Margaret usually entered unnoticed and immediately took her place in the corner with the other wallflowers, where she would be ignored all night. And she wasn't sure she liked this sudden attention. The same could not be said for her mother, who was positively glowing with happiness. She nodded regally to the staring guests and Margaret expected her to start twirling her hand in a wave reminiscent of visiting royalty.

While her mother thought she was witnessing everyone giving due acknowledgement to a future duchess, Margaret knew exactly what they were thinking. They were wondering how a woman like her had managed to snag the most eligible man available, a man with a reputation as a rake, one it was assumed was unlikely to ever settle down with any woman and especially not an ageing wallflower.

The Duke walked across the room and bowed in front of them. 'It appears an official announcement will not be necessary as news has already spread of our forthcoming nuptials.'

'I only told Lady Chedmore and I swore her to secrecy,' her mother said, beaming with happiness.

'But she was obviously not to be trusted with such exciting news.'

For once Margaret was pleased to have a garrulous mother, because in the Duke's presence she was feeling unaccountably shy. What on earth was wrong with her? She was not shy. She did not blush. She was never coy. What was next? Was she going to become flirtatious and giggly as debutantes were expected to be?

'Well, I believe we owe them a show,' he said, bowing once more. 'Will you do me the honour of this dance, Miss Whitmore?'

Margaret knew she had no option but to accept as good manners demanded it, and she should also make some effort to pretend this was a real courtship. But it would be easier to get her fizzing nerves under control if she did not have to touch the Duke.

He held out his hand, those smiling blue eyes staring into hers as she continued to hesitate. Then, as if measuring the heat of a burning stovetop, she tentatively placed her hand on his, grateful that gloves were protecting skin from skin.

With everyone in the room watching, including the footmen and maids, he led her into the middle of the dancefloor. Perhaps that was all this was. Her nervousness had nothing to do with the Duke. It was simply because she was not used to being the centre of attention.

This realisation did nothing to stop her heart from beating faster when he placed his hand on her waist. She was sure she could feel the warmth burning through her gown, corset and chemise and straight onto her skin. Cautiously, she placed her hand on his broad shoulder.

He was dressed in a black swallow-tailed coat and crisp white shirt and Margaret knew it was not possible to feel his muscles through his clothing, but for one moment she was sure their coiled strength rippled under her fingers.

They moved off in time to the music, swirling across the highly polished parquet floor. He was a superb dancer. But given his reputation with women she would expect nothing less. She also had to admit being swept around the room by him was far from unpleasant. He was a much better partner than all of the men she had danced with over the last three Seasons. They'd generally been clumsy oafs, either young men who were presumably practising with her before they moved on to court the young ladies who really interested them, or old men who took pity on the wallflower but were so past their prime they could do little more than shuffle along out of time to the music's beat.

With such men, she knew she was never given a chance to display any dancing skills she might possess, but in the Duke's arms she felt poised and elegant as they moved in perfect harmony with each other and the music.

'You are an exquisite dancer, Miss Whitmore,' he said as he spun her around.

'You sound surprised. Did you think because I spend most of my time sitting in the wallflowers' corner that I'd have two left feet and the lightness of an elephant?'

He laughed, and she knew she was being ungracious.

'I'm sorry, that was rude of me. I did have an excellent dance instructor and I do enjoy dancing. It's just I don't often get the opportunity.' *Especially to dance with a man as accomplished as you*, she could add, but saw no need to add to his already high opinion of himself.

'Then we must dance together often during our courtship.'

Margaret had decidedly mixed opinions about that. Yes, he was a fabulous dancer, but when her mutinous body was forgetting she was in the arms of a man who held no attraction for her whatsoever she wasn't entirely sure dancing together often would be such a good idea, particularly when her mind was becoming clouded by the warmth of his body, his sandalwood cologne and that underlying, infuriatingly attractive masculine scent.

'Do I take it you had all the requisite training of a debutante?' he asked.

'Again, you sound surprised,' she said, pleased that her voice betrayed none of her inner turmoil. 'Yes, I learnt all the correct etiquette, how to flirt, how to flatter a man, even what I was supposed to do with my fan to send men supposedly secret messages. As you have probably already gathered, I paid those instructions little heed.'

'I'm pleased to hear it and do not feel any obligation to flatter me. Feel free to be as rude as you wish and insult me as often as you choose.'

She knew he was teasing her, but she did have rather an unfortunate reputation for doing both those things when in men's company. Although usually that was because the men were just so exasperating she felt she had no option.

'You may live to regret saying that.'

'I doubt it. I have very thick skin.'

She looked up at his flawless skin with the hint of dark stubble on the angular jawline. For one second, she imagined running her finger along his cheekbone, discovering for herself whether his skin really was thick or soft to the touch. She blinked rapidly to force that image out of her mind.

'And believe me, it is refreshing to meet a woman who does speak her mind,' he said, as he once again spun her around. 'I've lost count of the number of debutantes who have complimented me on my engaging conversation when I've done nothing more than wonder aloud whether it might rain, or those who have declared me most enterprising because I'm able to light a candle without setting fire to my cuffs.'

The edges of Margaret's lips curled at his description of the inane conversations that took place throughout the Season, before she mentally chastised herself.

'Debutantes are under enormous pressure to marry. That's why they compliment you instead of saying what they really think.'

'I am aware of that. Painfully aware. But it doesn't make it any easier to be treated as if you have the wit of Oscar Wilde, the intelligence of a philosopher, the charm of Sir Lancelot and the looks of a Greek god. Especially as you know none of it is true.'

Margaret bit her lip, remembering how she had intended to draw him and was once again relieved she had instead depicted him as a peacock. 'All right, I admit that might be tedious so I promise I will never flatter you.'

'What we should do is agree to never indulge in false flattery.'

'Agreed,' she said with a quick nod.

'So, in light of that contract, I should say you look lovely tonight. You've done something different with your hair and it suits you.'

Heat exploded on Margaret's cheeks. Damn. She did not want him to think she cared about such things, or wanted his approval.

'It was all Molly's doing,' she blurted out, tripping over her words. 'And my mother, who said I should try and look more like a duchess.' *And Gertrude's strong hands.*

'Well, this Molly person and your mother were right. You look positively majestic.'

Did his eyes briefly stray to her decolletage? She hoped not. And hoped even more that he did not think she was putting on a display for him. It would be beyond mortifying if he thought she'd chosen to wear a low-cut gown in an attempt to gain his attention, not least because given all the reputed beauties he had been linked with, such behaviour would be doomed to failure.

The music came to an end and she was still feeling somewhat flustered as he led her off the dancefloor towards her mother.

'I can see the Duke has managed to put some colour in your cheeks,' her mother said, doing nothing to help cool her burning face. 'I was just saying to Lady Tilsbury what an attractive couple you make.'

Her mother swept her hand towards a woman who was looking at Margaret's mother with barely concealed contempt.

Margaret's heart went out to her mother. She'd had

to endure so much snobbery and even mockery from the other mamas throughout the last three Seasons. They'd never let her forget for a moment that her daughter was failing at the one thing expected of a young lady. As annoying as she could be at times, Margaret knew this had not been easy for her mother. She now had a chance to shine, and perhaps Margaret should give her this moment in the sun.

To that end she placed her arm through the Duke's and leant in towards him, letting it be known they were indeed a couple, while ignoring the way being so close to him was causing her skittering heart to behave.

Her mother's smile grew even wider and she turned towards the group of watching mamas. 'Ladies, in case you have not already heard, the Duke of Rosedale is to marry my daughter.'

The mamas all nodded with matching expressions of pique, while Margaret's mother delighted in them getting their comeuppance.

'This is all rather sudden, is it not, Your Grace?' Lady Tilsbury said. 'Haven't the two of you just met?'

'Well, when Cupid's arrow strikes, we mortals are powerless to resist,' the Duke said. 'It was love at first sight and I knew immediately I had found my Duchess.'

Margaret gritted her teeth so she would not grimace at such a blatant lie, especially as the dubious expressions on the assembled mamas' faces proved he was fooling no one, apart from her mother.

'When will you be marrying?' Lady Chedmore asked with a disbelieving frown.

'We plan a long engagement,' Margaret answered before the Duke made any other outrageous statements. 'Even though it was…' she paused to clear her throat '…love at first sight, we thought it would be good to have a proper courtship before we marry and not rush into something so important.'

'They're to wed at the beginning of next Season,' her mother announced. 'It will be simply wonderful and so romantic to start the Season with a grand society wedding. And I'm sure once my daughter is a duchess she will become one of the leading lights of London society, hosting balls, soirees, salons. Oh, it is the life she was born to.'

Margaret struggled not to look pained as these lies continued to swirl around her. She had not been born to such a life, nor was she the type to fall in love at first sight. She could see trouble ahead when the life her mother hoped for her did not come to fruition, but she'd deal with that when the time came. First, she had to get through that expected long courtship with the Duke.

'Now, if you'll excuse me, ladies, I would like to dance with my future mother-in-law,' the Duke said, and reached out his hand towards Margaret's mother, who instantly blushed and adopted the behaviour of a coy debutante.

Margaret sent him a silent thank you. Most men would do anything to avoid her mother's incessant chatter, even, she suspected, those who really had been struck by Cupid's arrow, and dancing with the Duke would please her mother immensely.

The moment they left, the other ladies crowded around her and Margaret knew she was about to be on the receiving end of a barrage of questions, questions for which she would have no honest answers, so she quickly excused herself to make a hasty retreat towards her usual place in the corner of the ballroom.

Baron Edgeware halted her progress and bowed in front of her. 'Miss Whitmore, may I have this dance?'

For a moment she stared at the young man, certain she had not heard correctly, but his hand was extended, so she placed hers on top of his and still in a state of bafflement allowed him to lead her onto the floor for the polka.

Two dances in one night, this was all but unprecedented.

Was this the result of her being betrothed to a duke? It had to be. Nothing else about her had changed. They moved off to the lively tune and, despite herself, Margaret realised she was enjoying herself. She loved dancing but rarely got the opportunity.

Once the dance was over, Baron Edgware led her

back to her mother, who was twittering away to the Duke, while he listened with commendable patience.

When her mother paused to get her breath, the Duke turned to Margaret. 'May I have the next dance?' he asked with a bow.

Dancing twice with the same man would not usually be acceptable, but as the guests believed they were engaged there was no harm. That was, no harm to her reputation; her nervous system was another matter.

'Thank you,' she said as they took their places for the galop.

'No, thank you. Dancing with you is a pleasure,' he replied.

'I mean thank you for dancing with my mother. I know she can be a bit, well...'

'Not at all, and it gave me a chance to find out all about you.'

Margaret's breath caught in her throat. 'What? Me? What?' She hated to think what her mother had said.

'Don't worry. I'm sure all your deepest, darkest secrets are still safe.'

Margaret could assure him she had no secrets, deep or dark. Well, apart from one unfortunate incident in her first Season, but her mother knew little of the real details of what had happened with the Earl of Covington and, even if she did, was unlikely to have mentioned it to the Duke.

'So, what did she say?'

The Duke tapped the side of his nose. 'That, I'm afraid, is between your mother and myself.'

Before she had a chance to question him further, the music started, and they moved off at a pace even more energetic than that of the polka.

Once again, dancing with him was wonderful. The confident way he swung her around the floor made her feel as light as a feather. Part of her wanted to resist him, but most of her found it thrilling to be in the arms of such a commanding man and she soon lost herself completely in the galop's joyful exuberance, and even found herself laughing with giddy pleasure when the Duke lifted her up and twirled her around. Laughing at a ball, that was something else she had never before done.

'That was fun,' he said with a bow, when they came to a halt.

Still smiling, her breath coming rapidly, hopefully from the dance and not because she could still feel the warmth of his touch on her waist, she curtsied. 'Yes, it was.'

He placed both hands on the top of her arms. She froze, stunned by this act of possessive familiarity, but not entirely averse to it. 'I'm sure your dance card is filling up, but remember to save the last waltz for your fiancé.'

'Yes, yes. Um, now, if you'll excuse me, I need to talk to my mother.'

With that she rushed off. She did need to talk to her mother and find out what they had discussed during their dance, but it was also wisest to get away from the Duke so she would stop acting like an awkward ninny just because he had touched her in such a surprising manner.

Before she could reach her mother, Lord Templeton halted her progress, bowed in front of her and asked for the next dance.

Her interrogation of her mother would have to wait.

When that dance finished she found herself being led back onto the floor by yet another man. And so the night continued. While she was on the floor for every dance, each time with a different man, the Duke danced with each of the mamas in turn, and several times with her own mother.

As much as she was enjoying herself, she couldn't entirely shake off the anxiety that she would soon be back in the Duke's arms for the final waltz.

The last dance was announced. She waited on the edge of the dancefloor as he crossed the room towards her, his eyes fixed on hers. She did her best not to act like a coy debutante, waiting expectantly for the man she was enamoured with, a fight she suspected she was in danger of losing.

He bowed in front of her, sent her one of those disarming smiles then led her back onto the dancefloor.

'So, how is the engagement going so far?' he asked as they spun around the floor.

'Exhausting. I've never danced so much in my life,' she said with a little laugh, while trying to ignore the effect of once again being surrounded by his scent of sandalwood and the warmth of his body.

'Well, if that is how you look when you are exhausted, I recommend you tire yourself out more often.'

She gave a forced laugh. 'We made a contract, remember? No false flattery.'

'I assure you, it is the truth. You have a delightful flush on your cheeks and a pretty glint in your eyes. Anyone would think you really were a young woman in love.'

'Well, they'd be wrong,' she snapped back, horrified that he could say such a thing.

'Yes, they'd be wrong about the reason, but not wrong in thinking you look stunning. That is why these men all want to dance with you.'

'Nonsense. They just think my value has increased because I'm engaged to a duke.'

He looked at her, as if assessing her reaction. 'You don't like being complimented, do you?'

Margaret could say she'd had so little practice she didn't really know how she was supposed to react.

'Perhaps you should just accept that, no matter what the reason, tonight you are the belle of the ball. You danced with every man present, and the other young ladies were all looking at you with the greatest of envy.'

'Well, yes, I'm supposedly engaged to a duke. Of course they think they have reason to envy me.'

'Again she proves she does not like to be given compliments, even honest ones.'

No, again she proves it is something with which she is completely unfamiliar.

'I'm afraid I'm going to give you one more compliment, so brace yourself.'

Margaret did exactly that, dreading what he had to say, but also, annoyingly, hoping he would once again flatter her.

'I believe you are going to make the perfect fake fiancée and I look forward to our fake courtship.'

Margaret laughed in nervous relief. 'Under the circumstances, I'm not sure if that's a compliment or not.'

'Believe me, it is a compliment. So, let's enjoy this last dance at our first ball and promise to try and enjoy our fake engagement.'

Margaret nodded. He was right. Despite the turbulence of her confusing emotions, she had enjoyed the evening. She had smiled more than she usually did and had even laughed on occasion. She hadn't been anywhere close to the wallflowers' corner and had danced more at this ball than all the ones she had attended in the last three Seasons combined.

There were definite advantages to being betrothed to a duke, even if it was all fake. And that was the catch. Despite the fun she'd had, despite how much she loved dancing with him, that was something she must never forget. It would be a danger to her emotional wellbeing if she started to delight too much in the Duke's company and forgot he was using her to silence a scandal with another woman.

She moved slightly closer to him. Yes, it would be sheer folly to ever think any of this was real.

Chapter Four

Jacob woke the next morning feeling better about the world than he had since this self-imposed exile in the Kent countryside began.

The ball had been a great success, just as he'd hoped. He wouldn't be surprised if word had already spread to London that the Duke of Rosedale was to marry, the gossip mill being even more efficient than the telegraph system, and an engagement notice in *The Times* was hardly necessary as he was certain the mamas would spread the news throughout Society.

But for the sake of appearances, he would have to follow all the expected procedures. He would not want to rouse Baron Winterborne's suspicions. It was vital the Baron be convinced that Jacob had suddenly and unexpectedly fallen in love, and was about to settle down as a happily married man.

The first action required was a formal approach to Miss Whitmore's father to get his approval, something he was sure would be a matter of course. Jacob was a duke after all, and not many fathers would turn down an offer for their daughter's hand from a duke. And even if the father was not entirely in favour, he could not see any man being able to stop Mrs Whitmore from getting what she wanted, not if he desired anything resembling a quiet life.

Once he had the father's blessing, notice would go in the newspaper and they would begin their courtship, proving to the world, and Baron Winterborne in particular, that he was a reformed man. Winterborne would realise nothing was to be gained by dragging his own name, his wife's reputation or Jacob through the divorce courts and all would be right with the world.

Then, when the time came, he and Miss Whitmore would find some suitable reason why their marriage could not go ahead, a reason that ensured no harm was done to the young lady's reputation, and ideally one that enhanced it and increased her desirability as a wife in the eyes of other men. And judging from the attention she'd received at last night's ball, that would be an easily achievable outcome. Being engaged to a duke had certainly elevated her in the eyes of the fickle men present at this weekend's party, and there had been no signs of her attempting to escape through any open windows.

And the way she had looked last night had no doubt

been a contributing factor. The stern expression had mostly disappeared, as had the moue of disapproval on those lovely red lips, along with the wary tension in her posture. She'd actually looked like a pretty young woman capable of enjoying herself. Yes, he was certain this engagement would get her out of the wallflowers' corner for ever and be as beneficial for her as it was for him.

All in all, this was a more successful break in the countryside than he could have ever envisioned when he'd first fled from London.

Feeling decidedly pleased with himself, he climbed out of bed and rang for his valet to help him shave and dress, then headed downstairs to find the house in a state of turmoil, with hurrying servants preparing for the guests' departure.

He entered the breakfast room, where only Henry was still present, everyone else having presumably dined early so they could ready themselves to take their leave.

After such an eventful night Jacob had a hearty appetite, so served himself a generous plate of eggs, sausages and bacon from the silver tureens lined up on the sideboard and joined Henry at the table.

His friend stopped eating and looked at Jacob, saying nothing, his fork poised in mid-air, his silence and expression speaking volumes.

Jacob signalled to the footman to pour some coffee and commenced slicing up his sausages, deciding not to put his friend out of his misery immediately.

'Come on man, out with it. What's really going on?'

'I'm engaged to be married. That's what's going on.'

'Stop beating about the bush. What's the real story? No one changes that quickly and don't give me any of that rubbish about Cupid's arrow. You might have impressed the ladies with that romantic rubbish, but I don't believe it for a moment.'

'You don't believe in love at first sight, Henry? You surprise me.'

'Come on, I want the truth, the whole truth and nothing but the truth.'

Jacob laughed. 'Funny you should use a legal reference. That is what this is all about. Winterborne is threatening to divorce his wife and plans to cite me as the co-respondent.'

'So what? It's not as if the whole of London doesn't already know that his wife is your lover.'

'Yes, I suspect you are right,' Jacob conceded. Even Miss Whitmore had suspected he was in trouble with a married woman. If the debutantes knew then it really must be common knowledge, although Miss Whitmore was certainly not your typical debutante.

'Well? Why this sudden need to get married?'

Jacob lowered his knife and fork to his plate. Henry

was obviously not going to let him eat in peace until he had the whole story. 'Things are over between Helena and myself, but I still have a great deal of affection for her. I'd hate to see her dragged through the courts, her reputation in tatters and shunned from Society. It would all be so unfair, particularly as her husband had all but given his consent to her taking lovers in the past.'

Henry frowned at his friend as if he still couldn't understand what Jacob was talking about.

'Winterborne has never objected to any of Helena's other lovers, so I suspect the threat of divorce is more about me than about his wife's behaviour. So, if he thinks I'm besotted with another woman he might see no need for going through this ridiculous divorce which benefits no one.'

'But it's a bit drastic, isn't it? Marriage? Couldn't you find some other way out of this?'

'What have you got against marriage? Didn't you fill your house with debutantes this weekend so you could find a wife yourself?'

'That's different—family pressure and all that. My hideous cousin's even more hideous wife visited recently and was actually taking measurements so she could redecorate my house when her family inherits. I've got to marry and sire an heir so that never happens.'

'You are such a romantic, Henry.'

His friend gave him a long, questioning look. 'Is that what this is all about? You want to sire a son on Miss Whitmore.'

Jacob recoiled at the way his friend was talking. Did he always refer to women in such crude terms? Jacob was unsure, but they'd never had a discussion about marriage and children before, so it was hard to tell. And, unlike Henry, Jacob would be more than content for his cousin to inherit his estate. He knew what it was like to be the unloved product of a loveless marriage. His parents had married for duty and sired a child for no other reason than to carry on the family title. He would not inflict a loveless marriage on any woman and would certainly never be responsible for an innocent child experiencing such an unhappy childhood.

'No, I simply proposed to one woman to save another woman's reputation.'

'How self-sacrificial of you.' Henry's tone suggested he did not see this as admirable but more likely as a sign of madness.

'But of all the deliciously fresh and pretty young things I stocked my house with this weekend, why on earth did you have to pick Miss Whitmore? A woman who has been overlooked Season after Season?' Henry added, still looking at Jacob as if he had lost his sanity.

'That, I suppose, is a very good question and one

I'm not sure how to answer.' He looked down at his plate and tried to remember the sequence of events that had led him to this point. He was a duke. He *could* have selected virtually any young woman. So why had he picked Miss Whitmore?

He doubted he'd ever met another young lady who had such a low opinion of him. He'd certainly not met a young lady who could be as rude, forthright and downright prickly in his company.

And Henry was correct. As he so coarsely put it, she was not as young and fresh as the other debutantes present, young ladies who were about to embark on their first Season. Although last night she had looked surprisingly stunning. He certainly wasn't the only man at the ball who'd noticed her generous cleavage, and dancing with her had been a dream. But when he'd proposed it had not been because of her womanly body or her agility on the dancefloor.

He took a sip of his black coffee. If he had been aware of such features, perhaps he would not have made his impetuous proposal, but what was done was done. And the fact that she wanted this marriage as much as he did remained unchanged, so there was no danger of her holding him to his word and demanding they actually tie the knot.

The moment he had seen her glaring at him in the morning room he had known that to be the case. He might not have consciously thought it through, but that awareness had happened suddenly, almost as suddenly as love at first sight. This was a woman who could not abide him. That was why he knew he had picked the right woman.

'Because marriage to Miss Whitmore suits me very well indeed,' he said, before taking a large bite of his toast.

The sound of her name brought Margaret to a sudden halt in the middle of the hallway. As she was the topic under discussion, she refused to see anything wrong with eavesdropping on a private conversation, so she flattened herself against the wall, her ear turned towards the breakfast room's open door.

The deep male voice, rich with amusement, was obviously the Duke's, and Margaret was curious to hear what he had to say and to whom he was speaking.

'Why?' came the response, the disparaging tone revealing it to be that of the Earl of Northwood. 'She's hardly a beauty, is she? And my goodness, there were some beauties here this weekend. You could have had the pick of any one of them.'

Margaret's jaw clenched tightly. This was not the first time she had been described as 'hardly a beauty'. She would not let it upset her, but she braced herself for the Duke's response, which undoubtedly would be a hearty agreement with this assessment.

'Miss Whitmore has all the qualities I am looking for in a wife,' came his unexpected reply.

Margaret held her breath at this encouraging response and leaned in slightly closer to the open door.

'And what would those qualities be?' the Earl said. It was the very question she wanted answered. 'A sharp tongue? A fiery temperament? They're not exactly qualities most men look for in a wife, hence the fact she was heading straight to spinsterhood.'

'She has a quick wit and knows her own mind. I believe those are admirable qualities.'

Margaret frowned. Did he really think those qualities admirable? They had never been described in such a manner before.

'Admirable qualities in a politician perhaps, but in a wife? I think not.'

'Perhaps I want a wife who challenges me?'

The Earl's laugh was tinged with derision. 'I find that hard to believe. Surely you want a nice compliant wife who will let you do whatever you want, with whomever you want. I can't see you wanting to give up wine, women and song after you marry. Nor can I see that formidable wench letting you continue to live the lifestyle you enjoy. Once you're married, she's going to put you on a short leash, of that I am certain, and you will be miserable.'

The Duke said nothing, but then, what could he say? He was not going to change. And, more to the point, they never were going to marry anyway so it mattered not how long or short a leash she might wield.

'I beg you, Jacob, reconsider this foolishness,' the Earl continued, a note of desperation in his voice. 'Find some way out of this. Any of the other debutantes present this weekend would happily let you keep as many mistresses as you want, and you'd never be on the receiving end of that supposed quick wit when you did stray.'

As offensive as that was, the Earl was correct. Debutantes were well aware that when they married they were expected to turn a blind eye to their husband's affairs. He was also correct to suppose that it was something Margaret had never approved of, and never would, although in these unusual circumstances what she thought was of little consequence.

'All you'd have to do is get whichever chit you choose with child a few times,' the Earl added. 'And while that is never an arduous task, doing so with one of the prettier, more compliant debs on offer this weekend would make it even less arduous. Then you could return to your old way of life, knowing you'd done your duty as the Duke of Rosedale.'

The Earl laughed while Margaret simmered with rage, not just for herself but for every debutante who was depicted in that appalling manner.

'While Miss Whitmore may not be to your taste,

I see a lot to admire,' the Duke continued, annoyingly not telling the Earl how offensive his attitude was. 'She has a boldness that makes her striking, and by contrast all the other debutantes appear simpering and weak-willed. She showed a great deal of elegance on the dancefloor last night, and I would say her beauty, while not demanding attention like many other young women, is more alluring because of its subtlety.'

Margaret's hand covered her mouth as she listened in disbelief. Was he really talking about her? Did he actually mean what he was saying? Or did she hear some sarcasm in his words?

'You can't be serious!' the Earl gasped, once again that odious man saying exactly what Margaret was thinking.

'I have never been more serious in my life.'

'I beg of you, Jacob, reconsider your actions. It's not too late. No official announcement has been made. You can still get out of it if you act quickly.'

There was a long pause, while Margaret continued to hold her breath.

'All right, Henry, promise me this will go no further,' the Duke said in a lowered voice. Margaret drew in a much-needed breath, held it once again, and leaned in even closer to the open door.

'Neither myself nor Miss Whitmore has any intention of going through with this marriage,' the Duke continued. 'She means nothing to me. This engagement gets me out of a sticky situation with Baron Winterborne. It will save Helena's reputation and save Miss Whitmore from having to endure another Season as a wallflower. At some stage we will call it off and go our separate ways.'

Margaret stiffened, gripped with an unexpected pang of disappointment, even though the Duke was simply speaking the truth in a private conversation with his friend. And what had she expected? That he would continue to extol her charms and beauty as if he really had been struck by Cupid's arrow?

'Oh, thank God!' the Earl said with evident relief. 'For a moment I thought you'd lost your mind.'

'Believe me, my friend, I am completely sane and know exactly what I am doing.'

Of course he did. He was using Margaret to save his mistress's reputation. She had always known that and had no right to feel the rage boiling up inside her. And the second part of his statement was equally true. That was what she should focus on. She, too, was using him, to save herself from enduring another Season stuck in the wallflowers' corner.

It was all just an amicable arrangement.

Margaret strode off down the hallway to prepare for a hasty departure, telling herself she was not angry, but instead grateful to have overheard their conversation. It meant that any lingering delusions she'd harboured regarding the Duke following the attention he had paid her at last night's ball had been well and truly swept away.

Chapter Five

London

Jacob had expected to see Miss Whitmore again before she left Henry's estate, but mother and daughter were gone by the time he'd finished his breakfast.

He was sure such a breach of etiquette was of no consequence. She *was* an unusual woman who cared nothing for convention, and such peculiarities would no doubt continue to reveal themselves as their so-called courtship continued.

Now he was back in London, he needed to make this arrangement formal, or rather, give it the appearance of formality. To that end, his first duty was to visit Miss Whitmore's father and ask for his daughter's hand.

He arrived at the Whitmore's Kensington household certain it would be a quick visit, a shake of the hand and then he would be off. The footman ushered him into the father's study, where he surprisingly found both father and daughter waiting for him.

Again, he decided to put no stock in this additional breach of the usual protocol. He already knew Miss Whitmore was somewhat unconventional, which was another reason why she was his ideal co-conspirator.

Mr Whitmore emerged from behind his desk and indicated for Jacob to take one of the deep leather buttoned armchairs. He sat in the one beside Miss Whitmore, sent her a quick smile, which wasn't returned, while Mr Whitmore took the chair facing the couple.

The older man stared at Jacob over his half-moon glasses, like a judge considering how harshly he should sentence the recalcitrant in the dock.

'My wife tells me you proposed to my daughter after having known her for no more than a few days,' he finally said.

'That's correct, sir. We both knew it was what we wanted.' Jacob resisted pulling at his stiff collar to relieve the discomfort caused by the older man's unflinching stare.

'Is that correct, Margaret?' he asked, turning to his daughter.

'Yes, Father. More or less.'

Jacob doubted he had ever seen a woman who looked less in love. On the night of the ball her demeanour had been delightfully light-hearted, but now those brows were once again drawn together and her lips were tightly pursed, just as they had been when he proposed.

The father waited for his daughter to explain further.

'It's an arrangement,' she said on a sigh, shocking Jacob with her honesty, but causing the father to nod as if he'd suspected that all along. 'We're not in love but this suits us both.'

'That is unfortunate,' the father said, causing Jacob's heart to sink. Why couldn't she have just used the same line he'd used, about Cupid and his arrow? 'But you would not be the first couple to marry for reasons other than love, although a love match was what I had hoped for you, Margaret.'

He looked at Jacob, who did not know what to say. Miss Whitmore had already informed her father that there was no love between them; to claim otherwise would be foolhardy.

'I do, however, have the greatest respect for your daughter,' he said instead, hoping that would suffice. He waited, like the awkward suitor he now appeared to be, for the older man's response.

Mr Whitmore finally nodded, still staring at Jacob as if trying to figure him out. 'So why did you choose to make this arrangement with my daughter and not some other young lady?' It was the same question Henry had asked, albeit in less crude terms, but he had not expected it from her father.

'Because, as I said, I respect your daughter. I also admire her,' Jacob said, scrambling for words. 'She is intelligent, talented and has a marvellous sense of humour.'

Father and daughter exchanged raised-eyebrow looks as if unsure what he was talking about.

'You should see the cartoon she drew of Henry's weekend party,' he continued. 'It was hilarious, worthy of publication in *Punch*.' He looked from father to daughter, neither of whom appeared impressed by his declaration, and an uncomfortable silence descended on the group.

'You wish to marry my daughter because her cartoon made you laugh?' the father finally said.

'There are worse reasons to marry,' Jacob mumbled, wondering why he was having to defend himself. Had they forgotten he was a duke?

'Hmm,' was the father's non-committal response, before he turned to his daughter. 'So, Margaret, why do you want to marry this man?' He looked Jacob up and down and frowned as if he personally could see no logical reason, then turned back to his daughter. 'Are you entering into this arrangement freely? Or are you being put under pressure, say, from your mother?'

Miss Whitmore sighed again, and they both waited for her response. Jacob had assumed this whole thing would be quickly settled and this meeting was simply a formality, but it seemed with Miss Whitmore, it was best to assume nothing.

'Mother is ecstatic, as expected, but no, I have not succumbed to any pressure. I *am* entering this arrangement for my own reasons and of my own volition.'

Mr Whitmore nodded slowly. 'Then I suppose I have no option but to agree.'

Finally. Was that so difficult?

Jacob placed his hands on the arms of the chair, but was halted from rising and taking his leave by the father, staring him firmly in the eye.

'I am willing to agree to this arrangement, but there is something I want you to never forget. I love my daughter more than life itself. You will treat her with the utmost respect at all times or else I will do whatever it takes to ruin you, even if I ruin myself in the process.'

Jacob was somewhat taken aback by the strength of the man's assertion but nodded his agreement.

'I don't wish to spell it out in front of my daughter,' the older man continued. 'But I read the newspapers, and I do not want to read anything that in any way reflects badly on Margaret, nor do I want to see your name mentioned in any scurrilous publications.'

Again, Jacob nodded. Staying out of the scurrilous publications was what this arrangement was all about.

'And it would be best not to mention that this marriage is an arrangement that has nothing to do with love when talking to my wife,' Mr Whitmore added in a slightly more conciliatory tone. 'She has always been, and remains, a hopeless romantic. Let us not ruin her happiness.'

'Of course,' Jacob said. 'Now that I have your...' he paused; *blessing* was perhaps not quite the right word '...your consent, can I assume you will soon place an announcement in *The Times*?'

And as soon as possible, so I can avoid being hauled into the divorce courts, he could add, but suspected that would not go down well with a man who had just threatened to ruin him at the first sign of any scandalous behaviour.

Father and daughter gave matching nods, making it apparent that the conversation was at an end. So, with that, he said goodbye and departed from a meeting that had been nothing like what he'd imagined.

If he had chosen any of the other debutantes at Henry's weekend party he was certain to have been greeted by a deferential father, eager to give his blessing, overwhelmed with joy at the prospect of his daughter becoming a duchess and elevating the family's status in Society.

But if that had happened this morning, right now he would be feeling like a charlatan who was deceiving his intended's parents, even if it was for a good cause. Perhaps it was all for the best that the father possessed the same forthright manner as the daughter. And there was no doubt that he had just witnessed a close relationship between the two, one based on mutual respect and genuine affection.

As he entered his carriage and signalled for the driver to take him home, he couldn't help but wonder what it would be like to have two parents who cared about you so much. One showed her love in her desperate and misguided attempts to find her daughter a husband. The other was prepared to threaten a duke and sacrifice himself in order to protect her. Jacob doubted if parents more different from his own would be possible to find.

While the carriage rolled through the leafy streets back to his Mayfair townhouse, he continued to muse on that strange encounter and the mystery that was life in a happy family.

Would he be a different person if he'd had parents who had loved him the way Miss Whitmore's parents loved their daughter? And what kind of man would he be? A respectable man? A family man? One who really was capable of falling in love? One who really did want to settle down with one woman for the rest of his life? That was impossible to imagine and as there was no way he would ever know, there surely was no point even speculating over a question that had no answer.

Once home, he roamed around the house, wondering what he was to do now. How did engaged men occupy their time? All those of Jacob's acquaintance continued to live the same way they always had—a life that involved constant parties and a non-stop round of pleasure—and that did not come to an end after they married. Nor did they cease keeping company with their mistress or mistresses.

But those engaged men did not have a future father-in-law who had threatened to ruin them no matter what the cost. Perhaps he should have thought this through a bit more and selected a woman whose father didn't care how he behaved. Perhaps a father who was blinded by his title would have served his purpose much better after all. But how was he to know that Miss Whitmore's father loved his daughter quite so fervently? Such familial love was not something with which he was acquainted.

But it was too late for that now and he would have to find a respectable way to pass the time for the duration of this engagement. But how? He supposed going to his clubs would still be acceptable, but what fun would that be if he could not go on to a party afterwards?

There was nothing for it. He drafted a note, handed it to the footman and asked him to deliver it immediately. It looked as if he was about to become a respectable man courting a respectable young lady, whether he liked it or not.

* * *

'You must change your dress immediately and get Molly to do something about your hair!' her mother cried out, rushing into the parlour and causing her paintbrush to slide across the canvas, leaving an annoying line of red paint.

'Why?' Margaret asked, dabbing at the damage with a damp rag.

'The Duke has sent a card, inviting you to take a ride in his carriage this afternoon. In Hyde Park.'

'I've already made plans for later this afternoon. I intend to visit Alice and Primrose to inform them of my...' she took in a breath '...engagement.'

'Those wallflowers can read all about it in the newspaper like everyone else,' her mother said, pulling the paintbrush out of Margaret's hand.

She swallowed her annoyance. 'Neither is a wallflower.'

Not any more. That was another reason why she'd been dreading the Season. She'd be all alone in the wallflower corner, without her two friends providing support and good company. 'Primrose is now a young lady of independent means and Alice is a countess.'

'A countess?' her mother said, adopting a facetious tone as if such a title was something to be sniffed at. 'Not as good as a duchess. But you're not a duchess yet, and until you're married you must do nothing to upset the Duke. So, get ready. Now.'

Her mother tossed the brush onto the table, took hold of Margaret by the shoulders and pushed her towards the door. 'And I hope you weren't wearing that dreadful paint-splattered smock when he came to ask your father for your hand?'

'No, I was wearing—'

'Why your father chose that time to meet the Duke, when I was attending my Ladies Benevolent Society meeting, I'll never know. I should have been present,' she added, as Margaret was pushed down the hallway towards the stairs.

Margaret could say her father knew exactly what he was doing when he chose that time, but for the sake of family harmony said nothing and walked up the stairs as commanded. Molly was waiting for her in her bedchamber, heated curling tongs at the ready, presumably already having received instructions from her mother.

'He said he'll be here at three o'clock, so that gives you plenty of time to get ready. Molly, you know what to do.' With that, her mother thankfully departed.

'Right, miss, let's make you beautiful,' Molly said, gesturing towards the seat in front of the dressing table.

Margaret admired her lady's maid's optimism but said nothing and sat down so she could attempt the impossible.

Once she'd been curled, backcombed, plaited and

heaven knew what else, Margaret changed from her sensible grey skirt and dark blue blouse into a cream linen skirt and jacket and a lacy white blouse.

She stood up so Molly could perform an inspection and, once deemed acceptable, her lady's maid handed her a cream parasol and white gloves.

At least her mother had not insisted she be tortured by the strong-handed Gertrude, but it was still a lot of entirely unnecessary fuss. It mattered not how much effort went into her appearance; she was nothing to the Duke. She had heard him say so with her own ears.

Nothing, she reminded herself as she walked down the stairs, trying to fight off those annoying and irrational nerves making her stomach churn.

This drive in his carriage was simply a continuation of the pretence they'd started while at the Earl of Northwood's Kent estate. It was no reason to get flustered. She just needed to keep in mind at all times what the Duke had said to his friend. *She means nothing to me.* All the ornate hairstyles in the world would not change that.

She entered the drawing room and momentarily halted in the doorway, her heart doing another of those vexing flips, just as it had continually done while the Duke was going through the motions of asking her father for her hand.

She lifted her head higher, determined that at all

times she would retain an outward appearance of composure, regardless of what was happening inside her traitorous body.

He stood up and smiled at her. A smile she refused to return, lest she revealed how unsettled his blue eyes could make her feel, and how easily he could undermine the defences she had built up around herself.

She bobbed a quick curtsey, then turned her full attention to putting on her gloves and doing up the small buttons at the wrist, as if such a task demanded her utmost concentration.

Once each button was secure, she looked up to see her mother smiling at her in an exaggerated manner, like the Cheshire cat, presumably as an instruction as to how she was supposed to comport herself in the Duke's company.

Margaret stifled a sigh. This outing was going to be stressful enough without her mother's relentless and not so subtle hints as to how she should behave so the Duke did not *slip through her fingers.*

'I thought I'd take Molly with me as my chaperone, Mama,' she said, just as her mother picked up her own gloves. 'She's been so busy lately.' *Trying to turn me into something I'm not.* 'And I'm sure she would appreciate being out in the fresh air.'

'Oh, well…yes, I suppose that would be acceptable,' her mother said.

She hated disappointing her mother, but being with

the Duke again was going to be enough of a strain. She did not need her mother adding to her discomfort.

'But do come and see me the moment you return and tell me all that you saw and everything you did.'

'Yes, Mama, I will,' Margaret said, giving her mother's cheek a kiss.

The Duke bowed to her mother and she performed a low curtsey, almost reaching the ground, as if being presented to Queen Victoria herself.

Once her mother was upright, the Duke offered Margaret his arm and led her out the house and towards the open-topped carriage waiting for them at the end of the garden path.

'Have you timed this so as many people as possible will see you courting your intended?' she said as he helped her into the carriage.

He smiled, and she'd rather he didn't. He was handsome enough when his face was in repose. When he smiled he became devastating. And devastated was how her nervous system was starting to feel. Why, oh, why did her pulse have to skip at the sight of his eyes crinkling at the edges? And life would be so much easier if her stomach didn't do that ridiculous flip as she watched his high cheekbones lifting and those cheeky brackets appearing on either side of his lips.

He'd said he appreciated her sense of humour, but she could see it would be advantageous to say or do nothing to make him smile or laugh.

'Well, I thought a ride in Hyde Park would be pleasant, and yes, at this time of day almost all of London Society will be present, so there is a good chance we will be seen behaving like a terribly respectable courting couple.'

He took her hand and helped her into the open-topped carriage, and she said a silent thanks to her gloves for keeping his warm skin from touching hers.

To the accompaniment of the horses' hooves clattering on the cobblestones, they left her family's Kensington townhouse, down the tree-lined streets, the soft breeze lightly touching Margaret's cheeks and going some way to cooling them.

They turned into Hyde Park and through the ornate wrought iron gates, the carriage crunching over the gravel. Margaret breathed in deeply, loving the scent of the newly cut grass which had driven out all lingering smells of the crowded city, and hoping it would soothe her frazzled nerves.

She had to admit that it really was a pleasant day to be in the park. And the Duke was correct when he said all of London Society would be present. It certainly appeared that way. Men were exercising their horses, groups of young ladies in fashionable attire, accompanied by their lady's maids or mamas, were walking and giggling together, and couples were strolling arm in arm.

Over at the Serpentine she could see young boys

floating toy boats, little girls were rolling hoops or playing with their dolls, and nannies, walking large black perambulators, appeared to be everywhere.

'I know you want us to be seen by as many people as possible,' Margaret said, turning to face him. 'And that would best be achieved by remaining in the carriage, but I really would like to walk.'

'Then walk we shall,' he said, leaning forward to tap the driver's shoulder.

The carriage rolled to a halt. The Duke helped her down then took her arm and they joined the line of people strolling along the path, Molly following at a discreet distance.

It appeared that Margaret was wrong. They did not need to be in a carriage to draw attention. Almost everyone they passed looked at them with interest. Quite a few women smiled at the Duke, and she was certain several even winked.

She told herself not to be surprised and not to react. That was what this was all about. He needed her to provide him with a respectable veneer. That was what she was doing and the only reason she was here.

'You'll be pleased to hear that Father has already sent off the notice to *The Times* so all of Society will know by tomorrow that we are to marry,' she said.

'Excellent,' he replied as he nodded a greeting to a passing couple. Margaret attempted to ignore the way the lady looked her slowly up and down with a curious expression, as if to say, *Why her?*

That was a look and a question she suspected she was going to have to get used to. Even her father had asked it, and nobody would think her more deserving of capturing the heart of a duke and becoming a duchess than him.

'I must say I was surprised that you told your father what we were up to,' he said, breaking in on her disconsolate thoughts.

'What do you mean?'

'Well, it isn't every father who would accept his daughter becoming involved in such a ruse.'

'Ruse? Oh, you mean telling him it is an arrangement? Well, my father knows how bad my first Season was, how much I hated all the subsequent Seasons and how much I am dreading being dragged to another. Neither of us can stop my indomitable mother, who won't cease throwing me at men until she finds one who doesn't throw me back. Father has simply accepted that I have found an effective way out of an unwanted and difficult situation.'

'That statement has raised so many questions I hardly know where to start.'

'Well, we have a long walk ahead of us if everyone is to see how respectable we are. What do you wish to know?'

'Why was your first Season so bad?'

Margaret huffed out a sigh.

'If you don't wish to tell me, that is perfectly all right.'

'No, it's not that. It's just a tedious story that has probably been told many a time before.'

He waited. Margaret was unsure that she wanted to reveal anything about her past, although she did want him to know what being out in Society was like for a debutante, something he not only did not understand but saw as a source of amusement and ridicule.

She took a deep breath and plunged on before she could falter. 'I thought I had fallen in love,' she said matter-of-factly, as if this was not the most devastating thing that had happened to her. 'I actually thought Cupid's arrow really had struck me and I had fallen in love at first sight, just as you described it to Lady Chedmore.'

'And?'

'The man was…' She hesitated. 'The man was a charmer, a notorious rake and someone who took pleasure in seducing debutantes.'

She felt him stiffen beside her.

'But don't worry. I saw through him before anything untoward happened. I remain completely respectable and still suitable for your purpose.'

Instead of causing him to relax, his body grew tenser. 'Men like that should be horse-whipped.'

She looked up at him in disbelief. 'What? Rakes? Seducers?'

'Yes, men who prey on the innocent.'

'Is that not a case of the pot calling the kettle black?'

He came to a halt and looked down at her, his jaw tense. 'No matter what you may think of me, Miss Whitmore, I am not a seducer and until now have never been associated in any way whatsoever with a debutante.'

She noticed that he did not deny being a rake. But as that was well documented in those newspapers her father thought she did not read, it would be foolish to try and do so. And she would have to take his word regarding his claim not to be a seducer of the innocent. Not that it mattered because he most certainly would not get a chance to seduce her, even if he wanted to, which she had ample evidence to prove he did not.

'So, what happened to this blaggard?'

'Well, he did try to have his wicked way with me, as they say in all the best melodramas.' She laughed off what had been far from funny at the time. 'And let's just say the man discovered a woman can sometimes wield a parasol as effectively as a fencer his sword.'

To prove her point, she gave a quick jab in the air with her closed parasol.

'Good for you. But did your father not do anything about it? He's already threatened to ruin me if I harm you. Surely he did the same with this scoundrel?'

'At first, I chose not to tell Father, and he put my change in mood down to being thwarted in love, which in a way I suppose I had been. But when I saw the man behaving in the same solicitous manner towards another debutante I was so furious I told Father everything before he could cause further harm to another young lady.'

'And?'

'I'm not entirely sure what Father did, but no one saw...' She paused, not wanting to mention that vile creature's name. 'No one saw him again during the Season as he had departed for Australia. I heard rumours that his eminently respectable family were so horrified at their son's behaviour they sent him out there with instructions never to return. I believe in such cases the reprobate is paid to remain on the other side of the world, with the threat that the family will financially cut him off entirely if he ever sets foot in England again.'

'Yes, remittance men, but such a fate is far better than he deserved,' the Duke mumbled. 'I am so sorry you went through such a terrible ordeal. Is that why you hate the Season so much, because you think all men are like that?'

She shrugged, not knowing the answer to that question.

'That does make perfect sense,' he said, as if to himself. 'So why do you keep attending each Season? I would have thought no one could make a woman with your strength of character do anything she did not want to.'

Again, she shrugged, not entirely sure herself. 'For a while I suppose I still foolishly lived in hope of meeting a man who would be all that I wanted in a husband.' She huffed out a derisive laugh. 'But mostly it's because it's just easier to go along with what Mama wants.'

She could have added that it did not take long for her foolish hope to be replaced by cynicism. Despite, or because of, her mother's increasingly desperate efforts to find her a husband, no man showed any interest in her during her second Season. By the third Season she was well and truly confined to the wallflower corner and knew that was where she would find herself during her fourth.

'Am I to assume you never told your mother about what happened?'

'You assume correctly. While Father and I have a relationship based on honesty, with Mother things are slightly different and we do try to protect her. Although, because I never told her what really happened, Mother thinks it was all my fault and I allowed a suitable husband to get away.'

'I see, but your relationship with your father is not *entirely* honest either.'

She stopped walking and stared up at him. 'How can you possibly say that? I never lie to Father.'

'But you did not tell him the entire truth regarding our arrangement.'

'Hmm, well, no, I felt it best, given the reason why you need this engagement, to keep some of the, well, sordid details back from my father.'

'Yes, a good idea, but it is not what I meant. You can't deny that you told him that we plan to marry, which we don't, and never have.'

'If you'd listened more closely to what I said, you would have heard me make it clear this was an arranged engagement. That's all I ever said.'

'But an eventual marriage was certainly implied.'

'I thought it prudent to leave that somewhat vague. What inference my father took from my words is up to him. I never said I intended to marry you.'

He laughed loudly, drawing the attention of several passing strollers. 'With a mind as sharp as yours and your gift for twisting words to your own advantage, I do believe you should be a politician or a lawyer.'

Margaret tensed, remembering what the Earl of Northwood had said, that a quick wit and knowing one's own mind were admirable qualities in a politician, but not in a wife.

'Except, like illustrators for *Punch*, they are two more occupations that do not welcome women,' she said with more bitterness than she intended.

'Well, that should certainly change.'

'On that, we are in complete agreement.'

They continued walking in silence, and Margaret admonished herself for once again becoming upset by that overheard conversation between the Duke and the Earl and wished she could stop going over and over it in her head. It mattered not that he had said she meant nothing to him. He meant nothing to her either. And that was as it should be.

And yet she had revealed more about herself to this man who meant nothing to her than she had intended. Was it because she wanted him to know that once she had been like those debutantes the Earl of Northwood saw as ideal wife material? Was that why she had told him about her horrid first Season? So he would see she had not always been quite so disillusioned? That she had once optimistically hoped that love, marriage and happiness would come her way?

Was she trying to convince him that she had not always been a wallflower but had first retreated to that corner after her unpleasant experience because it felt safe? Then, as she'd become increasingly invisible to the courting men, or in some cases the topic of cruel ridicule, she'd become more guarded, putting that reputed quick wit and sharp tongue to effective use against those offensive dullards, all the while having to deal with the increasingly desperate behaviour of her mother.

They were among the reasons why she was twenty-four and unmarried, but she could only wonder why he had not taken a wife. As the Earl had said, many a debutante would be happy to let him live however he chose in exchange for becoming a duchess. And dukes were expected to marry and to sire a child or two, as the Earl had so crudely put it. There was only one way to find out.

'Tell me, why have you not married? Aren't dukes expected to do so? Didn't your parents insist you marry, have children and carry on the family line?'

'My parents are both dead, so what they expect of me is irrelevant as they're in no position to make demands,' he said with a laugh that did not sound entirely amused.

'Yes, I did know that both your parents had died and I should not have mentioned them. I'm sorry and did not mean to be flippant,' she said quietly.

'Don't be sorry. I'm better off without them.'

She looked up at him, shocked at his statement and certain it could not be so.

'Did you ever meet the late Duke of Rosedale?' he said, registering her expression.

She shook her head.

'Lucky you. The man was a brute, and that was when he was in a good mood.' Once again, he said this with a laugh that appeared to cover a wealth of pain.

'That must have been very hard for you when you were a child,' she said quietly.

'Not really. I hardly saw the old monster. He packed me off to boarding school when I was seven and when I came home during the holidays I stayed out of his way as best I could.'

'And your mother?'

'She died when I was little more than a baby, so I don't really remember her.'

'That's sad, to lose a mother so young.'

'Not according to what my late father said. On the odd occasion he did mention his wife he did not refer to her in the most flattering of terms. Cold and heartless were among the more affectionate words he used to describe her. He never failed to rail against her for breeding such a useless son and feckless heir.'

Again, he punctuated this with a laugh, as if recalling an amusing anecdote, but there was nothing funny about this tale of neglect and cruelty.

Just as she had done, he had tried to make light of something that must have been painful, and that pain had presumably shaped him into the man he now was. And she was sure he would not want her to pry any further into areas he did not want to discuss. She could also tell he would not want words of comfort or sympathy from her, so she squeezed his arm gently and they continued to walk in silence, his revelation giving Margaret much to consider.

While she would never be so deluded as to think the Duke of Rosedale anything other than a libertine, it was apparent that he was a man who had suffered his own share of life's cruelties and had not always lived the life of a pampered peacock, as she had first thought. However, that did not detract from the fact that he was a man with completely different values from her own, even if those appalling values might have been the result of a lack of love and guidance from the two people who should have cared for him when he most needed it.

Jacob never discussed his parents with anyone at any time, and was unsure why he had just done so with Miss Whitmore. Perhaps it was her candid nature that made him feel comfortable doing so. He knew she would not coo over him or shower him with false sympathy, the way so many women would if he discussed his unfortunate childhood.

Perhaps it was her openness about what she had suffered during her first Season that made him talk of things he usually did not even allow himself to think about. Or perhaps it was seeing her happy if slightly imperfect family that made him remember what his own had been like.

Jacob found it impossible to imagine growing up in a family where you were wanted and loved. Maybe if that had been his childhood, he would not have so recklessly pursued warmth and affection in the arms of a stream of women from the time he'd become a young man.

He shook his head. This was getting far too deep and he was in danger of overthinking things. Something else he never did.

Miss Whitmore was lucky to be part of a warm, loving family, even if she might not realise it. And yet having a loving family and a father willing to sacrifice himself for his daughter had not saved her from nearly becoming the victim of a scoundrel who preyed on the innocent for his own twisted gratification.

He had little doubt that she had been referring to the Earl of Covington as he knew of no other rogue who had suddenly departed for Australia. The man was beneath contempt. Jacob could recall many a time when Covington had boasted about young women he had deflowered, as if it were a sport at which he excelled. On more than one occasion Jacob had let the man know in no uncertain terms what he thought of him, but obviously to no avail as it hadn't stopped him.

He hated to think that Miss Whitmore put him in the same class of men as that low-life. Anger at Covington was quickly overcome by a guilty little voice gnawing at his conscience. Was he not also using Miss Whitmore for his own ends, just as that scoundrel had done? Did it make it all right because it was mutually beneficial? And was it really? This engagement could be depriving her of the opportunity of meeting a man whom she did want to marry. A man who would be worthy of such a spirited and engaging young woman.

And she did deserve to be with a man who could love her and make her happy. A man who appreciated all she had to offer and wasn't after some chit of a girl who would make a compliant wife, as his friend Henry and so many of the men who attended the Season were seeking.

If she met the right man, a man who knew how to give and receive love, a man unlike him, he could easily imagine her as a happily married woman and a protective, loving mother. She should not be denied that opportunity.

'Miss Whitmore,' he said, knowing he had to broach the subject of love and marriage, even though both those topics made him as uncomfortable as discussing his childhood.

'Yes?' she said, looking up at him.

He coughed to clear his throat. 'I believe we should discuss the terms of our engagement.'

'Terms?' She frowned.

'Yes, terms. And one term I believe to be important is that should you meet a man you wish to marry, this arrangement should not prevent you from doing so.'

'I see,' she responded, her voice terse. She walked on in silence, her head lifted high, her lips once again pursed tightly together, and he suspected she did not see at all. 'Am I to take it that was a polite way of saying you wish to be free to associate with other women while we are pretending to be engaged?' she finally said.

'No,' Jacob shot back. 'You really do have a low opinion of me, don't you?'

'Do I?' She frowned at him, as if challenging him to prove her wrong. Something he suspected might be beyond him.

'Are you not the duke who has been linked with countless women, including several well-known actresses?'

That was well documented and required no answer.

'Have you not been mentioned repeatedly in the newspapers as being part of the Prince of Wales' Marlborough House set—a group known for its wild parties and salacious behaviour? Is it not correct that you are facing the possibility of being cited in divorce proceedings because your last lover was a married woman? And am I mistaken in saying—'

'Yes, all right. That is all true. But—'

'Well, then, as this engagement is not real it would be unreasonable of me to insist on fidelity on your part and no doubt pointless. I would, however, caution you to be more discreet in the future than you were with Baroness Winterborne, as my father's threat was not an idle one.'

'Have you finished listing my faults?'

She looked upwards as if in consideration. 'Yes, for now.'

'Good, because I meant what I said. During our engagement, should you meet a man with whom you develop an affection, I will raise no objection to you following your heart,' he said in a stilted tone; this conversation was not a comfortable one.

'Oh, I see,' she said looking slightly abashed, and he hoped this time she really did see.

'And several men showed considerable interest in you during the Earl of Northwood's ball,' he added.

'Hmm,' was her only response.

'Not to be too indelicate—'

'Oh, please don't let me stop you—be as indelicate as you wish.'

He ignored the implied insult. 'Not to be too indelicate, as you alluded on the night of the ball, being engaged to a duke will elevate your status in men's eyes and you may receive a lot more attention.'

She made no response.

'Am I wrong in assuming you still want love and marriage?'

'What one wants and what one gets are not always the same thing.'

'Miss Whitmore, I'm sure such things are still within your grasp. If you just made a bit more of an effort.'

She stopped walking, turned slowly and looked up at him, her eyes blazing. 'If I did what?' she said, enunciating each word slowly.

'I'm not blaming you,' he rushed on, trying to undo the damage. 'After that terrible experience in your first Season, I can see why you want to keep men at arm's length, and that is why you have developed a reputation for having a sharp tongue. But not all men are like that blaggard. There are some good men out there who would make an ideal husband.'

'Men like you?' she asked, fire still burning in her eyes.

'Well, no, obviously not.'

'Like the Earl of Northwood?' Her words were full of derision.

He flinched, remembering how Henry had talked about the debutantes he had invited to his house.

'Well, no, not Henry. Better men than me and my friends.'

'Then there's Edgeware and Templeton. They're not rakes, but can you really imagine me married to a man who can talk about nothing other than how much game he managed to bag during the shooting season?'

'All right. Yes, these are all among the list of men I wouldn't advise you to marry. I'm just saying, despite what you seem to think, my entire sex is not completely useless.'

'I didn't say that.'

'It certainly sounded like it.' Jacob wasn't sure why he was being so defensive, especially as part of him agreed with her. Aristocratic men did tend to fall into one of two groups; the men he associated with, who could perhaps be described as rakes if no other label was available, and the men whose company bored him. The ones who did indeed spend all their time talking about shooting game on their estates or boasting about the bloodlines of their hounds and horses.

'Let's just say that with each passing Season the wallflowers' corner has become more and more attractive,' she said with finality, once again resuming their walk.

'A pity,' he murmured. 'Well, if you're not going to marry, and you can't become a politician, lawyer or cartoonist for *Punch*, do you have any idea what you will do with your life?'

'Fortunately, my father has made it clear that, no matter what my fate, he will always support me.'

He nodded, relieved to hear that. 'And what will you do with your time?'

'I always have my art. That is my passion and it consumes me. Once my mother finally accepts my status as a spinster, I intend to spend my days painting and providing art lessons so I am not a complete financial burden on my father.'

He could point out that most art teachers were male, but that was no doubt something of which she was also aware.

'Have you taken art lessons yourself?'

She sighed. 'Yes, like all young ladies I learnt how to paint watercolours of pretty flowers and trees in the same manner that young ladies have been painting pretty flowers and trees since time immemorial. My art teacher seemed oblivious to all the changes that have taken place in the art world, and certainly did not think young ladies should dabble with anything as messy as oils or draw anything other than—'

'Pretty flowers and trees,' he finished for her.

'Exactly. My teacher had seemingly never heard of Impressionism, never mind the modern movements that have developed out of Impressionism.'

'That's terrible,' Jacob said, not entirely sure if he had either.

She sent him a questioning look and he laughed. 'Oh, all right. I have no idea what you're talking about, and I can see you will have to educate me about art. In our forthcoming outings we will visit London's art galleries, where you can expose me to the wonders of these Impressions.'

'Impressionism, and yes, I'd enjoy that,' she said with a smile which filled Jacob's heart with unexpected pleasure. Despite their earlier disagreement—or was that disagreements?—he still found her company stimulating. As long as he kept off the subjects of love, courtship, marriage, the dearth of good men available each Season, infidelity, the way he lived his life, the people he mixed with and his unfortunate reputation, he was sure they were going to get along splendidly.

Chapter Six

Despite herself, the following day it was an excited Margaret who walked arm in arm with the Duke up the wide stone steps towards the grand entrance of the National Gallery. She loved to visit as many times as possible during each Season. It almost made the London Season worthwhile. Almost.

Usually, these visits were in the company of her mother, who, like an annoying child, would be constantly asking when they could leave and go shopping, or a distracted Molly, who would meander along slowly, doing little to hide her boredom.

Molly accompanied them today, once again following on behind, paying little heed to the couple she was supposed to be chaperoning, and Margaret would not be surprised if she soon managed to lose herself in the labyrinth of rooms.

'So, where should my art education begin?' the Duke asked, looking around the entrance hall and adopting the same lowered voice as everyone else, as if they were now inside a place of worship. That reaction was something she always found appropriate because, for her, being in the presence of so many masterful artworks was akin to a spiritual experience.

'Education?' she asked.

'Yes, I know nothing about art and if you're thinking of becoming an art teacher when you give me the old heave-ho then you should practice what you're going to say to your pupils.'

'If it's an education you want then it's an education you'll get but you might come to regret saying that. This is a rather large gallery.'

'Then it's lucky for you that I am a wastrel duke with all the time in the world. Let's get started.'

Still arm in arm, they crossed the high-ceilinged entranceway, their boots quietly echoing on the marble floor, towards the rooms housing the Renaissance artwork. The deep red-and-green walls, the soft light coming in through the large skylight and the religious nature of many of the works always filled Margaret with a sense of wonder, as if each artist was connecting directly with her soul.

She led him to her favourite paintings and explained why she loved each one, what she thought the artist was trying to achieve, the techniques used, and how the world in which each artist lived affected their subject matter and approach.

Showing none of Molly's boredom or her mother's impatience, he stood in front of each painting and listened attentively to what she had to say, and to her surprise even asked intelligent questions. They slowly strolled past each work, taking in their beauty, but when they walked past Raphael's *Garvagh Madonna* the Duke came to a sudden halt. Margaret stood beside him, saying nothing, knowing from his expression that the depiction of the loving mother and her child had touched him deeply on a level that went beyond just admiring an impressive painting.

As he continued to gaze, transfixed by the painting, Margaret remained silent. There was something about him in this moment, something touching and vulnerable, that made her heart ache for him in a way she would never have expected.

As if emerging from a trance he looked at her, his expression still soft and contemplative. She placed her hand lightly on his arm and was sure that gesture said more than her inadequate words ever could.

They slowly strolled through to the next room, featuring the Dutch masters, then on to the somewhat more modern British painters. The Duke continued to ask questions and listen attentively, but no other painting caused him to react the way *The Garvagh Madonna* had. Something about that painting had touched his soul. It was apparent that Margaret would have to once again reassess her opinion of him. Did this suggest he was not just a dissolute rake, but a man who might be more complex and sensitive than she had previously imagined?

While the Duke never seemed to tire, eventually Margaret started to feel the effects of what was a long walk, and the beauty on the walls could not distract her from how hot her feet had become in her ankle boots.

She removed her pocket watch from her reticule and realised that several hours had passed, and the afternoon was all but over.

'Shall we leave it there for today?' the Duke said as they entered a room containing works by Spanish artists.

She nodded her thanks.

'Although there's still a lot to see and we haven't come across any of those Impressionist paintings you were talking about,' he added, looking around.

'No, they're all a bit too modern and controversial for a public gallery, I'm afraid. We'd have to go to private galleries to see them.'

'Then we will add private galleries to the list of places to visit. I'm sure my art education will not be complete unless I see the very latest and most controversial of works.'

'It will be my pleasure to show them to you,' she said, knowing it would be.

They strolled back to the entranceway and found

a bored Molly waiting for them, seated on a wooden bench.

'At some stage you should visit my estate in Northumberland,' he said as they walked back down the stone steps, followed by Molly. 'Various ancestors have collected artworks over the years, usually while they were indulging themselves during their Grand Tours of Europe as young men.'

'Oh, what works do you own?' she asked, trying to focus on the discussion of art and not on the fact that he had just invited her to his home.

'No idea. I spend as little time at that estate as I can, and I never looked at the paintings when I was a child. Although I remember a few that were dark and gloomy and rather scary.'

From what he'd said of his childhood, Margaret suspected it wasn't just the paintings that were dark, gloomy and rather scary.

'Then maybe you should fill your home with Impressionist paintings. They're so colourful and full of joyful life. Your children would never be scared of them.'

A blush tinged her cheeks and she hoped he was not thinking that she harboured any ambitions of them actually marrying and having children. They'd had a lovely day together, but that did not change a thing about their situation. And she would do well to remember that.

* * *

Jacob opened the carriage door and helped Miss Whitmore and her lady's maid up the steps then took his seat on the bench across from them. He was in a strangely subdued mood, which was not entirely unpleasant. The gallery had been a revelation, and he could not get that image of the Madonna and Child out of his mind. It captured the essence of maternal love. The soft, gentle expression on the mother's face, the baby's complete trust had stirred up something he found impossible to explain.

It could not be a personal recollection. He hardly remembered his own mother and, from all that he had heard, she had not been blessed with maternal instincts.

Jacob could not recall another time in his life when he had spent the best part of a day in quiet contemplation. Quiet and contemplation had little place in a life that involved almost non-stop parties. But he had actually enjoyed himself, and was pleased he'd experienced this rare sense of stillness with Miss Whitmore, particularly as she was so well-informed and had such a passion for art. Not to mention that she was rather delightful company.

He smiled to himself as the carriage wove its way through the busy London streets. Perhaps he was in danger of becoming genuinely respectable, not just acting in that manner. If this continued, by the end of this engagement he might have joined the Temperance movement, sworn off women entirely and become a regular attendee at Sunday church services.

He stifled a laugh. No, not even Miss Whitmore's influence was that powerful.

'What's so amusing?' she asked.

'Oh, nothing. I was just thinking what a surprise today has been and how much I'm looking forward to seeing more art galleries.' It was the truth, just not entirely the truth.

'Yes, I enjoyed myself as well. Thank you for today,' she said and beamed a full, glorious smile at him. He'd seen her smile before, hadn't he?—but not like this. How she looked now was worthy of being captured by a talented artist. While her frown seemed designed to keep everyone at a distance, she now radiated a warmth that made her invitingly approachable.

She definitely should smile like that more often. With her hazel eyes sparkling and her cheekbones flushed a sultry shade of rose she was transformed. Why had he not noticed before what a rather enticing young woman she was? Probably because she'd previously gone out of her way to disguise how tempting she could be, with a cool demeanour and a disapproving glare.

If she'd looked at more men the way she was looking at him now, she most definitely would never have made it to the wallflower's corner and many other men would have seen just how desirable and alluring she was.

He looked out of the window. Apparently, the threat of genuine respectability was still a long way away.

He might have acted like a proper gentleman while in the gallery, but there was nothing gentlemanly about the way he was now thinking of Miss Whitmore. A gentleman would never wonder what those lovely red lips felt like, tasted like. A gentleman would not imagine releasing the clips holding her chestnut hair in place and watching it tumble around her shoulders—shoulders that were preferably naked. And a gentleman most certainly would never, ever contemplate what it would be like to bed Miss Whitmore.

One visit to an art gallery had certainly not changed him from the reprobate he'd always been. If anything, it had stirred up trouble and caused him to forget that Miss Whitmore was most definitely out of bounds. It mattered not how attractive her smile might be nor how tempting her lips. She was a debutante. She was untouchable. He swallowed a groan. And he must spend a year in her company, resisting temptation, acting the paragon of virtue he had never been.

It was that glorious, unfettered smile that had done it. It had brought out his baser nature, which was always just below the surface. Should he ask her to refrain from smiling and return to scowling at him, as he no doubt deserved? Perhaps the problem was that after today's outing she was starting to think he really *was* a respectable man, one deserving of that enchanting smile. He had to make her see that she was wrong.

The man she had just seen, the man she had bestowed that smile upon, was not the man he truly was. Under normal circumstances he did not frequent art galleries. That was not the real Jacob Ashford. He was still the man whose antics regularly made it into the tabloid newspapers. He was a man she thoroughly despised. If he was to survive this courtship, he had to remind her of that.

'Perhaps tomorrow we could visit some of the private galleries and see those Impressionist paintings I was talking about,' she continued, excitement in her voice.

He looked over at her. Those large hazel eyes still shone, those ruby-red lips were still curved, her cheeks still bore an alluring flush. In those few seconds in which he had looked away she appeared to have grown even more striking, more enticing.

What on earth was wrong with him? He was not, and never would be, attracted to Miss Whitmore. That was why he'd proposed to her. Their mutual dislike made her perfect. They could maintain this deception without having to deal with the complication of desire creeping in where it was not wanted.

Why did she suddenly have to start radiating passion and warmth? It was all because of those damn paintings. And now she wanted to expose him to art yet again. It was time to nip this in the bud before she tested his self-control beyond its limits.

'Yes, we should do that. But perhaps tonight you'd like to accompany me to the theatre.'

She frowned slightly as she considered his suggestion and the tension in his body uncoiled.

That would do the trick. In such an environment she would see the real Jacob Ashford. The man who spent his time carousing with actresses. The man who, as she'd pointed out, was part of the Prince of Wales' fast set. The man who did nothing quiet nor contemplative but instead was noisy and louche and not worthy of her smiles.

'The theatre?' she said, her brows knitting together. 'Well, yes, I suppose.'

That was better. As long as she did not smile at him or look at him with anything bordering on approval, he would be safe. It would be even better if she went back to berating him with her sharp tongue and making it clear she saw him as beneath contempt. Hopefully, after a visit to one of his usual haunts, her disdain for him would return and all would be put to rights.

'Which theatre do you have in mind?' she asked.

Well, it wouldn't be anything morally uplifting, that was certain. A visit to the music hall, perhaps. No, that would be taking things a bit far and might fall into the area of behaviour her father deemed worthy of causing his ruination.

'Perhaps we should take in a comedy. Something light-hearted.'

'Oh, yes, that would be pleasant,' she said, and that infuriatingly captivating smile reappeared.

Hopefully, that would be the last time he saw that smile. A trip to the Gaiety Theatre would surely be something Miss Whitmore would not approve of. Nor would she like the fact that he was known to many of the actresses and dancers who appeared on stage.

Yes, seeing him in his own environment would remind her that he was not a man who strolled round art galleries, and certainly not a man who could become so affected by a bunch of brushstrokes on canvas that it left him in a state of awe and wonder.

Then she would go back to snipping and snapping at him, and everyone would be happy.

Chapter Seven

'Don't fuss.' Margaret flicked her head back to stop her mother from once again trying to rearrange the surprisingly springy ringlets Molly had so artfully created.

She knew she was being fractious and was aware that her mother thought she was being helpful, but she *was* fractious, and her mother was *not* helping.

Yet again, an exhaustive amount of time had gone into making her as pretty as possible. Molly had got to work on her hair the moment Margaret had announced her evening plans to her parents. Alterations had been made to her pale green silk gown, and Gertrude, along with her strong hands, had been summoned, despite Margaret's objections.

Given the time and attention that had gone into dressing her, she was starting to feel like an offering who had been prepared for the Duke's approval.

She closed her eyes and placed her hand on her

roiling stomach as an unsettling vision invaded her mind, one where she was a sacrificial virgin, bathed and bedecked with flowers for presentation to a worshipful god.

She shook her head to drive out that unwanted imagery. That was the last thing she wanted to think about if she was to retain a shred of composure tonight.

Margaret stood up and frowned at her mother as if this was all her fault. She was sure she would not be quite so flustered if her mother wasn't still hovering around her bedchamber, filling the air with her contagious anxious energy.

Her mother smiled, lifting up her hands at the sides of her face, to indicate how Margaret was supposed to comport herself. Margaret's frown deepened.

Tonight was not about courtship. It was not about impressing the Duke. This visit to the theatre was just another chance for them to be seen together in public. That was all. Many of the people the Duke associated with would frequent art galleries. It made sense that he would escort her to the theatre, where they could present themselves to Society as a respectably engaged couple.

Yes, it was very sensible. She glanced at herself in the full-length looking glass and patted her hair. And hopefully it would also be an enjoyable evening. Margaret loved the theatre but rarely got a chance to attend, neither of her parents having any interest in the performing arts. This evening would merely be a pleasant outing and had nothing to do with sacrificial virgins or Greek gods.

Her hand dropped from her hair and she clenched her fists tightly together to steady her nerves. Why did she have to think of gods and virgins yet again? He was just the Duke of Rosedale, for goodness' sake. A man who needed a fake engagement to save his lover from the divorce courts. Not a god. Not even close. And sensible women like her did not let men like him affect their equilibrium.

With that firmly in her mind, she pulled on her elbow-length white evening gloves and did up the small pearl buttons, then paused, her fingers toying with the last undone button.

But he was also the man who had gazed at *The Garvagh Madonna* as if it had touched him deeply in the core of his being. No, that was an aberration she thought as she quickly did up that last button and picked up her reticule. Most of the time he was a frivolous, superficial peacock who flirted with every woman he encountered and led a dissolute, completely soulless existence.

Fighting to keep that at the forefront of her mind, she descended the stairs, her mother following behind, still attempting to further fluff out her train, then entered the drawing room.

The Duke stood up and smiled at her, and she was certain that if a statue of a Greek god could smile, this would be exactly how he would look.

'You look divine,' he said almost reverentially. Was he gazing at her in that manner for her parents' sake? Of course he was. Her nerves were already frayed; the last thing she needed was to start thinking the Duke was seeing her as a woman to be admired.

'Doesn't she just?' her mother gushed, once again giving a ringlet a light pull, causing Margaret's head to flinch backwards. 'As pretty as a picture. She's going to make such a beautiful bride and a dazzling Duchess.'

'I think we should leave now,' Margaret said before her mother could cause more embarrassment. If that was possible. 'We should not be late.'

The Duke bowed to her parents and said his goodbyes, but that didn't stop her mother from following them out into the hallway, still trying to make last-minute adjustments to Margaret's hair and gown.

'I believe tonight you won't be needing Molly as your chaperone,' her mother said, causing Margaret's heart to sink. Would her mother be accompanying them?

'As you're officially engaged to be married now,' she continued as a disappointed Molly retreated up the stairs, 'I believe it will not breach propriety if you go to the theatre unaccompanied.'

Thank goodness for that.

The Duke once again bowed goodbye and to Margaret's relief they escaped from her fussing mother.

'I'm so sorry about my mother,' she said as the carriage drove through the night-time streets.

'Nothing to be sorry about. Your mother loves you. That is something to be treasured. And isn't a mother supposed to take pride in her daughter?'

Margaret could have said that he wasn't the one who'd had to endure several hours of having his hair styled and restyled and undergoing the ordeal of being cinched into a corset so tightly he thought his ribs were going to break, all so that he could make his mother proud. Nobody subjected him to such tortures so *he* could look attractive for *her*. And yet he managed to do exactly that. Dressed in evening attire of black suit, white shirt and tie, with a gold brocade waistcoat, he was the one who looked divine, and it was all so effortlessly achieved.

'What theatre are we going to?' she said instead, not wishing to think about his effortless good looks for a moment longer.

'The Gaiety Theatre.'

Margaret's head tilted slightly as if she had not heard correctly. She'd expected the Theatre Royal perhaps, or maybe St James's Theatre, but the Gaiety? 'I've never been there. It's not a theatre Father entirely approves of for young ladies.'

'Well, your father's not here tonight, so it's a chance for us to be a bit wild and reckless.'

'Perhaps,' Margaret answered, her nerves not soothed by the thought of doing anything that could be classed as either wild or reckless.

The carriage came to a halt in front of the well-lit building. The footman quickly lowered the steps and the Duke jumped out then held out his hand to help her down. Margaret looked up at the ornate façade of the three-storey building, topped with a domed roof. It certainly did not look like a den of iniquity, not that she actually knew what a den of iniquity looked like.

His carriage moved off and was quickly replaced by the next in the jostling line. Margaret and the Duke joined the other elegantly dressed men and women shuffling through the doors towards the foyer. They entered the building and the hubbub of countless voices greeted them. Excitement replaced nervousness as Margaret found herself caught up in the crowd's anticipation of the night's entertainment.

On the Duke's arm, she walked up the sweeping staircase and he led her to a private box. She stood at the entrance and couldn't stop herself from smiling with delight. It really was like being a princess. On the few occasions she had attended the theatre with her parents they had always sat in the ground floor seats. She had never for a moment imagined she would ever be one of the people sitting high above the crowd in a private box.

Like a queen, she took her seat on the plush velvet chair and, leaning forward, her gloved hands on the gilded balustrade, she looked out at the auditorium. The stalls below were filling up with women in beautiful gowns and men in evening suits. She looked up to the gallery, which was packed full of people one rarely saw at the more exclusive theatres, presumably also dressed in their finest clothing, even if they were rather shabby compared to the wealthy patrons below them.

But one thing they all had in common was that they were all abuzz, eagerly awaiting tonight's performance.

The gas lights lowered. The multitude of voices silenced and the red velvet curtain lifted to reveal a row of young women standing on the stage dressed in scandalously short skirts, showing not just their ankles but most of their calves, their tight bodices cut so low that Margaret wondered how they avoided falling out of them.

The audience erupted into thunderous applause, seemingly not as shocked by their appearance as Margaret. She joined in with polite clapping as the dancers began their routine by kicking their legs high in the air, exposing more than just their calves. Despite her discomfort, Margaret did have to admire the precision of their footwork, their energy and artistry. But still, she hated to think what her father would say if he knew the Duke had taken her to such a place.

When the energetic dance came to an end, the theatre once again filled with riotous clapping and even some whistling and stamping of feet. Several men in the stalls stood up, their hands raised above their heads as they clapped enthusiastically. Margaret was aware that some aristocratic men took young ladies from the theatre as their mistresses and had to wonder if that was what she was witnessing, men showing approval for their mistress's performance. She took a quick sideways look at the Duke. He too was a man known to associate with actresses and chorus girls. Had any of those young women she had just witnessed performing that risqué dance been, or still was, his lover?

He was clapping politely, rather than standing up, whistling or stamping his feet, but he was hardly likely to show his enthusiasm for his lover when he was supposed to be passing himself off as a respectable engaged man.

Margaret grimaced as a band tightly gripped her chest, and her sudden shortness of breath could not be attributed entirely to her constricting corset.

What she was experiencing was jealousy, that much was clear. What she didn't know was why. It was a ridiculous and inappropriate emotion. It mattered not whether he was or had ever been involved with any of those beautiful and decidedly athletic young women.

She had always known he was a rake. She, along with most of Society, had read the scandalous reports on what he and his friends got up to. He'd been linked to numerous well-known actresses and was presumably on intimate terms with many of those dancers as well. She knew this. Had always known this. But such knowledge had no effect on what she was feeling, as irrational as it might be.

Damn it all, she wasn't just jealous of the Duke, but also of those beautiful young women. They were women who were not restrained by the rigid rules of Society. They were not trussed up in tightly fitted whalebone corsets that made their movements stiff and rigid. They could dance freely and take lovers should they choose.

And worse than that, she was jealous of any of those young women who had discovered what it was like to be held by the Duke, to be kissed by him, to be caressed by him, to know what it was like to be made love to by such a devastatingly handsome man. That was something she would never experience. That was what was making her miserable, and angry with herself for feeling destructive emotions.

The last of the applause finally settled and the curtain raised once more. This time the actors on stage performed a light-hearted musical comedy that had the audience reeling with laughter. Margaret forced herself to keep smiling as if she too was amused by their antics so she would not reveal her sudden despondency.

When the play came to an end, and after several curtain calls, the lights rose for the intermission.

'Is everything all right?' the Duke asked, and Margaret mentally castigated herself. She did not want him to think she cared one single fig for the way he lived his life or was affected in the slightest that he regularly took women to his bed. Or even worse, that he might realise she was pathetically burning with jealousy over what those women had shared with him—something they would never share.

'Yes, perfectly,' she said, sending him a fake smile.

His raised eyebrows suggested he did not believe her, so she smiled even brighter, which did not cause those eyebrows to lower.

'Shall we take a walk during the intermission?' she said in a deliberately cheerful voice. 'That is the point of this excursion, is it not? To be seen by Society as a respectable engaged couple.'

'If you wish,' he said, looking at her sideways as if she was showing signs of derangement.

He led her out into the corridor, which had filled up with well-dressed ladies and gentlemen, talking together in small groups, while liveried servants rushed around providing glasses of wine.

The Duke removed two glasses from a footman's silver tray and handed one to Margaret. She took a sip, then another one, then a quick third, hoping the crisp bubbles of the champagne would wash away all her ridiculous notions, drive out her embarrassing emotions and soothe her rioting nerves.

They didn't.

A group of young men swaggered over to them, and the Duke gave a low groan.

'Jacob, I hear you're engaged,' one young man said, looking at Margaret, a supercilious grin on his face.

'Yes, may I present Miss Margaret Whitmore, my fiancée. Miss Whitmore, the Earl of Penvale.'

'So it's true,' another young man said, staring at Margaret as if she were an exhibit in a curio cabinet.

'It is,' the Duke said, and introduced Margaret to the other young men, who all bowed, with matching smirks on their faces.

She could hardly blame them. Their engagement had been sudden and for many people would be completely inexplicable. Margaret knew what they all must be thinking. If he had to marry, then why her? And she suspected they were coming up with explanations that did nothing for either her or the Duke's reputation.

One of the men, whose name she had forgotten,

leaned in to whisper in the Duke's ear. 'After the performance we're going on to a party at Penvale's townhouse. It should be a riot. You must join us if you're not otherwise engaged.' He looked at Margaret and laughed, as if he had made the funniest of puns.

The expression on the Duke's face suggested he found the man's attempt at humour as funny as she did. 'Not interested,' was his quick reply, before he took Margaret's arm and led her away.

'I'm sorry about that,' he said once they were out of earshot of his friends. 'They can be rather boorish at times.'

'And yet they are your friends.'

'Yes,' he said, drawing out that one word as if admitting to something he'd rather not.

'And if you wish to go to that party, don't let me stop you. That was our agreement, was it not? We won't stop each other from living our lives however we want.'

'Yes, that was our agreement,' he said, and that tight band gripped her chest with greater ferocity. No doubt there would be actresses and those pretty, high-kicking dancers at the party, and one would spend the night in his arms.

'But I do not wish to attend a party tonight, particularly not a riotous one.'

The gripping band of jealousy loosened slightly and Margaret was more pleased than she should be.

'Oh, no,' the Duke muttered, just as she was about to take another sip of her champagne.

She followed the direction in which he was looking and saw a couple walking towards them, arm in arm. The man was slightly shorter than the woman, flushed of face, and bore the expanding girth common in middle-aged men, but the woman was nothing less than stunning.

Perhaps she was an actress; her elegant demeanour and confidence suggested that. And she was certainly attractive enough to grace the stage, with her dramatic flame-coloured hair, her striking good looks and a smile that could light up any theatre.

Margaret doubted she had ever felt more frumpy or insignificant in comparison and hoped the couple would do no more than say good evening and move on.

Instead, they stopped in front of them and both looked at Margaret, the woman bearing the same questioning expression as the Duke's friends.

'Baron and Baroness Winterborne, may I present Miss Margaret Whitmore,' the Duke said. 'My fiancée.'

That tight iron band clamped her chest again like a torture device, making breathing all but impossible. Hoping to cover her shock, she bowed her head and made a low curtsey, praying her unsteady legs would not give way beneath her.

With as much composure as she could summon, Margaret rose to standing and made herself smile at that vision of beauty as if her name meant nothing to her.

'Yes, I read in the newspaper you were to marry. My congratulations,' the Baron said to the Duke, then nodded to Margaret. 'It's a pleasure to meet you, Miss Winterborne, and I wish you every happiness for the future.'

Margaret's jaw started to ache as she continued smiling. Was the man serious? He was talking to his wife's ex-lover, the man he had threatened to drag through the divorce courts, as if they were old friends.

The Baron bowed his head once more, then the two sauntered off and joined another group of chatting patrons and the Duke released a long, slow, audible breath.

'Again, I am so sorry about that,' he said.

'No need,' she said crisply, as if she was not still reeling from that disturbing encounter. 'It looks as if this visit to the theatre has achieved its purpose. We've been seen by the very people you want to convince this is a real engagement, and the Baron's behaviour suggests you have had a lucky escape from the ignominy of the divorce courts.'

'But I didn't wish to subject you to that.' He inclined his head towards where the Baron and Baroness were standing, chatting and laughing with their friends.

'Really? I thought subjecting me to *that* was the whole point of our engagement and the point of coming here tonight.' Margaret knew she was sounding ill-tempered, despite having no real reason to be, but it was better than sounding jealous, and that was undeniably what she was feeling.

'Would you like to leave?'

'Not at all. I'm sure there are many other people you need to parade me in front of so you can convince them of your new-found respectability.'

'You are angry. We should go.'

Before she had a chance to object, to convince him she was not angry, not jealous, not shocked, all the things she actually was, he was leading her down the stairs and out into the cool evening air towards his carriage.

Without waiting for his help, she climbed inside, telling herself to stop acting like a petulant child. She knew what he was like. She knew he was the type of man she should never, ever be attracted to. But, unfortunately, she also knew that no one felt jealousy unless they were being subjected to a powerful attraction, whether they wanted to be or not.

She was tempted to punch the lush velvet upholstery of his carriage in anger and frustration. She had done exactly what she had told herself not to do, what she had thought she was far too sensible to do—she had fallen under the Duke's spell.

As he took his seat on the bench beside her, she stared straight ahead and made herself breathe slowly and deeply. What was done was done. She *had* fallen completely and hopelessly under the Duke's spell. It was foolish. It was irrational, but there was no point continuing to pretend otherwise.

What she needed to do now was settle down, think clearly and work out what on earth she was to do about this entirely unwanted emotional insanity.

Chapter Eight

Jacob should be pleased. He had got exactly what he'd hoped for. This trip to the Gaiety Theatre was supposed to be a way of reminding Miss Whitmore of the sort of man he really was. He wasn't a man who wandered around art galleries. He wasn't a man who was touched by the beauty and wonder of art. He was a man who attended riotous parties with men like Penvale. He was a man who had a series of lovers, including Helena Winterborne.

She had seen exactly what he was like tonight. The way she was now looking at him held not a hint of the undeserved admiration he'd seen earlier in the day. Her expression had returned to the one he was used to seeing, her jaw lifted, her lips once again turned down in a frown, her body stiff with disdain.

And yet he was not pleased. The discomfort he was feeling was more akin to shame and regret.

He'd liked the way she had looked at him earlier

today—more than liked it. It was as if she'd seen him as a man worthy of her respect and admiration, as a better man than the one who regularly appeared in the gutter press. When she'd smiled at him with such warmth and affection it had terrified him, and he'd wanted to make it stop. Now, he wanted to see that smile again.

He should have taken her to a different theatre, one his friends did not frequent, somewhere he was unlikely to cross paths with a former lover. If such a place existed.

Instead, he had ruined everything. Now she hated him. He had to make this right.

As the carriage jostled its way through the still busy streets, he tried to think of something to say that would undo the damage caused by tonight's encounters with his friends and Helena. But what? *I'm sorry for being the man I am? I'm sorry that I am not, have never been and never will be a better man? I'm sorry I am not a man you could ever respect or admire?*

The carriage came to a halt outside her family's townhouse and still they had exchanged not one word. His footman opened the carriage door and Jacob reached over and closed it. They could not part like this. He had to say something.

'Miss Whitmore, I can tell you are angry with me and I believe we should discuss what happened at the theatre before you leave.'

'No, not angry. There is nothing to discuss.' She shuffled across the bench and reached out to the door handle.

He placed his hand on her arm to stop her progress. She froze, slowly looked down at his arm, then just as slowly raised her head and released a slow sigh.

'Oh, all right. Yes, I was angry about meeting Baroness Winterborne. And yes, I have no right to be. And it's hardly news to me that the woman is your lover.'

'*Was* my lover,' he said quickly, although that made no real difference. 'And I had no idea she was going to be at the theatre.'

'Nor should I care what your friends obviously think of me,' she continued.

'I wouldn't worry about them, and thinking is not something they do much of.'

That caused a slight curl at the edges of her lips, for which he was disproportionately grateful. But the smile disappeared as quickly as it had appeared.

'But you are correct. We do need to talk about what happened tonight.'

'Good,' Jacob said, although, apart from apologizing, he was unsure what he could say.

'It is apparent that tonight achieved the purpose you intended.'

He nodded, then frowned. How could she know his intention had been to show her just what a cad he really was? An intention he had achieved but now regretted.

'So I can see no need for us to have any future outings together.'

'What?' he blurted out in unaccountable panic. 'No, Miss Whitmore, I can assure you that in future—'

She held her hand up to stop his words. 'You needed an engagement so Baron Winterborne would not continue with divorce proceedings. Tonight, he could not have looked less like a man who intended to divorce his wife. Your ploy has achieved its aim. All we need to do now is to find a way to end this pretence.'

'No, we can't do that.' The words were out before Jacob could stop them. What was wrong with him? He should be relieved, not crestfallen. He should not feel as if something treasured was being ripped away from him. But he did not want this engagement to end, especially not like this.

Her eyes widened and she shook her head as if waiting for him to explain. But how did he explain when he didn't know himself why he had made such an objection. Hadn't he now got exactly what he'd wanted? Helena's reputation would not be destroyed in the eyes of Society. Life had returned to normal. He could now get back to his old life. She had offered him a chance to escape. Shouldn't he take it?

A thought occurred to him. 'Putting paid to those divorce proceedings was only part of our agreement,' he said quickly, before he could question the wisdom of what he was doing. 'In exchange for your help, I was to save you from the horrors of the Season. If we end this arrangement now, you'll be back on the market.'

A pained expression crossed her features and he knew she could see the truth in what he was saying.

'And after a failed engagement, your mother will be even more desperate than ever to get you married off.'

That was a somewhat underhand tactic, but it achieved its aim. She closed her eyes tightly as if the thought of another Season was even more unbearable than the thought of spending more time with him.

He waited for her response as eagerly as a real suitor seeking encouragement from the woman he wished to court. Why he was reacting like this he could not say. All he was prepared to admit was that it was the right thing to do. They had made an agreement, and just because that agreement had already resulted in a reconciliation between his ex-lover and her husband, that did not mean he could weasel out of his obligations and abandon her to the strutting roosters and the torment of her embarrassing mother. Yes, that made more sense than any other possible explanation as to why he was acting so out of character.

'Are you sure you wish to continue?' she asked quietly.

'Yes, I can think of no woman in the world I would rather have a fake engagement with than you.'

This resulted in another slight smile, and after all that frowning it was a glorious sight. Jacob's gaze moved to her lips, before quickly flicking back up to her eyes.

What on earth was wrong with him? Wasn't stopping her from looking at him in this manner the very reason he'd taken her to the Gaiety Theatre tonight? Wasn't he trying to make her disapprove of him? So why was he now trying to make her smile? Why did he want her to think well of him? And worse than that, why did he want to spend time with a woman who meant nothing to him and would never mean anything to him?

This was all getting very confusing. It was so much easier when he associated with women like Helena Winterborne or with any of the stream of other lovers he'd had in his life. With them he never had to indulge in all this aberrant soul-searching, nor had he ever felt the need to question his motives or what it was he wanted. His motives and what he wanted were always very clear and as lacking in complexity as it was possible to get.

'So, what do we do now?' she asked. 'You no longer need to parade me in public to give you an appearance of respectability.'

That was true, but wouldn't being in public be a lot safer than spending time alone together?

'I believe we should spend time together out in Society, just to keep your mother happy and make her think we are courting. Perhaps we can attend a ball or two together, or go to the theatre on occasion.'

Her arched eyebrows rose up her smooth forehead.

'Respectable theatres,' he added quickly. *Ones my friends and lovers never frequent,* he could have added, but he did not want to bring the conversation back to the source of her anger with him. 'And we still haven't seen those new impressions.'

She smiled at his deliberate mispronunciation. He did love that smile, the way her lips curved slightly at the corners, and a soft flush bloomed on her high cheekbones.

'No, you wouldn't want to miss out on those impressions, would you?'

Like a genuine courting couple, they continued to smile into each other's eyes, while the flickering carriage lantern bathed her with a soft golden glow and made her eyes appear to dance.

'Visits to the galleries would be wonderful, and I would like to attend the theatre again, but are you sure you want to accompany me to balls?'

'I believe I owe it to you after all you've done for

me. And who knows, maybe you'll meet a man during the Season, one whom you'll want to have a genuine courtship with,' he added, trying to ignore his resentment towards that man.

And looking the way you do tonight, so achingly lovely, how could any man resist you?

'It hasn't happened so far, so I doubt it will happen this year either.'

'And I believe that it is very likely to happen,' he said softly.

'Yes, well, being engaged to a duke does increase my attractiveness in men's eyes,' she said with a small laugh that sounded fake.

'No, because you are a beautiful, enchanting woman and sooner or later some man is going to realise that.' He knew he shouldn't do it, but he couldn't resist moving back a stray lock of hair and tucking it behind her ear, lightly stroking her soft skin as he did so.

Her lips parted as she gazed into his eyes, her chest rising and falling quickly as she gasped in quick breaths. He had made a mistake. He should have kept his thoughts to himself and he most certainly should not have touched her.

Despite the intimacy of their surroundings, they were not lovers. Hell, they were barely friends. They were simply two people who had come to an arrangement for their mutual benefit.

'Just don't choose a man like me,' he added, trying to make his voice jovial, and annoyed that it held a strained quality.

She said nothing, just continued to gaze at him, her eyes shining, those full red lips still temptingly parted.

'Choose a man you can love and who can love you in the manner you so rightly deserve.'

His words were hardly out when, as if he was being granted a wish he knew he should not ask for, those beautiful, soft lips were lightly kissing his.

Margaret's hand snaked around the back of the Duke's neck and she cursed her evening gloves for keeping the touch of his skin from her fingers.

She should not have kissed him, should not still be kissing him. Margaret knew that, but his gentle words had stripped away the last of her resistance until she no longer knew what was right and what was wrong. All she knew was what she wanted.

And this was what she wanted.

She'd wanted his kisses so desperately that every inch of her body burned for that forbidden intoxicant. And now that she'd had one taste, like any drug, she wanted more—so much more.

Oh, yes, this was what she had to have.

She kissed him harder, loving the smell of his expensive sandalwood cologne, that underlying masculine scent, the feel of his rough cheek against her smooth one, but mostly loving the taste of him. A taste she could not get enough of.

Her hand ran through his hair, weaving possessively into the curls as her lips continued to taste his.

She'd fought hard enough to deny the effect he had on her. When jealousy had consumed her on meeting his ex-lover, she'd tried to be appalled by him. When she'd imagined him taking one or more of those high-kicking show girls as his lover she'd tried to tell herself she was not envious but outraged. When the truth was that she longed to feel what those women had felt when he took them in his arms.

Now she did and it was glorious.

If he'd tried to seduce her, she knew she would never have kissed him. Her guard would have come up immediately. Her notorious sharp tongue would have lashed out at him. Instead, he made her feel beautiful, desirable, a woman who was sure to find a man who would love her, but right now that was not what she wanted.

She wanted no other man. Just him.

'We shouldn't,' he said, his voice a husky growl, before his lips trailed a line of kisses down her neck, each kiss sending waves of warm pleasure cascading through her body.

He was right. They shouldn't. But each touch of his lips on her sensitive skin further stoked the fire burning inside her and she knew she would not be stopping until he quenched it.

'Yes, we should,' she murmured, and angled her head, exposing more of her neck to his nuzzling lips.

Oh, yes, we most certainly should. But she wanted more than just his kisses, as glorious as they were. She wanted to feel his caressing hands on her body, wanted to explore the skin and muscles under his shirt. She wanted to lose herself to every pleasure this magnificent man could give her.

To that end, she wrapped her arms around his back and sank down onto the carriage bench, taking him with her.

His body covered hers, the delicious weight and warmth seeping into her, and his kisses once again found her lips. Both hands encircled his head and she kissed him with a fervour which she could not control.

His tongue moved tantalisingly over her bottom lip, and she parted her lips wider in response. When his tongue entered her mouth she released a sudden gasp of surprise, then gave herself over to the exquisite sensual pleasure as he kissed her harder, deeper, with more insistence.

Writhing beneath him, she returned his kisses and rubbed her soft breasts with their tight sensitive peaks against his firm chest, each stroke sending ever increasing heat pounding through her body.

Margaret knew she was lost. Lost to him. Completely.

'Unhand my daughter, you scoundrel,' an angry male voice burst into her dazed mind. The Duke sat up immediately, taking her with him.

Unsure what was happening, she looked towards the open door and her enraged father glowering at them. Behind him, peeking over his shoulder, her mother was beaming like a child on Christmas Day who had received every present she had ever wished for.

Margaret's hand shot to her mouth to cover the gasp trying to escape, and her body, which seconds before was tingling with pleasure, now burned with embarrassment.

'Winifred,' her father said, 'take your daughter inside while I have words with the Duke.'

'No, Father. You don't understand…' Margaret said, finally finding her voice and fully taking in the seriousness of what her parents had just witnessed. Feeling mortified at being caught by her parents in a passionate embrace was really the least of her problems.

'I understand perfectly,' her father snapped. 'Get inside, Margaret. Now. I will deal with this situation.'

'No, you've got it all wrong.' She turned to the Duke. 'It was all my—'

The Duke lightly placed his finger on her lip. 'It's all right. Do as your father asks. We'll talk later.'

No, it was not all right. It was all wrong and it was all her fault. But she could see her furious father was not going to listen to reason, so, with her mind a tempest and her body heavy with embarrassment, she stepped down from the carriage and followed her mother up the pathway.

'There's going to be wedding bells a lot sooner than we planned,' her mother trilled as they entered the house.

'What?'

'After what your father and I just witnessed, there's no other option.'

'Oh, no!' Margaret gasped, moving quickly towards the nearest chair and collapsing into it before her legs gave way beneath her. 'This is a disaster.'

'No, it's not. It just means things will happen a lot more quickly than you had inexplicably insisted and we'll get the Duke up the aisle before there's any chance of anything going wrong.'

Margaret looked up at her mother, who was still smiling fit to burst.

'Did you plan this?'

'How could I possibly do so?' her mother said, trying to look the picture of innocence but failing miserably.

'Is that why you sent us off together without a

chaperone, because you expected this to happen? Is that why you waited before coming out to the carriage, and came yourself rather than sending a servant to escort me inside?'

Her mother giggled. 'Margaret, dear, what do you take me for? As if I would put my only daughter's virtue in such jeopardy by sending her off to the theatre alone with a man if I had even the slightest inkling that any of this might happen? And yes, perhaps I should have instructed a servant to escort you inside, and not waited until I saw the carriage start to rock before insisting your father go out and see what the delay was, but what's done is done and there's no point thinking about any of that now.'

The two women stared at each other, one smiling, one scowling, then Margaret collapsed back into the chair. She had been played and her mother had won this round. But she still did not have her victory and Margaret would be doing everything in her power to make sure this marriage did not take place.

Her father entered the drawing room, his face like thunder. 'It's all settled. The Duke will apply for a special licence and the two of you will be married within the week.'

Margaret jumped to her feet while her mother clapped her hands.

'What? No!' Margaret shouted over her mother's squeals of joy. 'No, Father, that's not fair!'

'It is fair,' her father replied, pacing up and down as if trying to walk off his rage. 'And at least he had the decency to suggest the immediate wedding before I demanded it of him.'

'No, you can't force him to marry me.'

'I am not. You were already going to wed, but his actions mean it must happen a lot sooner than planned. My God, he has known you for less than a week. You've been officially courting for only a few days and already he's taking liberties.'

'It wasn't like that. He didn't take liberties.'

Both parents watched her intently, her father's face still red with anger, her mother still looking triumphant.

'I know what I saw, Margaret,' her father said.

The last thing Margaret wanted was to have this embarrassing conversation with her parents, but the Duke could not be punished for something that was not his fault. 'He didn't kiss me. I kissed him.'

Her father's brow furrowed more deeply. 'You kissed him?'

'Yes,' she said, relieved that he had understood so quickly.

'Then you'll have no objection to marrying him sooner than you intended.'

'What? No! That's not fair. I kissed him, so he should not be punished by being forced into a marriage he doesn't want.'

'He's not being forced into marriage. The two of you are engaged.'

Margaret drew in a deep breath and gritted her teeth together to steady herself for a conversation she did not want to have with her father. 'Yes, but we never intended to marry,' she said quietly.

Both parents stared at her and her mother finally stopped grinning.

'It was just a mutually beneficial arrangement between the two of us, but we never intended to actually go through with the marriage,' Margaret continued, forcing her voice to remain steady. 'The Duke hoped an engagement would make him look respectable and save him from…' She paused, knowing what she was about to say would not redeem the Duke in her father's eyes, but also knowing she now had no choice but to tell the entire truth. 'An engagement would hopefully extricate him from a scandal with Baroness Winterborne, whose husband was threatening to divorce her and cite the Duke as her lover.'

Her father's hands curled into fists, making it clear that such honesty was not really helping. 'And what do you get in exchange for saving him from a husband's justified wrath?'

'I wouldn't have to go through another Season.'

Both parents continued to stare at her as if trying to grasp what she was saying, then her father nodded slowly while her mother's beaming smile returned just as bright as before.

'None of that matters now, Percival,' she said to her husband. 'The Duke kissed her, remember? He took liberties. He has to marry her.'

'He didn't kiss me, Father. I kissed him,' she said, driving home her point.

'Why?' her father asked.

'Why what?'

'Why did you kiss him?'

'What?' she repeated.

'It's a simple enough question. If you don't want to marry the Duke, why did you kiss him?'

It might be a simple question but Margaret had no idea how to answer it. Should she tell him that something about the Duke made her ache with desire? Should she tell him about the jealousy that had consumed her at the theatre when she had met his ex-lover? Should she mention how he'd looked when he'd gazed at *The Garvagh Madonna*? Would her father understand? Did *she* understand?

'I don't know,' she said instead.

'Well, it matters not. You will be married within the week and that is the end of the matter,' her father said, causing her mother to once again clap her hands, and for Margaret to sink back into the nearest armchair, completely defeated.

Chapter Nine

After such a dramatic evening Jacob had not expected to sleep a wink, but he had easily fallen into a deep slumber, and would still be there if a loud knocking on the door of his bedchamber had not roused him.

'Come,' he called out and his valet entered.

'There's a young lady waiting downstairs, Your Grace. She says it's vital that she speak to you.'

'What time is it, Bates?'

'Just gone eight-thirty.'

Jacob rubbed his hand across his face and huffed out a breath. There was only one young lady who would arrive at his house at such an ungodly hour, uninvited. His future bride.

He climbed out of bed and pulled on his silk robe.

'Hot water is on its way so I can shave you, Your Grace. And should I lay out the grey suit?' Bates moved towards the wardrobe.

'Don't worry about that. If Miss Whitmore has turned up at this ridiculous hour uninvited, then presumably it is a matter of some urgency and she's not going to care whether I'm unshaven or what I'm wearing.'

'Very good, Your Grace,' Bates said, showing no reaction to this impropriety.

'It's not what you think,' Jacob said, not entirely sure what his impassive valet ever thought. 'Miss Whitmore and I are now to be married within the week and not at the beginning of next Season as… er…planned.'

This did get a slight reaction from Bates, whose eyes briefly grew wide, before he quickly recovered and his face once again adopted the mask of a well-trained servant.

'Very good, Your Grace,' he repeated, an answer he would no doubt give to any statement Jacob made, no matter how surprising or outlandish. 'Would you like coffee served in the drawing room?'

'Excellent. Yes, black and strong, please.'

Pulling his robe tightly around his naked body and knotting the belt at his waist to make certain he was completely covered, he headed towards the stairs, not entirely sure what was about to greet him.

Last night's kiss had certainly changed everything, and not only because he was now locked into this marriage. He had seen a side to Miss Whitmore he had suspected might exist but now knew for certain. A passionate nature that was simmering just beneath that tightly controlled surface. And soon that simmering woman was to become his wife. What he thought about that he was unsure, but there was one thing about which there could be no doubt. He would have to accept a forced marriage, just as many men had done before him, and he was sure many other reckless fools would have to do in the future.

Marriage was a state he most certainly was not champing at the bit to enter, far from it, but, as Mr Whitmore had said last night, he knew the consequences of his actions. He would just have to accept his punishment for that one fateful lapse in judgement.

But that one fateful lapse in judgement had also given rise to many confusing thoughts he couldn't even begin to sort out. So he had gone with the easiest option and chosen to leave those thoughts to a later date—a date which hopefully would never come.

But one thing required no thought whatsoever. He knew Miss Whitmore wanted this marriage even less than he did. If the events of last night had occurred with any other young lady, he would suspect it had all been intentional. But when her mother had all but dragged her away from his carriage, she did not have the appearance of a woman who had got her wish. Quite the contrary.

He entered the drawing room to find Miss Whitmore pacing up and down on the Oriental rug.

'To what do I owe this unexpected honour?' he asked.

'We have to do something,' she stated, not stopping her frantic pacing. 'We have to find a way out of this.'

He crossed the room and gestured towards an armchair, a gesture she ignored.

'You know there is no way out of this,' he said, watching her pace. 'Your father caught me kissing you. We both know the penalty for that.'

He frowned, wondering if describing their forthcoming nuptials as a penalty was appropriate, but Miss Whitmore's expression did not change, so presumably she thought the same.

'It's all your fault, you know,' she said, momentarily stopping in her pacing to glare at him.

Of that Jacob had no doubt. He had kissed a debutante. Every man knew what happened if you were caught kissing a debutante. You were up the aisle before your feet had time to touch the ground. That was one of the many reasons why he had always avoided such women. Until now.

'Yes, I apologise,' he said, genuinely sorry for what he had done for more reasons than he could mention, although among them was the strange way that kiss had affected him. That was something he was struggling to understand, especially as it had been little more than a brief kiss. It had aroused the usual physical reaction of course, but it had stirred up something else as well, something indefinable. But that too could be consigned to the list of things to be thought about at a much later date.

Bates entered with a coffeepot and two cups. Quietly placed them on an end table and just as quietly departed.

Jacob poured the coffee and held a cup out to Miss Whitmore. She flicked her hand in the air and frowned, which presumably meant, *No, thank you. I do not wish to drink coffee.* Nor did she take a seat, so he would have to drink his much-needed pick-me-up while standing.

'I gave you the option to call this whole engagement thing off,' she continued. 'Why on earth did you not take if? If you had, none of this would have happened.'

Jacob took a sip of the thick black coffee then placed the cup on the mantelpiece. 'That's why you're angry with me? For agreeing to continue our fake engagement for the rest of the Season?'

'Yes.' She paused in her pacing to scowl at him. 'If you had not, we would not be facing the prospect of a forced marriage.'

That was debatable, but he suspected Miss Whitmore was in no mood for a spirited debate. 'I believe it was your father catching me kissing you that sealed our fate.'

She stopped pacing, closed her eyes briefly and then looked in his direction, a blush tinging her cheeks. 'Yes, I'm sorry about that.'

'You're sorry? What on earth have you to be sorry about? We both know I should not have kissed you, and I should be the one asking for your forgiveness. So, once again, let me say I am truly sorry for my behaviour last night.'

He picked up his coffee cup then placed it back in the saucer. Was that true? He regretted being caught and he certainly regretted having to get married, but could he say in all honesty that he regretted kissing Miss Whitmore? Kissing her had been unlike anything he had experienced before, and that was why he had not listened to the commands of that underused sensible part of his mind. He'd ignored that little voice reminding him that he had a debutante in his arms and instead had given in to what he knew to be madness.

'You didn't kiss me,' she said, causing his eyes to widen and his brows to rise.

'You appear to have a very short memory. I definitely kissed you. I remember it well.' Too well.

'No, I was the one who kissed you.'

Yes, that was right. Her lips had touched his first. It had been as surprising as it had been welcome, but surely, who'd kissed whom first was an irrelevant technicality, and it hadn't taken long before he'd most certainly been kissing her back, and for that he now had to pay the price.

'I am truly sorry,' she added.

'No need to apologise,' he said with a laugh. 'I for one enjoyed it.' And her behaviour last night made it patently obvious she'd enjoyed it as well, although her severe expression today would contradict that claim.

'Well, yes, it's not that I didn't...' She bit her lip, a surprisingly shy gesture for such a forthright young woman. Jacob watched on, rather enjoying seeing her like this. 'I just mean if I hadn't kissed you, we would not be in this mess now, and that is what I am apologising for.' Her expression was once again stern.

'Well, whoever kissed whom first, whoever is to blame, it hardly matters. Your father caught me, now we are to marry.'

'We don't have to.'

He took another sip of his coffee and waited for her to explain.

'You could refuse.'

'What? I could tell your father that I refuse to do the honourable thing?'

'Yes.'

'Apart from that being the appalling behaviour of a cad—' *which you obviously think I am* '—your father has already said he will ruin me if I do anything to harm you or take liberties with your good name. And I believe he would define last night's behaviour as taking liberties.'

Her brow crinkled as if pained. 'Yes, there's that. He can be so annoyingly honourable at times. But you could refuse to marry me and tell him if he tried to make you then you are prepared to ruin our entire family, leave us penniless and living in the gutter. That might make him listen to reason.'

'So you want me to be a cad and a bounder, not to mention an unforgivable scoundrel?'

'Well, we have to do something.'

'I suspect even the threat of ruin would not get your father to back down when he thinks he is doing what is best for his daughter.'

This perhaps was the downside of having parents who loved and adored you. Something Jacob had never had to personally contend with.

The furrows in her brow deepened. 'Well, maybe if we both go to him together, and tell him how much we don't want to marry?'

'Which will probably beg the question: so why were we kissing?'

She released a deep sigh and sank down into the nearest chair. 'Yes, that's what he said to me last night when I told him it wasn't your fault and I was the one to kiss you.'

Jacob could ask her the same thing. Why did she

kiss him when she had such an objection to him? But he thought it best not to further stir up the hornets' nest by asking.

Instead, he took a seat across from her. 'It might not be that bad,' he said in his most consoling tone.

She looked at him as if he were a simpleton. 'It is *that* bad. You don't want to marry me and I don't want to marry you.'

'We're certainly not going to be the first couple who have found themselves in this predicament and I suspect we won't be the last. Perhaps we should just make the best of it.'

She continued staring at him as if he was proving himself to be a greater disappointment with every word he uttered.

'Nothing much will change,' he continued. 'We can both continue living our lives as we do presently.'

That had been the case for many of his friends. They'd married out of a sense of duty, to increase their family's fortune or to advance their place in Society, and then continued living lives not much different from the ones they'd lived when they'd been single. He and Miss Whitmore could surely do the same.

'In fact, your life might even improve,' he continued, warming to the idea. 'I have a townhouse in London which will be at your disposal whenever you wish.' He waved his hand to encompass the three-storey home reputed to be one of the finest in Mayfair. 'I have a vast estate in Northumberland, along with another estate in Yorkshire and a smaller one down in Devon.'

She still did not look convinced.

'You can convert rooms in any or all of my homes into a studio should you wish.'

This caused her expression to soften. Slightly.

'As a married woman, you will be able to visit art galleries without a chaperone, and you'll be able to have those proper art lessons you want so much. No tutor would turn down a request from a duchess. You'll be able to work with oils and whatnot and paint things other than pretty-pretty flowers.'

The expression softened slightly more. Jacob could hardly believe the absurd situation in which he had found himself, listing the reasons why she should marry him when marriage was the last thing he wanted.

'But what about you?' she asked.

'What about me?'

'What will you get out of this marriage?'

That was a good question. He sipped his coffee and gave it some consideration.

'Exactly,' she said, before he could formulate an answer. 'Nothing.'

That was probably what he would say as well, but

he doubted it was what she wanted to hear, so he continued drinking his coffee.

'And you don't want to get married, do you? You are being forced into an arrangement you do not want.'

Again, that required no answer as she was simply stating a fact.

'Well, I won't do it. I will not marry a man who does not want to marry me.'

'I'm afraid, like many other debutantes, that is exactly what you are going to have to do.'

'No, I am not,' she said, standing up, her expression defiant, her hands planted on her hips. 'I can see you are going to be of no help whatsoever, so I'm going to have to put an end to this nonsense all by myself.'

With that she turned and stomped out of the room.

He raised his coffee cup to her retreating back and wished her good luck, but suspected the next time he saw Miss Whitmore it would be as she walked up the aisle towards the wedding altar.

The man was absolutely hopeless. Margaret would have slammed the front door behind her if the butler had not been standing politely at the open door, waiting for her to leave. As she stormed past him, she could only wonder how many other young women he had held the door open for in the same manner.

Women who were departing in the early hours after having spent the night in the Duke's bed.

Her fury increasing, she climbed back into the waiting hansom cab and gave the driver another Mayfair address. She still hadn't visited her friend Alice to discuss the fake engagement. Now she would visit her and discuss how to get out of this unwanted marriage.

Alice had recently arrived in town, accompanied by her husband, the Earl of Thornwood, so she could visit the publisher of her children's books. She was a sensible woman and Margaret was sure that between the two of them they would come up with a solution to this dilemma.

She knocked on the townhouse door and the footman ushered her into the drawing room. Alice soon appeared and, like the Duke, was dressed in her robe, her long brown hair falling around her shoulders.

'Maggie, dear, what is it? What's wrong?' she asked, rushing towards her friend, her arms outstretched.

'I'm to marry.'

Alice stopped in her tracks, her expression making it obvious that she did not yet realise what a disaster this was.

'But your letter said it was not a real engagement, merely a convenience to get out of attending another

Season. Am I to assume from your expression that this has changed?'

'You assume correctly.'

Her friend called for a maid, then took her hands and led her to the settee. 'Tell me all about it over a nice cup of tea.'

So Margaret did. She told Alice everything, from their first meeting at the Earl of Northwood's weekend party to arriving at his house this morning to confront him. Although she did not mention that the Duke was still in his robe and she had momentarily allowed herself to be diverted by speculation as to whether or not he was naked underneath that thin garment. And had even, for one humiliating moment, wondered what the caressing silk fabric felt like against his skin.

'So you kissed him?' Alice asked, as if that was the most important part of her story.

'Yes, and my, have I come to regret that one impulsive action.'

But was that entirely true? She definitely regretted the consequences of her actions, but she could never really regret that kiss. It had been heavenly. No, that was not correct. It had been devilishly wonderful. The Duke had caused her body to feel things she had not thought possible, and if her parents hadn't interrupted, she no doubt would have urged him to continue giving her such wicked pleasure.

She looked at Alice, expecting her wise counsel, but she was staring at her in a peculiar manner.

'Maggie, I think I know you well enough to be certain you would not kiss a man lightly.'

'No, it wasn't lightly,' she said with a sigh. 'Well, it was to start with, when I first kissed him. Then it became much more...' She saw Alice's bemused expression. 'Oh, you mean it's an action I would not *take* lightly. Well, perhaps...maybe... I don't know.'

Alice waited for her to explain and she knew they would not get around to formulating an escape plan from this marriage until she got the matter of the kiss out of the way.

'All right, yes, I wanted to kiss the Duke. And yes, I find him extremely attractive, but I'm hardly the first woman to be bedazzled by him. The man is so damn handsome it should be illegal. He's a menace to all women.'

Alice looked unconvinced that none of this was her fault.

'I mean, didn't you hear what I said about why we were pretending to be engaged in the first place? Because he has a lover. A married lover.'

'*Had* a married lover,' Alice said, being unnecessarily pedantic. 'So that was the only reason you kissed him, because you were bedazzled by his good looks?'

'Yes. Well, that and because he is charming and

funny and he was being so lovely last night when we were sitting together in his carriage, making me feel, well…um…different, as if I wasn't my usual self.'

Her body seemingly remembering how it had felt before she'd kissed him, her skin warmed and a soft sigh caught in her throat.

'And then there was *The Garvagh Madonna*,' she said, her voice little more than a whisper.

'The what?'

'It's a painting we saw at the National Gallery. The way he looked when he was staring at that painting…' She closed her eyes, recalling the expression on his face. 'It was as if he was mesmerised. He looked like a different man, not the rake I had met at the Earl's party, but a man who could be touched deeply by beauty. A man who had depth to his character. A man who—'

'A man who you could love?'

Margaret's eyes sprang open. 'No one is talking about love,' she gasped out.

'Aren't we?'

'No, definitely not. I admit I rather fell under his spell last night. And yes, I'll also admit I was a fool to kiss him, but I would never be so much of a fool to fall in love with him. Please, credit me with some intelligence.'

'Well, if you're not prepared to admit to loving him, do you think he might just be in love with you?'

Margaret could hardly believe the words coming out of her friend's mouth. She had always considered Alice to be a sensible, rational woman. It would seem she'd been wrong.

'Alice. He is a rake,' she said, enunciating each word carefully and slowly so her friend would finally understand what she was talking about. 'Men like him do not fall in love, and certainly not with women like me.' That surely was so obvious it did not need to be stated.

'Maybe. But you gave him the option to get out of the fake engagement. He didn't take it. You've now given him the option to get out of this marriage. He is a duke and no one, not even your formidable father, can make a duke do anything he doesn't want to. Do you think there is a possibility he *wants* to marry you?'

'None whatsoever. He will go through this marriage because he has to and because he knows it will make no real difference to him. He knows he can continue to live exactly as he always has. That is what he said to me, that this marriage will change nothing. For him, that will mean he can take as many lovers as he wants, and there will be nothing I can do about it.'

Tears pricked at her eyes. 'Alice, last night, when I watched those high-kicking dancers I got so jealous at just the thought of him with another woman. When I met the Baroness I was so consumed by rage it was as if it was possessing me. Once we're married, if he takes a lover I'm not certain I will be able to bear it.'

Her friend held her close and those tears she had been fighting back began to roll down her cheeks.

'Maybe you should tell him how you feel,' she said quietly.

Margaret pulled back from her friend's embrace and furiously brushed away her tears with the back of her hand. 'No, never. It's bad enough that my reckless kiss got us into this situation. If I tell him how much I'm attracted to him he's likely to think this is all deliberate on my behalf. He'll assume I wanted to marry him.'

'But maybe honesty is the best approach.'

Margaret shook her head, as disappointed with her friend as she had been with the Duke. 'No, it is not.'

Alice looked at her with compassion, but compassion was not what she needed. She needed ideas, suggestions, plans, before she found herself trapped in an unwanted marriage with a man who did not love her, who was not attracted to her, and had only kissed her because she'd all but thrown herself at him. What those plans, suggestions and ideas could be she did not know, but one thing she did know for certain—she would not be marrying the Duke of Rosedale.

Chapter Ten

Jacob was right. The next time he saw Miss Whitmore she was walking up the aisle towards him. He couldn't see her expression as it was covered by a lace veil, but suspected it was not a happy one.

Just as he had promised her father, Jacob had immediately applied for a special licence, allowing them to marry within the week. A small chapel near his London home had been chosen for the hasty ceremony. No invitations had been sent out, and only Margaret's family and her two friends acting as bridesmaids were in attendance.

Jacob had no family he'd wanted to invite, and did not wish to ask Henry or any of his other cohorts to be his best man, their attitude to marriage being even worse than his own.

Unbeknown to Miss Whitmore, he had visited her father prior to the wedding day and tried to convince him that this marriage was not in his daughter's best interests and something she wanted even less than he did. He'd apologised profusely. Had assured the man that no one would hear of what had happened. He'd even suggested they continue with their fake engagement so his daughter could meet someone she really did want to marry. Someone who could give her what she surely deserved—love and a happy home. Unlike her, he had no experience of such things and he had no idea how a good husband would behave. She deserved to be with a man who wanted children, not one who flinched at the mere thought.

It had all been to no avail. Mr Whitmore had stated repeatedly that he knew his daughter better than anyone. That she would not kiss a man she did not wish to marry. Nor would she allow any man to kiss her unless she wanted it. Presumably that was a reference to the attack on the Earl of Covington with her lethal parasol.

So, here they were, one week later, standing at the altar. He was dressed in a dove-grey morning suit which his tailor had quickly made for the occasion, and Miss Whitmore was dressed in the white gown she had presumably worn at her coming out, and gripping a bouquet so tightly she was in danger of ripping the pink flowers to shreds.

The two bridesmaids stood behind her, looking as surprised to be in this chapel as everyone else. Only a smiling Mrs Whitmore gave the appearance of being exactly where she wanted to be.

The vicar conducted the service with the required solemnity. When it came to the vows, Jacob did as expected and promised to love and to cherish till death do us part, although in reality the best he could do was promise to try. The honour should not cause any problem. He admired Miss Whitmore immensely and held her in the highest esteem. He would also attempt to cherish her whenever it was needed, but love, well, that might be asking more of him than he was capable of giving.

Having never known love, the giving or the taking, he had no idea what it actually entailed. Unlike Miss Whitmore, he had not been raised by loving parents. One parent he hardly remembered but he'd been told she'd never wanted him. The other had made it clear at every opportunity that nothing about him was deserving of love.

The vicar turned to Miss Whitmore and asked the same questions, including a vow to obey.

The quiet chapel became completely silent as they all waited for her response.

'I will,' she mumbled.

Jacob expected her to add a defiant *not* at the end, or at least to enter into a debate over the *obey* part of the vow.

She did not.

The vicar then proclaimed them man and wife and informed him he could kiss his bride.

It was done. He was married. He lifted her veil tentatively and braced himself in preparation for the sight of an unhappy bride.

Instead of seeing an angry young woman's icy expression, as expected, he looked down on a woman whose beauty all but took his breath away. It was as if every time he saw her she became more attractive. How she managed to do that he had no idea.

She lifted her gaze to meet his. He looked into those hazel eyes, flecked with gold, and detected an unfamiliar shyness as she waited for the kiss that would seal their union. His heart yearned to do what he had just promised, to give her comfort, to make this better for her, but, not knowing how to love, he was uncertain how one achieved that end.

'It will be all right, I promise,' he said quietly, before leaning down and lightly caressing her lips with his.

Then he drew back but continued to gaze down at her, hoping he had not just told her a lie. All he could really do was try, and hopefully he would succeed in making this all right for her, although what *all right* would be he had no idea.

Neither of them wanted to be in the situation they now found themselves, but there was nothing they could do about it, apart from trying to make the best of things, and for him that meant doing nothing that would make marriage to him even more intolerable for her than it undoubtably was.

He gently took her arm and they walked out of the church, followed by her family. He exchanged a few pleasantries with the members of her family and was introduced to the two bridesmaids, Alice and Primrose, both of whom eyed him with suspicious, assessing looks.

No wedding breakfast had been arranged. There would be no speeches. Instead, with almost as much haste as they had been married, they were boarding the night train up to his estate in Northumberland to begin their life together.

Feeling as awkward as a teenage boy in the company of a girl for the first time, he led her to their private compartment. They sat on opposing benches and looked across at each other, her look of stunned disbelief no doubt mirroring his own.

'Well, Miss Whitmore...' Jacob began, 'although I suppose I should call you Margaret now that you are no longer a miss.'

'Yes, I suppose so.'

'And you must call me Jacob.'

'Jacob,' she repeated and the sound of his name caused an unexpected stirring in him.

That was something else he would have to come to terms with. He was becoming increasingly attracted to his new wife, and that would never do. Despite being married, they hardly knew each other, and she had made it abundantly clear on as many occasions as she could that she did not want to be with him. That kiss they'd shared in the carriage had surely been a momentary lapse in judgement, one for which she had been soundly punished, and now the feisty Miss Whitmore had turned into a timid Duchess of Rosedale, all because she had been forced into this marriage.

That was so unfair and would never do. It was time to address her fears and provide some of that comfort he had promised at the altar and put her mind at ease.

'Miss... Margaret, now that we are married, we should discuss the terms of this arrangement.'

'Terms?'

'Yes,' he said slowly, surprisingly embarrassed about what he needed to say. 'We both know you do not want this marriage.'

'I believe that is mutual, Your Grace... I mean, Jacob.'

'Hmm, well, yes.' He ran his hand around the back of his neck, unsure how he should phrase this. 'I dare say your mother gave you a talk about what to expect on your wedding night.'

A blush exploded on her cheeks and even moved down to her neck, making it apparent that such a conversation had indeed taken place.

'I can assure you, Miss... Margaret, that under the circumstances, I will not expect you to...' he swallowed, feeling ridiculously uncomfortable '... I will not expect you to perform your wifely duties in the bedroom and will never, ever put you under pressure to do so.' God, he sounded like a pompous old parson who saw sex as an abomination.

'I see,' she said, looking out of the window as if the passing scenery held much more interest than this conversation.

He could add, *unless, of course, you want to*, but suspected that might constitute putting her under pressure.

'So, we are to be husband and wife in name only,' she said, her cheeks still burning.

'Yes. I assume that suits you?' *Because if it doesn't, I'm more than happy to perform my husbandly duties, if such a pleasure could ever be described as a duty.*

'Yes, it does,' she said, still staring out of the window.

'I thought that would be the case, so I have booked separate sleeping compartments for tonight.'

She nodded without looking at him.

Jacob had never made love on a train, and suspected the rocking motion would add another dimension to the experience, but that was something he was not going to discover, at least not tonight and not with his wife.

'That is very respectful of you,' she said, still not looking at him.

'Good,' he said, for something to say, hoping this was not what marriage was going to be like, a series of stilted conversations as if with a stranger. He'd much rather go back to how they'd been when they were unmarried and sparring off each other.

Like her, he turned to stare out of the window at the passing countryside.

'Look, Margaret—'

'I know you're—'

They spoke at the same time. Jacob indicated for her to continue.

'I know you're trying to make things as easy for me as you can, with that talk about…well, duties and such…and I do thank you for that.' She looked down at her gloved hands, clasped in her lap. 'Because… well…from what Mother said, it is your legal right to expect me to perform…well…you know.'

'Oh, God, no, Margaret, no,' he said, shocked by her words, even though what she was saying he knew to be correct. 'Who cares what the law says? In this case the law is most certainly an ass and should be changed.'

'Thank you.'

'Oh, Margaret, you have nothing to thank me for. I know you think me a cad, but I am not like Covington.'

Her eyes widened. 'I never told you his name.'

'No, but I know of no other brute who was dispatched to Australia. What he did was unforgivable and your father was right to make him pay for what he did. If anything, he got off far too lightly.'

She gave a small humourless laugh. 'Yes, Father could have forced him to marry me.'

Jacob drew in a long breath through flared nostrils, hating that she could ever see him in the same light as Covington.

'I'm sorry, that was unfair,' she said, raising her eyes to look at him. 'And you're right. You're nothing like the Earl of Covington.'

Faint praise indeed.

'So, what were you going to say to me when we spoke together?' she asked.

'I was going to say that even though we are going to be man and wife in name only, perhaps we should try and be friends.'

She said nothing, as if considering his words, then nodded slowly and smiled. Once again, he was struck by how a smile transformed her face. It was so warm and genuine, containing not the slightest hint of artifice and all the more attractive because of it.

He wanted to make her smile as often as possible, even if the effect of that smile might challenge his resolve to just be friends.

The steward knocked politely on the door and informed them that dinner was now being served in the restaurant car.

Margaret stood up immediately, as if wanting to escape the confines of this small compartment, or perhaps it was him she was anxious to get away from.

Jacob wasn't particularly hungry, but dinner would provide a diversion from thoughts of what their marriage would and wouldn't be. And he too would be more comfortable if they were surrounded by others, although he would have to get used to them being alone together at his Northumberland estate.

That was something else her father had insisted upon, saying they needed to give this marriage a chance, and time alone together was the best way to achieve that. Jacob had no choice but to agree, certain that her father's opinion of him was so low that he suspected that if he was not sequestered away in the countryside, Jacob would go straight from the marriage altar to another woman's bed and completely humiliate his daughter.

He slid open the door of their compartment and as she brushed past him her feminine perfume wafted over him. His body instantly recalled what it had been like to hold her in his arms, to be surrounded by the scent of rosewater and her own feminine essence, to taste her sweet lips, to feel her soft body moving against his.

He coughed, while simultaneously trying to hold

his breath so he would not breathe in any more of that enticing aroma.

Just friends, remember. You are not a complete lowlife. You do have some redeeming features. Although at that moment Jacob was struggling to remember what they were.

She walked ahead of him down the narrow corridor. Was it the movement of the train that made her hips sway from side to side in that seductive manner? Whatever it was, that was a part of her body that should not be drawing his gaze.

They approached the restaurant carriage and he reached out to slide open the wooden door, remembering not to breathe in so her scent could not cause inappropriate thoughts to invade his mind.

The train made a sudden lurch. She stumbled backwards. His arm encircled her slim waist, pulling her in towards him to stop her fall. The train continued its steady progress. Neither of them moved. His arm remained around her waist. Her body remained pressed up against his.

Under his hand he could feel the rise and fall of her breath and the warmth of her skin through her dress. His chest was flush against her back and his heart was beating so hard he was certain she must be aware of its pounding.

He glanced down at the curve of her neck. So close.

So tempting. All he had to do was lean down and he could kiss that soft, delicate skin.

The sliding panel was pushed aside and an elderly man stood in the doorway to the restaurant carriage.

'Excuse me,' he said, causing Jacob to drop his arm. They both stepped back as the man edged past them.

Attempting to act as if nothing untoward had just happened, Jacob swept his hand towards the open door to signal for her to enter.

He followed behind her and they took their seats. Their marriage had only just begun and already it was abundantly clear that thinking of Margaret as *just a friend* was not going to be easy. But it was a challenge he would have to rise to, and that would entail doing all that he could to ensure one impulsive body part did not do some rising of its own, no matter how great the temptation.

Chapter Eleven

Margaret tried hard to compose herself. He was just saving her from a fall. That was all. It meant nothing. Her mind knew that. Now she just had to convince her body of that fact. She breathed slowly and deeply, willing her heartbeat to slow down as she tried to ignore how it felt to lean into the hard muscles of his chest, how his arm felt wrapped around her waist and how his masculine scent had surrounded her.

This man does not want you. Yes, he kissed you once, but only because you gave him little option. He only wants your friendship, nothing more.

To distract herself, Margaret looked around the restaurant carriage, pretending to take great interest in her surroundings.

'This is rather nice, isn't it?' she said in her best conversational voice as she took in the table laid in the manner one would expect in the best homes, with polished silverware, glinting crystal glasses and fine china laid out on a crisp white tablecloth. Still avoiding looking at Jacob, she glanced around the carriage, at the wooden panels and polished brass trim glinting in the soft light of the gas lamps. Her wandering gaze was arrested by the sight of the woman staring back at her from the darkened windows draped with maroon velvet curtains.

The woman smiling as if her life depended on it was her. She looked such a ninny, and that was exactly how she felt, like a complete ninny, one who had overreacted to a meaningless gesture. A ninny who had seen his behaviour as a gesture of affection, even of desire, and not just as a way of stopping her from falling flat on her face.

That rictus smile still plastered on her face, her gaze moved to her fellow passengers. Several returned her smile, presumably thinking she was just a friendly young woman and not one so racked with nerves that her face had become frozen and she was doing everything she could to avoid looking at the man who was now her husband.

The waiter handed them menus and asked if they would like champagne.

'Yes, please,' she said immediately, then just as quickly wondered if that was a good idea. Would champagne soothe or increase her nervousness? Before she had answered that question, the waiter filled their glasses with the bubbly liquid.

'Perhaps we should have a toast,' Jacob said, raising his glass.

Margaret raised her eyebrows but not her glass. 'To what? To forced marriage? To our plan for a fake engagement failing dismally? To finding ourselves in a situation neither of us wanted?'

'Yes, to all three,' he said, not lowering his glass but sending her a roguish smile that suggested he found everything, including this marriage, a big joke. 'Or perhaps to making the best of things,' he added.

'You want to drink to making the best of a bad situation, which is our marriage?'

'Yes. Or if that is too much to ask, then let's just drink to friendship.'

Margaret knew she was being ungracious, so lifted her glass and lightly clinked it against his. 'To friendship.'

She sipped her champagne as he opened his menu and scanned the contents. He really was making an effort to try and make things easier for her, and surely it would not hurt her to do the same. It was hardly his fault she was so attracted to him. He could hardly be held responsible for being so damn good looking, so charming, so irresistible.

Nor was it his fault he had found himself in this unwanted marriage. He could have refused to marry her, which so many other men would have done. Instead, he had willingly, or perhaps not entirely willingly, sacrificed himself for her and they were now tied together *till death us do part*, as the vicar had said.

And he was right. There was nothing they could do about it now and they should make the best of things.

'Thank you,' she said, determined to do just that.

He looked up from the menu, his expression questioning. 'For what?'

'Well, for marrying me, I suppose.'

That questioning look did not go away.

'I'm sorry I've been so ill-tempered, blaming you for something that is not your fault.'

'It's been a shock for both of us. It's only been a few weeks since we met. Everything has moved so fast, I think a bit of ill-temper is to be expected, from both of us.'

He really was being so much more gracious than she was, and *he* had not shown a hint of ill-temper at any time, even though he had ample reason to do so. Perhaps she should take her lead from him.

'I apologise if I have ever suggested that you are a cad. You are most certainly not. And you couldn't be more different from the Earl of Covington. If you were, you would never have let Father force you into this marriage.'

'That is the nicest thing anyone has ever said to me,' he replied, that roguish smile once again quirking the edges of his lips.

She smiled back at him.

'And I meant what I said when we made our vows,' he added, causing her smile to fade and her brow to furrow in question. He could not possibly mean that he intended to love and cherish and certainly not the last of those three.

'When I promised you at the altar that it will be all right, I meant it and will do everything in my power to make it so.'

She nodded. Of course he didn't mean that he took his marriage vows seriously.

'Thank you,' she said, knowing she had no right to expect more than that. 'And *I* will try to make this marriage as tolerable for *you* as I possibly can.'

He laughed. 'Perhaps we should suggest that be added to the wedding vows.'

'Hmm, it might be a bit more honest than the ones we just made.'

His eyes grew comically wide. 'What? Are you telling me you really won't be obeying me? I am shocked.'

She smiled at his teasing. 'That one, I'm afraid, I won't even attempt.'

'And thank goodness for that. If you did it would make me very worried indeed. So, these are our new wedding vows: we are going to make things as tolerable as possible, neither is going to obey the other, and we are to be friends.'

'It's agreed.'

She reached across the table to shake his hand. He took her hand in his and gave it a decisive shake. They continued to smile at each other, her hand still in his. She looked into his deep blue eyes. Had she noticed before what an arresting shade they were, reminding her of clear skies on a long summer's day, or drifts of forget-me-nots, and they were certainly captivating enough to make one forget one's train of thought.

'May I take your order?' the waiter asked, and she quickly released his hand.

'I don't know,' Margaret said, still flustered by thoughts of his eyes. 'You can order for me.'

'You're not about to start obeying me, are you?'

'Certainly not,' she responded, then realised he was teasing, so smiled to soften her words.

'My wife and I will have the consommé, followed by the sole, and fruit for dessert.'

He looked at her over the menu for her approval. She nodded, hardly registering what he'd ordered, only aware that he had called her *my wife*. That was who she now was. The wife of Jacob Ashford, the Duke of Rosedale, even if it was in name only.

The waiter collected the menus, bowed and departed.

Margaret made an effort to pull herself together. Despite her inner turmoil, she needed to start abiding by her promise to make things as tolerable as possible. To that end, she made polite conversation, asking about his estates, and he in turn asked her questions about art, a subject she was more than happy to talk about.

The dinner passed pleasantly enough, as if they really were friends, giving Margaret hope that they could do this. They *could* make things tolerable for each other.

When they arose from the table she discovered their fellow diners had all departed. She'd been so caught up in their conversation she had not noticed the other passengers leaving and that they were alone in an empty carriage, nor had she realised it was getting late.

'Your berths have been prepared for you,' the steward informed them, and Margaret could tell that, like the dining car waiters, he was eager for Margaret and Jacob to depart so he too could get to his own bed.

They followed the steward down the swaying corridor and he stopped outside the sleeping compartments, indicated which two were theirs, then departed.

'Well, goodnight,' Jacob said.

'Yes, goodnight.'

They remained standing in the corridor.

'I hope you have a good night's sleep,' he said.

'Yes, you too.' She knew he would not depart until she did, so that was what she should do.

She waited. He waited. This was silly. She needed to leave or they would be standing in the corridor all night.

'Goodnight,' she repeated and lifting herself up onto tiptoes kissed his cheek, in the manner that parting friends would surely do.

Her lips grazed across his skin, his stubble rough under her touch, his masculine scent and taste once again wrapping itself around her. Her lips lingered a moment too long for a kiss between friends, then she quickly lowered herself, turned and fled into her sleeping compartment, leant against the shut door and exhaled slowly.

Never, ever, ever do that again, she admonished herself.

Even a friendly gesture such as a kiss on the cheek was fraught with danger. This marriage would only be tolerable if she kept any feelings completely bottled up and hidden from his view. And that was not going to happen if she went around kissing him willy-nilly.

She remained leaning against the door as she looked around the cabin, which had been transformed into a sleeping area. What she had to do now was get some sleep and try to face the next day with a greater degree of self-discipline and restraint than she had shown this evening.

She took a few more moments to compose herself,

then pushed the service bell. When the steward returned, she asked him to summon her lady's maid. Molly soon arrived and helped her out of her clothing and into her nightgown, then departed. Margeret climbed into the bed, determined to sleep and put this long, confusing day behind her.

Sleep didn't come. Instead, she stared at the ornate ceiling, knowing that behind the wooden panels that divided their compartments he was sleeping. The man she had married had no doubt drifted off into a trouble-free sleep while she lay wide awake, feeling like a complete fool.

She absolutely should not give him even a friendly kiss ever again, she told the ceiling. She must do nothing to remind herself of that fateful kiss that had led to this unwanted marriage. She should avoid getting so close to him that she could smell his expensive cologne or feel the warmth of his body. And she must never, ever give a moment's thought to what it felt like when his arms were around her and his body covered hers.

She gently ran her finger along her bottom lip, still tingling from the touch of his rough skin. It had been a seemingly innocent gesture but there was nothing innocent about the memories it had evoked. Her hand ran lightly down her neck, following the path his lips had trailed the night he had taken her in his arms.

At the time she had wanted his kisses and caresses

to explore more of her body. Her hand tentatively moved across the mounds of her breasts, knowing that was where she had wanted his kisses to go. Her hand cupped her breast and she sighed, remembering what it had felt like to rub herself against him, to feel the sensitive buds tighten against his chest.

That was what she had wanted him to do when she had been in his arms. For him to relieve the exquisite tension building up in her body. Her fingers lightly stroked the tight peak, causing her burning body to grow hotter as she imagined his fingers touching her in such an intimate way.

The pounding in her body increasing with each stroke, she gasped loudly. Her hand flew from her breasts and covered her mouth. She looked towards the wall that separated her compartment from his. How thick were those mahogany panels? Could he hear her? Did he wonder why she had cried out in such a manner? Would he know what she had been doing? What she had been thinking? Would he know what she had been imagining him doing to her?

Her body once again burned furiously, this time from the embarrassment of him knowing how much she hungered for his touch. The wallflower he'd been forced to marry against his wishes because she had thrown herself at him was now fantasising about him caressing her in an intimate manner, while he was unlikely to be giving her a second thought.

It was all too mortifying. The sooner this enforced time together at his Northumberland estate was over and done with, so that he could return to his old life in London and she could begin her separate life as the Duchess of Rosedale, the better.

Chapter Twelve

Jacob watched the light creep around the edges of the thick velvet curtains. His sleepless night had finally come to an end and they would soon be pulling into the final station of their journey.

He pushed the bell to summon the steward and asked him to call for his valet to help him dress and shave.

Margaret's father had given him no indication of how long they were expected to remain cloistered together at his estate. All he had said was that it would be a chance for them to get to know each other, but what more about each other did they need to know in order to maintain this pretence of a marriage?

A knock on the door signalled Bates's arrival, so he climbed out of bed. He'd leave such speculation to a later date.

Once shaved and dressed for the day, he felt somewhat better. Usually, he slept exceedingly well on trains, but usually he did not have a tempting but off-limits woman in the next compartment. Jacob could not remember ever having to spend time of any significance with a woman who was neither his lover nor one who soon would be. Nor had he ever been friends with a woman before. He gave a small laugh. Then again, he'd never been married before either—everything about his relationship with Margaret was a first.

The rhythm of the train changed as it slowed down. A low hiss erupted from beneath the carriage and a gush of steam filled the air, clouding the windows, then slowly dissipated to reveal the busy station.

Whistles shrilled, accompanied by a burst of noise and activity in the corridor. Jacob left his compartment and found Margaret and her lady's maid discussing the organisation of the luggage with a porter.

'There's also…' she paused, pointing towards Jacob '…my husband's luggage, which you'll find in his compartment.'

Jacob could only wonder how long it was going to take her to get used to calling him thus. Perhaps that would be the sign that they had done as her father insisted and *got to know each other*. Once she could refer to him as *Jacob* or *my husband* without hesitating it might mean it was time for them to return to London.

'I sent a telegram before we left London so carriages should be waiting for us,' he informed the woman he now had to think of as *my wife*.

'Good, good,' she said, not looking in his direction, but watching the porter to make sure he had all the bags. The porter and the lady's maid departed, along with their luggage, and she quickly walked off down the corridor, still not looking at Jacob. She hesitated at the door, so he climbed down and held out his hand towards her to help her onto the platform.

Her eyes lowered, she stepped down. It seemed the shy woman had replaced the one who had kissed him goodnight. Perhaps these rapid changes in personality were something he was going to have to become accustomed to, and constituted part of the *getting to know each other* her father had insisted upon.

Taking her arm, he guided her through the swirling melee towards the iron gates at the end of the platform. Steam still hissed out of the stationary train, filling the air, along with the smell of burning coal. Trolleys pushed by uniformed porters and stacked high with piles of luggage rushed by, while passengers disembarked and were greeted by friends and family members, while others were saying their fond farewells and waiting to embark.

They made their way out of the station, but the forecourt beyond was no less hectic. Hansom cabs were waiting for passengers, the drivers touting for business. Newspaper boys were shouting out the latest headlines, while flower-sellers and boot-blacks were weaving through the crowd, plying their trade with cheerful persistence.

Jacob was relieved to see his carriage bearing the Rosedale crest waiting for them, with the driver and footman dressed in the family livery of red and blue.

While Bates and Margaret's lady's maid organised the luggage to be loaded into the second carriage, he helped Margaret up the steps to their carriage. The footman closed the door and they were soon off, driving towards the outskirts of the city.

'Is it very far?' she asked.

'No, not really. We should be there in an hour or so.'

He could add that it was not nearly far enough away. He rarely returned to this estate, leaving everything in the hands of his trusted estate manager, and would prefer to keep it that way. He looked out of the window at the passing scenery and wondered why he had chosen his Northumberland estate to begin this farce of a marriage.

Her father had merely insisted they spend time together on his estate, not specifying which estate. He could have gone to Yorkshire or Devon. Both those estates held bad memories for him, but none as bad as the Northumberland estate. Was he trying to punish himself? Was he trying to remind himself just how unhappy marriage could be by bringing her to the place where his parents had spent their miserable lives together? Was he trying to remind himself of why he would never have children by spending time in the location of his miserable childhood?

Perhaps that was it. He would never want any child to go through that intense loneliness he had suffered as a child, nor that crippling awareness of being unwanted. That was one of the many reasons he had vowed never to have children. And if anything could remind him of that vow, time at his Northumberland estate would do so.

He looked over at Margaret, who was watching him with a quizzical expression. He'd also never intended to marry, and yet here he was. But that was all that would change, and as he had a wife in name only, there was no danger they would ever bring any more unwanted and unloved children into this world.

He turned from Margaret to look out of the carriage window and fought to push memories of his childhood away, as he had done so many times before.

The scenery outside the window had changed from dense rows of soot-smudged houses to the sparsely populated countryside, with its green fields, hedgerows and stone fences. Such pastoral beauty should have provided a sense of calm, but it did nothing to lift Jacob's spirits.

The carriage finally drove through the gold-and-black wrought iron gates that opened up onto a long driveway which led to the house, and his spirits sank even further. This really was a mistake. He should never have come here and he most certainly should not have brought Margaret to this cursed place. If he wasn't careful, Margaret would see a side of him he tried to keep hidden—a morose, joyless man haunted by painful memories he'd rather forget.

The stone house came into view, its three storeys topped with jagged crenellations dominating the landscape, the turrets on each corner adding to its appearance of an impenetrable fortress.

'It's rather grand,' Margaret said, looking out of the window. 'It's almost like a fairy tale castle.'

He continued to stare at the house, at the multitude of windows staring back at him like blank eyes and the strangling ivy creeping up the cold brown walls.

'Fairy tale?' he asked, certain she could not be talking about the same building. 'Perhaps this is where the Big Bad Wolf would live, or the evil sorcerer.'

She looked at him with concern and he made himself smile, not wanting her to think he was doing anything other than making a joke.

The carriage crunched to a halt in front of the house, where all the servants were lined up, waiting to meet the new Duchess. Many of them had worked on this estate when his father had been alive, and

Jacob had no doubt that, like him, they were pleased the old tyrant was no longer in residence.

He led Margaret down the line. She smiled at everyone, asked each servant their name and exchanged a few polite words. That would be a new experience for many. Jacob doubted the former Duke had ever bothered to learn the names of the people who cleaned his house and prepared his meals, and certainly never spoke to them, unless it was to shout commands.

When they reached the end of the line, he took her arm and they walked up the stone steps that led to the forbidding entrance. As a child, these steps had always seemed mountainously high, but, in reality, the entrance was no higher than those at the country homes of many of his friends.

They walked through the entrance and a chill trickled down his spine. His father's portrait loomed over the entranceway in pride of place, where it could not be missed, staring down at everyone beneath with a look of contempt.

'Is that the late Duke?' Margaret asked, placing her hand lightly on his arm.

'It is indeed. That's the old devil, in all his glory.'

Not wanting to linger, he led her through the entranceway towards the stairs, his father's glowering eyes following, just as they had when he was a child.

'I dare say you'd like to have a bath and change out

of your travelling clothes,' he said once they were out of sight of his father. 'I'll leave you in the hands of Mrs Larkins.' He signalled to the housekeeper and looked towards the doors, the need to get out of this house pressing down on him like a heavy weight on his shoulders.

'Yes, and then perhaps you could show me around your estate. It would be good to stretch our legs after that long journey.'

'I'd be happy to escort you around *your* estate,' he said, making it clear that this was now her home, even if it would never feel like his.

'And I suppose I should also bathe and change my clothes,' he added, acknowledging that after the long journey he needed to make himself respectable, even though what he really wanted to do was escape this house before it swallowed him whole.

Something was wrong. From the moment they'd left the station, Jacob's countenance had shifted, and that shift had increased when the carriage had turned into the grounds of his estate. He still wore that charming smile, but somehow it didn't quite fit, as if he was forcing himself to remain light-hearted for Margaret's benefit.

And she couldn't fail to see his reaction when he'd looked up at his father's portrait. A visible shudder had run through him and his features had momentarily hardened, so she barely recognised him.

It was also apparent that he was anxious to get out of this house. So, instead of luxuriating in the warm bath, she quickly washed off the effects of the long train journey, wrapped herself in a thick white towel and went through to her bedchamber, where Molly had unpacked her clothing.

Her lady's maid helped her into a dark grey skirt and white blouse suitable for a walk in the countryside, then she sat on the bed as Molly tied up the laces of her walking boots.

'Do you think you should take your cloak?' Molly said, eyeing the discarded travel cloak, draped over a chair and bearing coal smuts from the train trip. 'I hear it rains all the time this far north.'

Margaret smiled at her lady's maid, who had never travelled this far away from London. 'I'm sure it will be all right. And don't worry, Molly, we'll be back in London soon.' How long that really would be, Margaret had no idea, her father not giving details on the exact time needed for her and Jacob to *get to know each other*.

'That's all right, miss... I mean, Your Grace. I think I'll like it here well enough. I've already met His Grace's valet. Mr Bates is a nice man and he says the servants up here are a friendly lot.'

Margaret was pleased that at least someone was

happy with this arrangement. But, as Jacob had said, they had to make the best of things, so, with that in mind, she headed downstairs to join him.

She passed through the entranceway and was once again struck by how beautiful and well-designed it was. The sun's golden light was streaming in through the expansive windows and the glass dome topping the ceiling two storeys above and reflecting off the black-and-white marble floor and crisp white walls, making it an open, light and welcoming space.

The scent of beeswax hung in the air, suggesting it had recently been thoroughly cleaned and someone had thoughtfully placed a bunch of daffodils in a blue-and-white vase atop a marble pedestal.

She looked up at the portrait of the late Duke. He really did look rather formidable and ruined what was otherwise a delightful space. Given his reaction when they'd first arrived, it was unlikely that Jacob would wish to meet her under his father's grim stare, so she walked out to the steps in front of the house and down to the forecourt, then turned back to admire the house.

It was one of the grandest Margaret had ever been in. She hadn't been joking when she'd said it was like something from a fairytale. From the outside it resembled a magical castle, built in warm honey-toned stone. Lichen and moss had burrowed their way into the stone over the years, giving it an ancient patina, and the ivy climbing up the north wall added to its romantic image.

While Jacob might not like this house, it was apparent that it had been designed by an architect with a masterful sense of proportion, symmetry and beauty.

She turned back towards the ornamental garden and could see that buds had started to appear on the rosebushes. To her right was a woodland, and to her left miles of rolling green countryside that seemed to stretch on forever.

There was no denying this was a magnificent estate.

The sound of boots on gravel caused her to turn towards the path that led around the side of the house and Jacob appeared, his gaze fixed somewhere beyond her and the surrounding garden, towards the distant horizon.

'Shall we?' he said, taking her arm as if anxious to be away from the house.

They walked in silence for a moment, his pace more rapid than one would normally take for a stroll in the gardens.

'Was this your family's main home when you were a child?' she asked, gently broaching the subject.

'Yes, I lived here until I was seven and sent away to boarding school,' he said, his voice matter-of-fact, but his stiff posture suggesting there was much more to that statement than he was disclosing.

'It's so sad the way parents do that. My brother has been sent off to boarding school. Mother cried and cried for days after he left, and I'm sure Father would have done the same if men were allowed to do such things.'

'I don't imagine many tears were shed over my departure,' he said. 'My mother was dead by then and my father was no doubt pleased to see the back of me, and I was pleased to get away.'

'Your father does look rather stern in that painting in the entranceway.'

He laughed, but it did not contain its usual humour. 'I thought the artist rather flattered him and made him look much less of an ogre.'

'I'd like to hear about your father' she said gently.

'I wouldn't want to ruin a decent walk,' he said, giving another of those mirthless laughs.

'You won't.' Without intending to, she moved in closer to him, wanting to do something, anything, to give him comfort.

'I hated him,' he finally said. 'I know that's a terrible thing to say about your father, but it's true.'

He continued walking for a few minutes in silence.

'My parents wanted an heir, or should I say they were duty-bound to produce an heir for the Rosedale line, but they never wanted children, and that was constantly made clear to me.'

He huffed out another humourless laugh. 'The ways

in which he let me know how unwanted I was are countless, but one minor incident came to mind when we first arrived. He caught me running through the entranceway, grabbed me by the arm, almost wrenching it out of its socket, and shook me until my teeth rattled, all the while informing me that all children were an abomination, and I more than most.'

Margaret closed her eyes, horrified that anyone could treat a child like that, just for being a child and doing what children loved to do—run and play. 'How old were you?'

'I'm not sure. It was before I went to school, so younger than seven.'

'And what of your mother?' she asked, her voice little more than a whisper.

'I have no memory of her, which is probably all for the best. Along with informing me that I was an abomination, my father often reminded me how much of a disappointment I was to my mother and that was why she had never been able to love me the way a mother should.'

'They were the ones who were an abomination,' Margaret said, rage at those long-dead parents welling up inside her. 'Children should be loved and cherished, and they should be allowed to be children, and that includes running through entranceways.'

She looked up at him. 'I'm sorry that you were cursed with such terrible parents.'

'Don't be,' he said, once again his lips quirking into a smile that did not look genuine. 'My childhood made me the man I am today.'

It was obvious he was trying to make light of what was a tragedy and she wondered how much of what he had said in jest was true. The more time she spent with him, the less like that strutting peacock he became. There were layers to him that she had not realised existed when she had dismissed him as a handsome rake who revelled in the effect he had on women. But had he turned himself into a man who hid behind a charming façade because he wanted to push away the dark shadows of such an unhappy childhood?

Maybe that was something she would discover during this imposed time together.

Chapter Thirteen

Once again Jacob had revealed more about himself to Margaret than he had intended, yet, strangely, talking about his father had not increased his agony. Rather, that unrelenting pain that had sunk its talons into him the moment the carriage had turned into the long driveway had eased somewhat.

They continued to walk, past the formal garden which, as always, was laid out with military precision, as if even the flowers and shrubs had to bend to his father's will, towards the path that led them through the woodlands.

'Finally, somewhere that brings back fond memories from my childhood,' he said as they entered a grove of oaks, beeches, elms and birch trees. 'This was where I would escape to as a child. It became Sherwood Forest or King Arthur's Camelot.'

'And can I assume you were always Robin Hood or King Arthur?'

'Absolutely,' he said, remembering those childhood games. 'Defeating enemies, saving damsels in distress, slaying dragons. I did it all. And there's something I want to show you. If it's still there...'

He led her deeper into the woodland, the canopy of trees growing thicker overhead so that only filtered light was reaching the soft, leaf-strewn ground below.

'There it is,' he said, coming to a halt beside a ramshackle hut built of rough-hewn stone and untreated timber, its slate roof draped in thick green moss so it almost appeared to be merging with the forest.

'What is it?' she asked.

'A hermit's cottage.' He led her closer to the small entrance. 'It was built during my grandfather's time, when it was fashionable to have an ornamental hermit living in your garden.'

She laughed as if he was making a joke.

'I assure you, it's true. Wealthy people would pay some poor old codger to live alone in a rundown cottage they had built for them.'

'Why?'

'They thought it romantic, or poetic or something.'

'I doubt if it was romantic or poetic for the poor old man living here.'

'Apparently, they were often unfortunate men who had returned from the Napoleonic Wars with their nerves shot to pieces and unable to return to their old lives.'

'How awful.'

'Yes, but my grandparents thought what they were doing was noble. They had weird notions about the dignity of living a simple life and being close to nature.'

'As long as they weren't the ones living the simple life or being this close to nature.'

'Exactly. Do you want to see inside?'

'Yes, I'd love to.'

He pushed back the weather-beaten wooden door. 'Excuse my bad manners, but on this occasion I think I should enter first.'

Lowering his head in a manner he never had to do as a child, he walked through the small doorway. He'd expected the cottage to be in a state of advanced dilapidation, full of spider's webs, with the floor covered in animal droppings, but it was just as he remembered from his childhood—rundown but livable. The rough limestone walls needed a coat or two of plaster, but it looked as if someone had been tending to the cottage in his absence. The flagstone floor had been swept. There was a copper kettle suspended from an iron hook above the hearth and piles of dry wood were stacked beside the fireplace.

Perhaps the gamekeeper or someone else employed on the estate had been using it as a place to shelter and make himself a cup of tea.

'This isn't so bad,' she said, looking around. 'Although I wouldn't want to live here.'

'When I was home for the school holidays I did virtually live here.' He indicated the straw mattress on the small cot in the corner where he'd often slept at night when he did not want to return home to the cold, unwelcoming house and his cold, unwelcoming father.

She scanned the bookshelves, which still contained books from his childhood, including, rather embarrassingly, some by the romance poets, a leftover from his sentimental adolescence.

He hoped and prayed she did not open any of them as even more embarrassing would be the poems he had penned himself and placed inside the books, believing them fit for publication. From memory, they were all odes to girls he'd never met and contained some excruciating rhyming.

'No, don't!' he cried out as she opened a book and pulled out a crinkled page, scanned it then looked up at him.

'Oh, girl of mine, you are so fine.'

Jacob groaned and sank onto the cot, his head in his hands.

'Am I to assume you composed this?'

'I was fifteen,' he pleaded. 'I thought I was the next Lord Byron. I should have thrown those poems away long ago.'

She grinned at him above the paper and continued reading.

'With hair of gold you make me bold, Like stars in the night, your eyes are bright, Big and round and such a delight.'

He groaned again, even louder. 'Please, stop this torture.'

Her teasing expression suggested she would show him no mercy. 'So, who was this fine girl with big, delightful eyes and golden hair?'

'A figment of my adolescent dreams.'

'Well, I'm sure any fifteen-year-old girl would be pleased to receive it.'

'A fifteen-year-old girl with no taste in poetry.'

'Are there any more poems?' She flicked through the pages of the book.

He quickly crossed the room, removed the book from her hands and placed it back on the shelf. 'Unfortunately, I think that was one of my better compositions.'

'You must have been a very sweet young man,' she said, looking towards the book.

'I think that's a contradiction in terms. Fifteen-year-old boys are seldom sweet. Now that you've seen the cottage and I've been completely humiliated, perhaps we should walk through more of the garden.'

He pushed open the door. Still smiling at his expense, she moved past him and stepped outside, then quickly stepped back in. 'Oh, it's starting to rain.'

He poked his head out of the door. 'It's probably just a passing shower, but it would be best if we shelter here.'

'Oh, good, we can pass the time with a poetry reading.'

'I didn't realise you had such a cruel streak.'

'And I didn't know you had a poetical nature. It seemed my father was right. We are getting to know things about each other.'

'Things we'd rather keep to ourselves' he said, taking her arm and leading her away from the bookshelf. 'There's something else about me you don't know and I'll show you if you promise to leave the poetry books alone.'

She looked at him, as if assessing which would provide her with the most amusement. 'All right, what?'

'I am a dab hand at making a fire.'

'Really? No, I don't believe it. You have a house full of servants who do everything for you.'

'I'm not quite the useless aristocrat you seem to think me. When I was a youth hiding out in this cottage, I didn't spend all my time writing bad poetry. The estate manager taught me all sorts of ways to fend for myself.'

Along with the other servants, the estate manager had taken pity on him and knew he often needed to escape from his father's wrath. The hermit's cottage had provided a refuge and the estate manager had taught him not just how to light a fire, but how to prepare the game he caught and how to cook it. If necessary, Jacob could have almost lived out here and become the hermit the cottage had been built for.

'Watch and be amazed,' he said as she sent him an incredulous look.

He piled up some dry leaves in the bottom of the grate, broke up some of the branches piled beside the fireplace into smaller pieces and arranged them on top of the leaves so air would circulate. Then he looked to Margaret for approval.

'Very good,' she said, still with that delightful teasing smile. 'You know how to lay a fire, but how are you going to light it?'

'Well, Robinson Crusoe, who, along with Lord Byron, was a boyhood hero of mine, used to rub two sticks together.'

'Off you go then,' she said, sitting down on the cot as if expecting this to take a long time.

'Or I could do this.' He crossed the room to the small cupboard in the corner, opened one of the drawers and was pleased to see a box of matches still stored where the gamekeeper had always left them. He struck a match on the side of the fireplace, put the light to the tinder-dry leaves and twigs, then watched as the flame caught the smaller branches and flared to catch the larger pieces. Once it was burning, he turned to Margaret.

'*Voilà*,' he said and made a bow.

'That's cheating,' she said with a laugh.

'All I said was that I could make a fire, and that's what I did. I didn't say I was going to do it in the style of a caveman or shipwrecked sailor.'

She stood up and placed her hands in front of the fire as if to check it was a real fire providing real heat.

To make things slightly more comfortable, he picked up the straw mattress and placed it in front of the fire. 'A seat for you, Your Grace.'

With exaggerated elegance, she lowered herself to the ground. He sat beside her and mirrored her action, holding his hands out to the now crackling fire as if in need of the warmth.

'It's rather cosy, isn't it? she said. 'I can see why a child would enjoy playing here.'

He added another piece of wood to the fire. 'It wasn't a playhouse. It was somewhere I felt I could breathe. Somewhere I didn't feel like I was constantly tiptoeing through a minefield.'

She sent him a consoling look. 'I'm sorry you had such a terrible childhood.'

'Well, I made up for all that misery later in life,' he said, trying to return the conversation to the playful mood it had moments ago.

She frowned slightly and he wondered if mentioning his later life was such a good idea when it meant reminding her of the man he had grown into.

'Was it because of your parents that you decided to never marry?' she asked, the question taking him by surprise.

'I am married.'

'I mean really marry.'

He threw a stick in the fire.

'And don't say *I am really married*.'

He picked up another stick and stirred the flaming fire. 'No, I don't think I can blame my parents. I just didn't want to get tied down, I suppose.' Although he had to admit there might be a kernel of truth in what she was saying. He had never wanted to become like his father or have a marriage like his parents'.

'Even to the fine girl with the starry eyes?'

He laughed. 'She was a figment of my imagination. But what of you? Did you ever want to marry?'

'I am—'

'Married,' he finished for her. 'Yes, but did you ever want a marriage that you weren't forced into? A happy marriage, like your parents'?'

'Well, like the fifteen-year-old Jacob, I too had my fantasies. And we have both learnt that fantasies are not real.'

She was right. He knew it, but right now, with the fire crackling, the light drumbeat of rain on the slate roof and a pretty young woman at his side, it did feel as if his fifteen-year-old fantasy had come to life.

Margaret hadn't exactly told a lie. She had never fantasised about sitting on the floor in front of a small fire in a hermit's cottage, the rain pattering lightly on the roof above them, with a man who affected her in ways she had not thought possible. Probably because such a scenario would be more romantic than she could ever have imagined.

But if she had fantasised about such a scene, the man she was sitting next to would be in love with her. He would want to be with her, not just making the best of a situation that was not of their choosing.

'That was a loud sigh,' he said. 'Are you going to tell me what caused it?'

Margaret had been unaware that she had sighed and she most certainly would not be telling him the reason. 'Sitting beside a fire always makes me sigh,' she said. Another half-truth.

'Yes, there's something rather romantic about a fire.'

She tensed, hoping he could not read her mind.

'Perhaps you could compose a poem about it,' she said, aiming to keep a teasing note in her voice.

'What rhymes with fire?'

'Dire, liar, conspire—'

'Ire, quagmire, pariah—' he added, laughing.

Margaret joined in with the laughter, while ignoring the first word that had sprung to mind. *Desire.*

But how could she not think of desire, when sitting next to the most desirable man she had ever met—a man who was her husband, a man with whom her mother had informed her she would soon be sharing the most intimate of experiences? A man who had told her that such intimacy would not be part of their marriage.

She shifted uncomfortably on the straw mattress. She would not think of that. She would just enjoy spending time with a man whose company was becoming increasingly pleasurable, a man with whom she would be friends, nothing more.

'So did you have any hiding places when you were a child?' he asked, and she suspected he too wanted to get off the subject of romance.

'Not as a child, but as an adult I've spent a lot of time hiding from my mother.' She pulled a comical face of horror and was pleased that he laughed.

'Well, you've made your mother happy now and hopefully you'll never again feel the need to wind your way up a pillar and flee through a window to get away from her. She was positively rapturous on our wedding day.'

Unlike the bride and groom.

'I wonder what your parents would think of this marriage?' she asked.

He huffed out a breath and poked the fire with a stick. 'I believe their marriage was an arranged one, so I suspect they would see nothing wrong with people being made to marry against their will. Apart from that, I have no idea what they would think and care even less.'

Margaret picked up a stick of her own and joined him in poking the fire.

'My father certainly disapproved of the man I grew into,' he continued, as if talking to the fire. 'And I have to admit that upsetting him gave me enormous pleasure. While he was alive, every time my name appeared in the gutter press I could picture him storming around his empty house in a state of apoplexy. Even after he died, I could still imagine him turning over in his grave in self-righteous fury at the way I was disgracing the precious family name.'

'But who were you really hurting?' she asked in a barely audible voice.

He stopped poking the fire but said nothing in response and they both sank into a thoughtful silence.

'I think the rain has stopped,' he said a few moments later, looking upwards.

She followed his glance. The patter on the roof had indeed stopped.

He pushed the remaining pieces of wood apart so they would quickly burn out, then stood up and reached out his hand to help her to her feet. 'We should make a move in case it starts again. We wouldn't want to be trapped here all night.'

He sent her another of those devastating smiles that always caused her to quiver inside. 'Although it would provide me with the opportunity to show you my skills in catching and cooking game.'

'It's tempting, but I think I'd rather see what Cook has prepared for us.'

'Very sensible. I have to admit my cooking skills never got much better than my poetry writing.'

They emerged from the hut to a world made fresh by the rain. The canopy of trees had kept the ground almost dry, but water still dripped from the leaves and a lovely clean scent filled the air.

He took her arm and they retraced their path back through the woodland towards the open lawns and past the ornamental garden towards the house, chatting amicably about the gardens and the surrounding countryside.

Margaret was pleased the tense posture he'd adopted when they'd first begun their walk had left him and, rather than moving at a cracking pace, his stride was now more relaxed, his manner more in keeping with a stroll around the tranquil grounds of a country estate.

When they entered the house, they both stopped and looked up at the stern man who had caused Jacob such grief during his childhood. The portrait dominated the entrance and managed to exert an unpleasant influence, as if he was still present in the house and still terrifying his young son.

'You know what we should do?' she said, still staring up at the portrait. 'We should banish your father from this house.'

'What an excellent idea. I should take down that eyesore and put my boot through the old tyrant's face.'

'No, don't do that,' Margaret gasped out in shock, causing him to frown in surprise. 'An artist toiled over that painting and, despite the subject matter, it really is quite a masterpiece. It would be a sin to destroy it.'

'All right, let's just send him off to the attic, where he can join my mother.'

'Your mother?'

'Don't worry, I haven't imprisoned her in the attic. Father put all her things up there, along with her portrait, after she died, and they've never seen the light of day since.'

He stopped a passing footman and asked him to bring a stepladder. When it arrived, she expected Jacob to give instructions to the servant, but instead he climbed the ladder, removed the portrait and handed it down to the waiting footman.

'Right, to the attic,' he said, taking the portrait from the servant. She followed along behind, up two flights of the grand sweeping staircase, then to the narrow uncarpeted stairs that led past the servants' bedrooms, up another even narrower flight and through a small door that led to the attic.

'Right, let's put the two portraits together so they can continue to torment each other for an eternity,' he said, looking around the dusty room, with its boxes, trunks and piles of old ledgers piled against the sloping walls.

'Where is she hiding herself?' He crossed the creaking wooden floorboards, lifted several boxes and moved them aside, then turned around a portrait.

'Here she is.'

He lifted up the painting so Margaret could see. She crossed the room to join him, surprised by what she saw. It was obviously the work of the same artist who had painted his father, but instead of depicting a morose subject, as Margaret had expected, the woman in the picture appeared gentle and reserved. Wearing a ruffled pale pink dress, her hair parted in the middle and pulled back into a bun, she was the epitome of a fashionably dressed mid-century woman. The only ornamentation, apart from her wedding ring, was a gold locket around her neck.

Margaret gazed at her, finding it hard to reconcile what Jacob had said about her being a cold, unloving woman who'd never wanted her only child with the woman who was looking out from the canvas in such a pensive, wistful manner.

One hand was placed protectively over her stomach and Margaret wondered if she'd been pregnant at the time. If so, her gesture was not that of a woman who did not want her child, but that of a woman guarding something precious.

Jacob placed the portrait back against the wall and leant his father's against it, so the two would be staring at each other, but their faces would be hidden from the world.

She looked down at the boxes stacked beside the paintings. Several were full of gowns and day dresses.

'It's a shame all this expensive material is going to waste,' she said, picking up a silk gown bedecked with lace and intricately embroidered. 'Molly is such an expert with needle and thread. She even has one of those sewing machine things and can whip up a dress in no time. I'm sure she could use all this material and make clothing for the servants and your tenants.'

'Tell her to help herself,' he said with a shrug.

She lifted up another beautiful satin gown embellished with finely crafted embroidery. It was a crime that such intricate work had been abandoned to the moths and she knew that Molly would be able to work her magic and create something fashionable with what was left of the exquisite fabric.

She looked back in the box to see what other hidden treasures it contained and found the gold locket Jacob's mother had been wearing in the portrait. Pushing on the small clasp, she flicked it open. One side contained a miniature of the same young lady in the painting, the other was of a small child and a lock of blond hair was curled around inside.

'Jacob, I think this must be you.'

He looked over her shoulder at the contents of the locket. 'It's just a baby. They all look the same and that locket could belong to anyone.'

'No, it's the locket your mother was wearing in the portrait.' She pointed to where the portrait leaned against the wall.

'That proves it's not me. That portrait was painted before I was born.'

Margaret lifted up the lock of white-blond hair. 'But this has to be yours.'

'My hair is much darker than that,' he said dismissively.

'Hair often darkens as one grows older.'

He walked across the room as if suddenly interested in the pile of old books and ledgers stacked in the corner.

She looked back down at the locket and noticed that the miniature of the baby covered another picture. She gently prised off the top portrait and found a miniature of Jacob's dour father.

'She's placed a picture of you and a lock of your hair over that of her husband.'

'Well, we can hardly blame her for that. Even an unwanted child is better than having that ghoul glaring out at you,' he said, flicking through a book and not looking in her direction.

She sighed, let the locket's delicate gold chain curl gently in her hand, placed it to one side and lifted another gown from the box. Underneath, she found a haphazard pile of letters that appeared to have been tossed into the box. She picked one up and scanned the contents, hoping it would give her some insight into the woman Jacob had said never wanted him.

'Jacob!' she gasped out as she picked up yet another letter and quickly read through it.

He stopped what he was doing and looked over at her. 'What have you found now?'

'Letters to your mother. And they are about you.'

Chapter Fourteen

Jacob removed the letter from Margaret's hand and quickly read the contents, not sure if he wanted to hear his mother's cruel words, but determined to face the cold facts, no matter how unpalatable.

> *My dearest Charlotte, it is always a joy to receive your letters and to hear of little Jacob's latest exploits. Walking already! I think you might be right that he is the cleverest of children, although mothers always think their child is brighter, sweeter and more beautiful than any other child. Although, as you insist on telling me, yes, in Jacob's case, I'm sure this is correct...*

Frowning, he flicked to the signature and discovered that it was from his mother's mother, a woman he had never met.

He continued reading the letter, which then went on to discuss local gossip about people he had never heard of, and ended with the mother counselling the daughter on how she should be the one to temper her husband's bad moods and reminding her that it was the wife's duty to create a harmonious home so that her husband did not feel the need to constantly correct her and point out her faults.

Jacob winced inwardly, knowing that nothing anyone could ever do would have stopped that curmudgeon from finding fault with everything and everyone.

He picked up another letter and quickly read the contents to see if that one letter was an aberration. It wasn't. The next one, and the one after that, and the one after that, were all of the same nature. They began with the grandmother gushing over something supposedly remarkable he had done, such as learning to say a few words, or hugging the gamekeeper's dog, or trying to help the maid as she cleaned the steps, then went on to recount the local goings-on, and ended with further advice on how to turn a tyrant into a loving husband.

He placed the letter back in the box, picked up the locket and opened it. Had he been wrong about his mother all along? Those letters had not been sent to a cold, unloving mother, but one who had adored her child—a woman who'd had to live under the same tyranny which had made his childhood so miserable.

'I'm so sorry,' he said, looking towards the portrait

that had been dumped in this dusty room when she had died at a young age. Jacob wasn't sure what he was sorry about—for believing the lies his father had told him, which were obviously designed to hurt him, or for all that she had endured at the hands of his father, or for not cherishing her memory all these years but continuing to disparage an innocent woman.

He went over to the portrait of his mother and picked it up. He looked down at her gentle face, at that tentative smile, and once again whispered how sorry he was.

'Right, let's hang this where it belongs,' he said, heading out of the attic door, the portrait tucked under his arm.

They retraced their steps down the narrow attic stairway, onto the slightly wider stairway that led past the servants' rooms, then down the grand staircase that took them to the entranceway. The efficient footman had removed the stepladder, so he stopped a passing servant and asked him to bring a ladder and a duster.

A quick, bemused frown flicked across the man's face before he bowed and rushed off. The servant was right to look surprised. It was unusual for a duke to wield a duster, but his father had dumped this portrait in the attic and left it to gather dust. It was only right that her son would be the one to clean it and place it where it belonged.

The man returned, carrying the stepladder, followed by a maid with a duster. The footman placed the ladder in front of the empty spot where his father's portrait had been, and the maid moved towards the painting, cloth at the ready.

'Thank you,' he said, holding out his hand.

The maid looked towards the footman, who gave an almost imperceptible shrug of his shoulders, then she placed the duster in his outstretched hand.

'Right, off you go. I can manage.'

Still looking at him as if he might have gone mad, the maid bobbed a quick curtsey and the two retreated. Jacob set to work, removing the build-up of dust on the gilt frame and gently stroking the cloth across the portrait to ensure none remained on her lovely, kind face.

'So you dust as well as lighting fires,' Margaret said, an amused lilt in her voice.

'I am a man of many talents,' he said, stepping back to examine the portrait to assure himself it was spic and span. Then he climbed up the steps and hung it where it belonged.

Once he'd climbed down, he stood beside Margaret and they both looked into the eyes of a woman he wished he'd known.

'She's transformed this entranceway,' Margaret said. 'Instead of being confronted by a scowling man who appeared to be saying you weren't welcome in his house, you'll be greeted by a woman with a kind and gentle expression.'

Jacob nodded. She was right. Hopefully, generations to come would see his mother looking down at them and feel her love.

His eyes slammed shut. Where on earth had that thought come from?

There would be no generations to come, or if there were, they would be from a distant branch of the family, not his progeny. He looked over at Margaret, who was still gazing up at his mother, and sadness descended upon him once more.

This marriage really was a travesty. She too would make a wonderful, loving mother but this forced marriage to him had deprived her of that chance. She was trapped in a situation she did not want, just as his mother had been. He looked back up at that kind face and wondered what advice she would give him in this situation.

As expected, his mother said nothing, just continued to gaze down at him with that tender expression, leaving him to speculate what she would have thought if she'd known what kind of man her son had grown into.

Jacob was certain she would not have been impressed. He'd spent his entire adult life taking pleasure in horrifying his father with his dissolute ways. If his mother had lived, would he have become a different man? Would he have tried to make this woman proud of him? As pleased as he was to find those letters, or rather, that Margaret had found those letters, he now felt completely off-kilter, no longer knowing what to think and not entirely sure of who he was any more.

Margaret had expected Jacob to be buoyant after discovering that his mother was not as he had believed, but he was strangely subdued.

Was it because he was thinking of all he had missed out on? Was he wondering how different his life would have been if she had lived? He would not have been that sad, traumatised child who had to flee to the hermit's cottage. He would have had one parent who loved him.

'What's wrong?' she asked.

He turned towards her, his expression sorrowful. 'I let her down,' he said quietly.

Margaret shook her head slightly as he turned to look back up at the mother he had never known.

'I can't imagine what she would think of the man her son has grown into.'

'I'm sure she would be pleased her son became such a good, kind, thoughtful man.'

He looked at her sideways. 'We're talking about me, remember? The man whose antics regularly appear in the gutter press.'

'I'm not saying you're not without your faults,' she said with a smile to soften her words.

'That's somewhat of an understatement.'

'But, well, everything that has happened since we met would not have happened if you weren't good, kind and thoughtful.'

His brow furrowed and he shook his head in disbelief as if she were talking gibberish.

Margaret had now found herself in the bizarre position of defending behaviour that not long ago she would have seen as indefensible, but she hated to see him looking so downcast when he should be celebrating.

'You wanted to save your...' she paused '...your mistress from the disgrace of a divorce based on infidelity.'

'Ex-mistress.'

'Well, yes, but in doing so you were acting in an admirable manner. One could almost say you were being gallant.'

His eyebrows drew close and his expression suggested he thought she was losing her mind, and she had to admit she was pushing the definition of gallant somewhat.

'Then you married me because we were...' again, she paused '...caught in a compromising position. You didn't have to do that.'

'I did. Your father threatened to ruin me.'

It was her turn to send him a look as if he were talking nonsense. 'You're a duke. You could have got out of this, despite Father's threats.'

'But putting you in a position where we had to marry was not the behaviour of a good, kind or generous man.' He sent her a defiant look, as if challenging her to deny it.

'If I remember correctly, you did not put me in this position. I put myself in this position.'

'Hmm,' he said, looking back up at his mother. 'But you are now in the same position as my mother, stuck with a man you don't want to be married to.'

'Jacob, you are nothing like your father,' she said, lightly placing her hand on his arm.

'God, I hope not,' he said quietly.

Margaret drew in a long, slow breath before she continued. 'A man like your father would never tell his bride that she was...' she drew in another strength-giving breath '...was under no obligation to do her wifely duty. I'm sure a man like your father would not have tried to reassure his wife that they could just be good friends. I doubt a man such as he would do all he could to make the best of this situation and encourage his wife to do the same.'

'Hmm,' was all he replied as he continued gazing up at his mother's portrait.

'I know she would be proud of you, Jacob. I know she would have loved the man you grew into.'

Just as I do, she could add, that realisation breaking over her like a wave that had breached the cracks in her defences, washing away the last of her determined resistance to the truth.

She closed her eyes and breathed in and out, slowly and deeply, as she collected herself, then opened her eyes and turned to face him. He was gazing at her, and she was sure tears were glinting in his blue eyes. She took his hand and gave it a gentle squeeze.

'I believe it is you who are kind, generous and thoughtful,' he said, returning that gentle squeeze. He looked back up at the portrait. 'Another thing I have in common with my father is we both married women who were far better than we deserved.'

'Well, I'm not going to argue with you over that,' she said, adopting a teasing tone to mask the magnitude of what she was feeling.

'What? No argument?' he said in a similarly light vein. 'But it is what we do so well.'

'Oh, all right, you're wrong. You got exactly the woman you deserved.'

He laughed, as she'd hoped he would. Looked up at the portrait, then back at her.

'Right, now that we've transformed this entranceway and made it welcoming rather than gloomy and oppressive, there is another room I promised you we would transform.'

She angled her head in question.

'You need to find your perfect studio.'

She clapped her hands together. 'Oh, yes, let's do that.'

To that end, they took a tour of the house, looking into countless drawing rooms, music rooms, libraries, studies, a billiard room and a ballroom. The list seemed to go on and on, not to mention countless bedrooms on the second floor, and that didn't include the servants' quarters and their bedrooms.

Finally, she settled on a morning room that looked as if it had not been occupied for many years. Facing north, it had perfect light and not just in the morning. Once the heavy velvet curtains had been removed from the floor-to-ceiling sash windows, it would have good natural light throughout the day. It looked out over the gardens and the hills in the far distance, and Margaret was sure the ever-changing outlook throughout the seasons would be a constant source of inspiration.

'This is ideal,' she said to Jacob, who had shown no sign of tiring as she had led him from room to room, assessing each one as she went. 'The curtains will have to be taken down and those carpets rolled up and I don't need any of this furniture,' she said, looking around at the settees, chairs and side tables. 'I wouldn't want to get paint on them.'

'Excellent,' he said.

She looked around the room, her mind full of possibilities. 'Thank you, Jacob. This is wonderful.'

'My pleasure,' he said with a comic bow and a sweep of his hand. 'I just want you to always feel that you belong here, which is more than I ever felt as a child. Although, with you in it, I must admit this house is becoming a lot less like a dungeon and more like a home.'

'Well, I suppose that's a compliment,' she said with a laugh. 'But thank you. And I was right, wasn't I? You can be kind, generous and thoughtful.' She was tempted to give him a hug, to express just how grateful she was, then thought *Why not?* She reached up and kissed the cheek of the man she now knew she was in love with.

'If you keep doing that, my resolve for us to remain just good friends will be sorely tested.' The words held humour but his voice was soft, suggesting he too was reacting to the intimacy of her touch.

She looked up into his eyes, her heart hammering in her chest, her arms still holding his shoulders.

'Then let's test that resolve, shall we?' Her words were little more than a whisper.

'Test it?'

Heat tinged Margaret's cheeks. She was hoping he would not ask that question, would not expect her to spell it out, but she had come this far; she would not retreat now. 'You said you wouldn't expect me to do what you rather quaintly referred to as my wifely duty.'

Surely now he knew what she was saying, but he said nothing in response.

'Well, I want to. We can still remain friends, but… well, friends who are sometimes…well, a bit more than just friends.'

'Margaret, my God, I do want you in my bed, so very, very much, but I would never want you to think you have to do anything you don't want to. I don't want you to feel that you owe me.' He cast his hand towards the room as if suggesting she was offering herself to him in payment for providing her with a studio.

'It's not that. Whether we wanted it or not, we are now man and wife. I will not be marrying any other man, and well, I want to know what intimacy between a man and a woman is like.'

'You want me to satisfy your curiosity?'

Margaret knew that curiosity was among the many things she wanted satisfied, even if it was not the most pressing one, so she nodded. 'Yes, Jacob, I am asking you to show me what it is like when a man makes love to a woman.'

He said not another word but took her by the hand and quickly led her up the stairs towards his bedchamber.

Chapter Fifteen

The door closed behind them. Margaret's heart was beating so hard she was sure Jacob must be able to hear its pounding and maybe even see it thumping against the bodice of her dress.

She had no idea what would happen next. The only instruction her mother had given her was to let her husband do what he wanted and to take her lead from him. So, with nerves, excitement and expectation waging a war within her, she waited for him to do what he wanted and let her know what he wanted from her.

He leant down and lightly placed his finger under her chin, lifting her head slightly so she was looking into his eyes. 'Are you certain this is what you want?' he said, his husky voice almost unrecognisable.

Margaret was never lost for words, but the restriction in her throat made it impossible for her to say *Yes, this is exactly what I want*, so instead she nodded.

'Remember, if you change your mind at any time let me know. Ignore everything you've been told about wifely duty.'

Again, she nodded, wishing he'd hurry up and kiss her.

'I don't want you to—'

Her kiss interrupted whatever he was going to say. She didn't want words. This was what she wanted, to feel his lips against hers. To feel his arms holding her tight. To be so close she was enfolded in the warmth of his body, to lose herself to him.

His hand slid around the back of her neck and he kissed her, his lips hard, hungry and insistent. Oh, yes, this was what she craved. Her body moulded into his, wanting every part of him to be touching every part of her.

'Oh, God, I want you so much,' he murmured as his lips nuzzled her neck. 'I have to get you out of your clothes so I can have you. Now.'

With trembling fingers, Margaret undid the top button of the line down the front of her blouse.

'No.' He took hold of her fingers and lightly kissed them. 'I want to undress you.'

With expert fingers, he quickly undid each button. It was apparent she was not the first woman he had undressed, but she would not think of that now.

She would just surrender to the excitement pulsing through her and focus on the awareness that this intoxicating, handsome and oh, so desirable man was about to make love to her.

He pushed the top of her blouse off her shoulders and lightly kissed each one, then undid the buttons of her skirt and it dropped to the ground in a heap of fabric.

She stepped out of it and was now standing in front of him, dressed only in her undergarments. Part of her wanted to ask for her clothes back, to cover herself up, worried that he might not find her as attractive as the other women he had taken to his bed, but as he gave no sign that he was disappointed with what he saw, she continued to be bold.

'Turn around,' he murmured and she did as he commanded. His fingers pulled at the laces of her corset and that too was expertly removed.

'Lift your arms,' he whispered in her ear. She did as he asked. In one swift movement he pulled her chemise over her head and tossed it to the side, tucked his fingers into the edge of her drawers and pushed them over her hips.

She gasped in a breath as his hand lightly stroked over her naked buttocks.

'Beautiful,' he murmured, close to her ear. 'Turn around. I want to look at you.'

Her heart beating at a furious pitch, she turned to

face him, resisting the impulse to place her hands over her breasts to guard them from his view.

His gaze slowly moved over her body. 'You are so beautiful,' he said, the raw desire in his eyes removing all doubt. He wanted her, he had to have her, and with him looking at her in that way, with such hunger, she did feel like a beautiful, desirable woman.

He continued to admire her, as if savouring the sight. The beating of her heart intensified, throbbing through her entire body with wild anticipation as she waited for him to act, to show her what he wanted and what he expected her to do.

He reached behind her head and pulled out the clips holding her bun in place, then tousled her hair around her shoulders. 'You don't know how many times I've imagined you like this,' he said, curling one lock around her breast, his hand lightly caressing the nipple.

She gasped as desire shot through her.

'Touch me,' she murmured in an unrecognisable voice. 'Touch my breasts.'

When his hands cupped both breasts, his thumbs stroking the now tight, sensitive buds, she was sure she would melt with pleasure. This was what she'd imagined him doing when she was lying awake on their wedding night, this was what had caused her to gasp out. And now her fantasy was a reality.

'Yes,' she murmured, closing her eyes. 'Oh, yes,'

she gasped out again, as his stroking fingers sent waves of heat pulsing through her.

His lips found hers again, kissing her so hard it was as if he wanted to devour her, and that was what she wanted—for him to consume her and to satisfy her furious demand for him.

Still kissing her, he scooped her up into his arms, carried her across the room and placed her in the middle of the bed. His eyes never leaving hers, he ripped at the buttons of his shirt. His naked chest was exposed to her, and she lay back, drinking in the beauty of his sculpted muscles. She really had been right when she'd thought to sketch him as a statue of a Greek god. Every muscle of his chest was hard and delineated, just like a marble sculpture. That was what she had felt under his clothing and soon she would feel those naked muscles pressed against her own naked skin.

He pulled off his trousers and tossed them to one side. Her breath caught in her throat. She'd seen naked male statues before, but that had not prepared her for the reality.

'It's rather big, isn't it?' she asked, looking from the body part in question, standing strong and proud before her, up to his eyes then back again. 'And so hard?'

He laughed. 'You really know how to flatter a man, don't you,' he said, joining her on the bed. 'But I promise I will be gentle, and if I hurt you at any time, tell me and I'll stop.'

Margaret doubted anything he could do would hurt her and her body was so desperate for his touch she was certain she would be incapable of stopping him from doing anything he wanted, but she nodded her agreement and lay back on the bed, just as her mother had instructed, and waited for him to do what was required.

He lay alongside her, his body close, and traced a line from her cheek, down her neck and across the mounds of her breasts. 'I knew you'd be beautiful, but I never thought your body would be this captivating,' he said, before leaning over and kissing each waiting nipple.

That was something she had not fantasised about, had not imagined he would do, but, by God, it felt good. His tongue swirled around the tight peaks, sending the hot, throbbing intensity inside her to surge ever higher.

'Yes, yes,' she gasped out repeatedly in rhythm with his tormenting tongue.

A reckless need possessed her and she wrapped her hands around his head, holding him to her breast. He continued to nuzzle and suck while his hand cupped her other breast, the surging intensity inside rising higher and higher with each stroke of his tongue and fingers until she was certain she could take no more.

His lips left her breast and he lifted himself up onto one elbow. 'I want to watch you when you peak,' he murmured as his caressing hand moved over the mound of her stomach towards her most intimate place. 'Part your legs,' he said quietly.

Without hesitation, she did as he asked. Her hunger for his touch was so fierce, how could she do anything other than what he asked? Still holding her eyes with his, his hand moved between her legs, lightly running along the folds and parting her.

Unable to breathe, she looked up at him in appeal, not knowing what he wanted of her, what she should be doing.

'Don't worry,' he said, before lightly kissing her lips. 'If I do anything you don't like, tell me. I want this to be about your pleasure.'

She nodded, still slightly unsure about what was happening but trusting him entirely, and certain he knew how to do what he'd promised—give her pleasure.

His finger gently pushed inside her and she sighed lightly. This was not what she was expecting, but it felt good—very good. His palm rested against the very place between her legs that was throbbing with such a demanding insistence. He started to rub that pulsating core, softly at first, then with more and more pressure.

She released a loud sigh that was almost a cry. Yes, this was what she needed, what she had to have.

The pressure of his palm increased. The stroking intensified.

Not thinking, just reacting, her back arched in time to his rhythm as she rubbed herself against him, her cries coming louder and louder with each tormenting caress.

The fire inside her reached inferno level. Waves of pleasure rushed through her, the likes of which she had never expected or thought possible. She cried out loudly before collapsing back on the bed, luxuriating in the subsiding shudders that still rippled through her.

'My, oh, my, no one ever told me it was going to be like that,' she said when her heart returned to something resembling its normal rhythm.

'I knew you'd be magnificent when you came,' he said, nuzzling her ear. 'And there's so much more—we've only just started.'

Margaret moved sensually on the bed. 'Then I want it all.'

Her mother's talk had said nothing about what they'd just done. It had been little more than an anatomical lesson on what went where so marriage could be consummated and they could make babies. Now she wanted that as well. She wanted his what inside her where. And she wanted it now.

'I believe I am ready to finish doing my wifely duty now,' she said with a small giggle.

'As you wish,' he said, smiling down at her. His hand once again cupped her breast, his tormenting fingers stroking the tight nipple, causing that delicious pounding to erupt within her. 'But I meant what I said. If you want to stop, let me know. I don't want to hurt you.'

She remembered how big he was and briefly had some doubts, but she trusted him—trusted him explicitly.

'I promise I will,' she said, giving him the reassurance she knew he needed.

His body covered hers and he kissed her again. It was wonderful to feel him over her, naked skin against naked skin, the hardness of his muscles so different to the softness of her own body.

She wrapped her arms around him. Wanting to feel more of those muscles, her fingers stroked the contours of his back and down to those firm buttocks.

He moved one knee between her thighs and she parted her legs.

'Wrap your legs around my waist,' he whispered into her ear.

She did as he asked, opening herself up to him, offering herself to him, wanting him to fill her up and relieve her intense need for him.

She felt him hard against her cleft as he moved

towards her opening, slowly, as if afraid she might break, then he positioned himself at her entrance. She gripped his firm buttocks tighter, pulling him towards her, letting him know this was what she wanted, there was no need to hold back.

Slowly, he entered her, and she could tell he was exercising restraint. She waited for the pain she'd been told she'd feel. There was a slight burn, but who cared, a bit of pain was worth the pleasure.

'I want to feel you inside me,' she whispered into his ear.

He pushed slightly deeper, and she sighed, loving the feeling of joining with him as one.

Slowly, gently, he withdrew, then pushed inside her again, slightly harder, slightly deeper.

'Yes,' she murmured, as much to herself as to him. She looked up into his face and could see the desperate restraint on his face. 'Yes,' she repeated. 'I'm ready. I want this.'

The tension in his face relaxed. He leant down and kissed her lips, then pushed hard into her with a powerful thrust. She almost gasped at the fullness of him inside her and buried her head against his shoulder, so he would not stop for fear of hurting her.

'Are you all right?' he whispered in her ear.

'Yes!' she cried back. 'Yes, yes!' she repeated, all other words failing her, but fearful that he might stop if she didn't let him know how much she wanted this.

He withdrew from her and thrust into her again and again. The initial shock disappeared as her body reacted to the increasing tempo. Clutching his buttocks tighter, she moved her legs further up his back so he could enter her even deeper. Her back arching, she lost herself in his rhythm as he took her higher and higher, her sighs becoming pants, then moans, then cries.

Her body at fever-pitch, he pushed into her harder and faster, until spasm after spasm of pleasure ripped through her, each more insistent than last time, and she cried out loudly, her fingers digging into his buttocks as she shuddered beneath him.

He thrust inside her a few more times then withdrew, his release coming outside her body.

She told herself not to let that ruin something beautiful. He had made love to her. They had consummated their marriage. He had never said that he wanted her to bear his children. That had never been part of the deal and she had no right to even think it.

'Is your curiosity now satisfied?' he said, pushing a damp lock back from her face and tucking it behind her ear.

'Well, something was certainly satisfied,' she said, causing him to smile, as she'd hoped. 'But I am a very, very curious woman, so maybe I'll need a bit more satisfying.'

'I'm more than happy to oblige your curiosity whenever, wherever and in whatever way you want.'

Margaret sank back onto the bed in a state of bliss. That was what she would focus on. Not on the way she would never truly be his wife or the mother of his children, but the woman with whom he was making the best of things—and his best was simply wonderful.

Chapter Sixteen

Jacob watched Margaret as she slept, her head on his shoulder, her lovely body lying against him. After their repeated lovemaking he was exhausted and wished he could do the same, but too many thoughts were spinning around in his head.

He had no idea whether what they had just done was right or wrong and what the consequences would be of his actions. He had only known Margaret for a few weeks. Now he had not only made her his wife but he had taken her virginity. For a man who had always shunned responsibility, he now had to come to terms with the responsibility his desire for her had caused him to take on.

No matter what they'd agreed, they could not go back to being just friends now. When he'd made love to her he'd said he did not want to hurt her, and that had been the truth, but he hadn't just meant physically. He hoped he would never cause her any emotional pain, but he knew what he was like.

The longest time he had ever stayed with one lover was six months, then he'd moved on to the next tempting beauty. Fortunately, all the women in his past had been just like him, but Margaret was not like those women. His past lovers had all been married women who wanted a bit of fun while their husbands entertained themselves with their mistresses, or carefree actresses and chorus girls who wanted to extend the excitement they'd felt on stage by partying with any man who took their fancy. Like him, such women easily moved on to their next lover, and neither doubted, right from the start, that it was always a short-term relationship.

He lightly stroked Margaret's shoulder. And she was different in other ways as well. He'd never had a virgin in his bed, for so many reasons. Partly because he saw it as morally wrong, but mainly because, unless you were a complete cad—and while he *was* a cad, he hoped he was not a complete one—such liaisons could never be casual.

So, what would he do now? He had just made love to his wife, and he certainly wanted to do it again, often. There was nothing wrong with that, was there? In fact, wasn't it expected of him? And yet, deep down, he knew it to be wrong. He had known that when she had looked up at him with those beautiful hazel eyes and told him she wanted him to satisfy her curiosity. And yet he'd ignored his better judgement, all because he wanted her.

He ran his hand over her naked shoulder and along her beautiful full breast. He'd wanted her and had selfishly ignored what was best for her.

But should he judge himself so harshly? His eyes swept down her body, over her full tempting breasts, across her softly rounded stomach, to the mound of dark hair and down those long, slender legs. She was so breathtakingly beautiful—how could he resist her?

And he didn't just mean her appearance. There was something about Margaret that was different from all the other women he'd had in his life. It wasn't that she had been a virgin. He certainly wasn't the type of man who saw deflowering a woman as some sort of conquest. But there was definitely something—something indefinable. Just as there was also something indefinable in the way she made him feel. Making love to her had been unlike anything he'd previously experienced with a lover, and again it had nothing to do with her being a virgin.

It was as if there had been a deep connection between them. Something so all-consuming and indefinable. When they made love he felt so close to her, as if they were no longer two people, but had somehow joined as one on a level that was greater than just the physical.

This was all so baffling and somewhat disturbing, and nothing like the uncomplicated fun he usually had in bed with a woman. His stroking hand moved from her shoulder to her exquisite breast, lying against his chest. He circled the pink nipple and watched it contract under his touch.

Making love to her might have caused some complications, but, by God, it had certainly been fun. He'd had so many women since he'd lost his virginity at the tender age of sixteen, he'd long since lost count, and never expected any to surprise him, but Margaret had.

It wasn't due to any expertise she'd possessed. When she'd entered his bedchamber, she'd been a nervous virgin, unsure of what she was doing. Nor was it the way she had so quickly become comfortable with her body and the giving and receiving of physical pleasure. But whatever it was, it had left him wanting more—much, much more.

She opened her eyes and looked up at him. 'Mmm, that feels very nice,' she murmured as he continued to caress her tight bud.

She looked down at his arousal and sent him a cheeky grin. 'And I see you're rather enjoying it as well.'

With a growing boldness that never failed to surprise and excite him, she reached down, ran her hand along his shaft and lifted one leg over his thigh. 'Perhaps we need to do something about that.'

'No, you must be sore,' he said, running a finger lightly over her cheek. They'd already made love several times and he was loath to cause her any pain.

'A bit,' she said. 'But I don't mind.'

'I do,' he said. 'But don't worry. There's lots more we can do while we give your precious parts a much-needed rest.'

She smiled at him, a delightfully wicked smile that he'd seen several times during their lovemaking—a smile he had come to adore. 'Oh, I like the sound of that. I want to know everything.'

'Everything?' he asked, sure she couldn't mean it.

'Everything,' she said emphatically. 'I'm sure a man such as yourself has a lot to teach me,' she added and lifted herself up onto her elbows as if waiting for instructions.

He wrapped her in his arms and kissed her. 'Well, you can keep doing what you just started,' he said as he nuzzled her neck.

'You mean like this?' Once again, she took him in her hand.

'Oh, yes, I mean just like that.' He lay back, loving the way her fingers were working their magic, and loving the way he had unlocked her sensual, passionate nature, a nature he had always suspected existed.

And so they spent the rest of the evening, exploring each other's bodies and discovering the many ways they could pleasure each other. And she had not been lying when she'd said she wanted to learn everything he could teach her. Just as he had when he'd taken her virginity, Jacob made it clear at all times that she was completely in control, could stop at any time, but she was an eager student.

They did on occasion break for much-needed meals, which the servants left on trays outside his room, but neither had any desire to leave his bed, so they ate among the tangled sheets.

'What on earth must the servants be thinking of us?' she said after they'd finished another meal—breakfast, lunch, dinner—he wasn't sure what.

'They'll think we're on our honeymoon,' he said, gathering up the discarded empty dishes, placing them on the tray and depositing them outside the door.

'Mmm,' she said, and lay back on the bed, licking her lips, that simple action driving him wild with desire.

'No, don't come back to bed!' she said, sitting up and holding up both hands in a stop gesture. 'Stay just like that.'

'Have you had enough of me already?'

'No, I want to draw you.'

She jumped off the bed and he watched her naked body quickly retreat through the adjoining door that led to her bedchamber. He heard a trunk being opened and slammed shut, then she rushed back in, a sketchbook in her hand.

'I never travel without this,' she said, sitting on the end of the bed and flipping open the book. 'Right, adopt the pose of a Greek god.'

Jacob raised his hands, palms upward, having no idea how a Greek god posed.

'Just stand facing me, looking manly and commanding.'

He had no idea how one did that either, so he just stood the way he always did.

'Perfect,' she murmured, her black pencil moving quickly over the page, her gaze flicking backwards and forwards from him to her drawing.

Watching her at work, he wished he had some artistic ability because it would be wonderful to depict her as she looked right now, her exquisite body completely naked, sitting amidst the sheets tousled by their lovemaking, her lovely face a picture of concentration. There was something so erotic about a woman whose passions extended beyond the bedroom.

And she *was* so passionate, so sensual, so erotic. It was hard to believe that she had entered this room a shy, awkward virgin.

'Don't move,' she said, a laugh in her voice.

'I'm not moving.'

'Oh, yes you are.' Her eyes widened and she pointed her pencil at his groin.

He looked down. 'Well, that my dear wife, is entirely your fault, not mine. If you want to keep him still you shouldn't be so damn arousing.'

'Well, in that case, perhaps I'll finish this sketch later,' she said, tossing the sketchbook aside, moving back onto the bed and stretching her arms out for him to join her.

Margaret could hardly believe such happiness was possible. She was so besotted with Jacob it was making her constantly weak with longing. During their lovemaking she had so often wanted to whisper words of love in his ear, but each time she had thankfully held back just in time. Often those declarations had to be quickly turned into *I love it when you do that*, or *I love the way you make me feel*, or even *I love the way you smell and taste*, all of which were equally true. Even on occasion she had declared her love for whatever body part was giving her the most pleasure at that particular time, which again was true; she loved every inch of his magnificent body.

But most of all, she loved the way he desired her. Just as he was now, as if he could not get enough of her.

'Come here, my little vixen,' he said, joining her on the bed and covering her with kisses.

She lay back on the scattered pillows, loving the touch of his lips on her body, giving herself completely to their lovemaking and feeling loved and adored.

His kisses trailed down her body and she purred with pleasure, knowing from past experience where they were heading. 'I love it when you do that,' she said, parting her legs.

'And I love the way this makes you cry out my name,' he said, lifting one leg and kissing the soft skin of her inner thigh.

Thoughts drifted off as the passion of the moment consumed her, and soon she was doing exactly what he said she would, crying out his name again and again as he expertly brought her to a pinnacle of bliss and sent her crashing over the other side.

And this was how they spent the next few days. The only time they left the bed was when Jacob called for a servant to prepare a bath in her bedchamber. It was lovely to step into the warm water, and even more lovely when Jacob washed her, running the sea sponge over her body in a manner equally as erotic as their lovemaking. Then he towelled her dry, his stroking hand like an act of worship, as if she were a goddess being tended to by a devoted acolyte.

When they did finally emerge from his bedchamber, Margaret was unsure how many days later, she knew she was a completely different woman from the one who had arrived at his estate after that rushed wedding.

Holding hands, they walked down the stairs together towards the dining room, intending to eat their meal at a table for the first time since their arrival, instead of from trays in the middle of their large bed.

As the servants hurriedly laid the table and placed the breakfast tureens on the sideboard, Jacob and Margaret smiled at each other. 'I assume you remember how to sit at a table,' he asked as he pulled out the chair for her.

'Yes, I have a vague recollection,' she said, picking up a fork and looking at it as if it were an object she had not encountered before, causing him to laugh.

Then he looked around the room with the same confused expression she'd adopted when joking about the fork. 'This house looks different, somehow.'

'Different?'

'Yes, less...' he waved his hand in the air as if searching for words '...or more... Did the servants change the wallpaper and furniture while we were in bed? The room looks so much brighter.'

He continued to look around the room in wonder. His gaze returned to her. 'I know what it is. You've changed this house.'

'What? You think I sneaked out while you were sleeping and changed the wallpaper and furniture?'

He reached across the table, took her hand and

kissed it. 'No, but you being here has changed this house. You've made it... I don't know...more like a home.' He leant in closer and lowered his voice. 'I do believe that making love to you has driven out the ghosts in this house.'

A thrill of pleasure coursed through her. She hoped it was true and he was no longer haunted by those terrible memories of his childhood and the unhappiness he had experienced in this house.

'I'm happy to fulfil my role as exorcist any time you want.'

He kissed her hand one more time, his eyes holding hers, and if Margaret had a fanciful imagination she would believe that he was looking at her with love.

After breakfast they went for a walk around the estate. This time it was a slow stroll, their arms around each other, and Margaret hoped he meant what he said, that this really was their home now. The place where they would happily live their lives. Deep down, she knew that was a delusion, they had made no real commitment to each other, but it was a delusion she was happy to indulge in for as long as she possibly could.

And under that delusion, she enjoyed the next few weeks, revelling in a state of blissful desire, until the invitation arrived that changed everything.

Chapter Seventeen

'He certainly worked fast.' Jacob read the crisp white card with gold lettering, then passed it across the breakfast table to Margaret.

She stopped reading the newspaper and took it from his outstretched hand. They really were turning into a married couple—seated at the breakfast table surrounded by marmalade pots, coffee and teacups and all the other breakfast paraphernalia, him reading his correspondence, her the newspaper. Not long ago such an image would have filled Jacob with horror, but he had no objection to this turn of events, none whatsoever.

As much as he enjoyed their time in bed together—and enjoy it he most certainly did, more than his inadequate words could convey—he also enjoyed these quiet times they spent in each other's company. That was as much of a surprise as anything else about this marriage. Never before had he wanted to spend time with his lovers doing anything remotely domestic.

She looked down at the card, a teacup in her other hand, and read it aloud.

'Mr and Mrs Fitzsimmons would be honoured by the presence of the Duke and Duchess of Rosedale at the wedding of their daughter, Gwendolen, to Henry Larcomb, the Earl of Northwood.'

She lowered her cup. 'It's in two weeks.'

'Yes, as I said, Henry has worked rather fast. Do you know this Gwendolen Fitzsimmons? Was she at Henry's weekend party?'

'Yes, we did meet. She's about seventeen, pretty, blonde, petite, somewhat reserved, but very sweet and rather nice. She was quite excited about her first Season.'

'Exactly Henry's type then.'

'Yes, young, fresh and presumably compliant.'

He raised his eyebrows, questioning how Margaret knew what Henry's type was, especially as she'd summed it up to a T.

'I believe I overheard him stating his preferences,' she said with a slight blush.

He was tempted to ask when she had overheard Henry making such a pronouncement but thought it best not to dwell on the matter, especially as there was a danger that he'd been the one with whom Henry had that unfortunate conversation, and an even greater danger that his responses had been equally offensive. He certainly did not want to remind her of the man he had been when she had first met him.

She reread the card then placed it back on the table. 'Well, I hope they make each other very happy.'

'Hmm, I suspect happiness is not what this is all about. Mr and Mrs Fitzsimmons will be pleased their daughter is to become a countess and, given the haste, I suspect Henry has been put under some pressure to marry.'

'I don't think either of us is in a position to judge them on that account.'

'No, well, then I too hope that, despite the haste, they find happiness, the way we have.' He lifted his coffee cup. She raised her teacup and tapped his cup in a toast.

'It does mean we'll have to return to London within the next two weeks,' she said, stating what he already knew, and causing an unsettling feeling to burn up inside his chest at the thought of returning to London.

That was peculiar. He loved London. Usually, he couldn't bear to be away from the theatres, the parties, the excitement and hectic lifestyle. The only time he did leave London was when he had no choice but to do so, such as having to take a brief sojourn in the country to get away from an irate husband, as he had on the occasion of Henry's weekend party.

And yet he felt hesitant about returning there and

ending this time alone with Margaret. What he had to fear he was uncertain about. Was he worried he would revert to being the man he had been before they'd married? Was he concerned that it would mean this precious time with Margaret would come to an end? Or was he worried that if she saw him back in London, she would remember he was the man she'd never wanted to wed and had only done so under duress?

He picked up the card and reread the invitation. He was tempted to suggest they turn down the invitation, perhaps send a letter of regret and make some excuse. Then he could keep Margaret all to himself for much longer. But he knew that would never do. Henry, for all his faults, had been a good friend to Jacob over the years and it would be remiss not to attend his wedding, and especially for the selfish reason that he was racked with misgivings over his wife coming to her senses and remembering what the man she had married was really like. And he certainly couldn't keep her imprisoned up in Northumberland and away from her friends and family. Could he? No, he could not.

'Our return to London will give you a chance to see your friends again.' *And a chance for you to see me with all my reprobate friends.*

'Yes, it will be lovely to see them again,' she said, frowning at the card in his hand. Was she too having misgivings about returning to London? No, she had nothing to fear. There was nothing about her life that he had disapproved of.

'And your parents.' *Including your father, who always had his doubts about me and my suitability as a husband.*

'Yes,' she said, almost absentmindedly, still staring at the card in his hand.

'And you can organise those art classes you've been anxious to attend.'

She looked up at him. 'You mean stay in London?'

'Is that not what you want?'

Selfish cad that he was, he was hoping she'd say, *No, I want to stay here for the rest of my life, alone in the countryside, away from all my friends, away from my family, with only you.* It looked as if he still *was* that appalling man she had first met.

'Yes, I suppose so.' She looked at the card he had placed back on the table then up at him. 'It will be lovely to see my friends and parents again, and now that I'm a duchess I'm sure I'll have no problem finding a reputable art teacher prepared to put aside his objections to providing instructions to a woman.'

'Maybe you should put together a portfolio of the drawings you've done while you've been here.'

She sent him a wicked smile. 'Have you seen the drawings I've done recently?'

'That bad, are they?' he said with a mock frown.

She lightly swatted his arm and laughed. 'They're

all of you and they're scandalous, as well you know, and I won't be showing them to anyone. We'll just have to keep those drawings between the two of us as a memento of our honeymoon.'

Jacob made himself laugh at her jest, hoping the drawings would not become exactly that, a memento of a fleeting time they'd spent together, which would come to an end when they returned to their old lives in London.

Over the next two weeks he tried to put those misgivings aside and enjoy the remaining time they had together.

But those weeks passed much faster than he wished, and soon they were on the train returning to London, and whatever that city had in store for them.

While he had many questions that would have to remain unanswered until they got back to London, there was one question that had plagued him on their journey to Northumberland and he was hoping Margaret would help him provide the answer.

Sitting beside her in their private compartment, where they would later be sleeping, he took her hand, lightly kissing the palm. 'Darling, do you remember what you said to me the first time we made love?'

'I imagine I said a lot of things.' She sent him that now familiar cheeky smile. 'You'll have to be more specific.'

'You said you wanted me to satisfy your curiosity.'

'Hmm, and you most certainly did that.'

'Well, I'd like you to do the same for me.'

'Is there something you haven't yet shown me? You have me intrigued.'

'I'd like to discover what it is like to make love on a train.'

She gave a small laugh. 'Funny, I was wondering the same thing myself. Shall we call the steward to make up the bed? We could tell him we are in desperate need of sleep.'

'I'm in desperate need of something, and I have no intention of waiting for the steward.' He stood up and pulled the lever that released the bed, closed the blind on the window, locked the door and even pulled the blind down on the outside window, in case they pulled into a station at an inopportune moment or were seen in a compromising position by someone working in the passing fields.

They soon discovered the jolting of the train and the confines of their small compartment, with the bed taking up an inordinate amount of space, was not entirely conducive to a romantic encounter.

But after much giggling from Margaret, a lot of contortions from him, the occasional elbow in his face and a balancing act to stop them falling off the narrow bed, they managed to finally find their rhythm.

And he was right. Making love on a train, despite

the awkwardness, was sublime, but making love to Margaret was always sublime, as was the time they spent together afterwards, exhausted and lying in each other's arms, and, he had to admit, the time they were together outside the bedchamber.

'So, is your curiosity satisfied?' she asked, lying sated in his arms, as she ran her hand along the centre of his chest and curled her fingers through his damp hair.

'Hmm, it wasn't quite as smoothly done as it was in the fantasies I had during our trip up to Northumberland.'

She sat up and looked down at him, her eyes wide. 'You were fantasising about making love to me on the train?'

He pushed back the hair that was falling over her face. 'Yes. In my mind I had you doing all sorts of wicked things to me.'

'So was I. Well, I wasn't thinking about wicked things—I didn't know about wicked things then—but I was imagining you kissing me and touching me.'

'So, we were both lying in our separate compartments, thinking about each other and driving ourselves mad.' He ran his hand along her cheek. 'And now we're in the same compartment and you're still driving me mad, I'm pleased to say.'

With that, he kissed her again. 'And I don't think

my curiosity is entirely satisfied,' he added, pulling his giggling wife on top of him.

Throughout the journey they never left the compartment. Jacob was determined to make the most of these last precious hours with Margaret, before they faced whatever awaited them when they arrived in London, where he hoped and prayed nothing would change between them. That she wouldn't remember all those reasons why she had originally dismissed him as a strutting peacock, a superficial rake and a man no sensible woman would ever see as worthy of marriage.

Chapter Eighteen

When she stepped off the train at King's Cross Station, Margaret looked around, hardly able to believe it was a mere two months since she'd been at this very station, about to start her married life. It felt as if she had been away for a lifetime, and yet at the same time as if she had only just left.

And she felt different. She was no longer that naïve young woman worried about the future, unsure what her new husband really thought of her, yet convinced he did not find her attractive and did not want her for his wife.

She wove her arm through his and leaned against his strong body. After what they had shared during their time together at his estate, and that delightful time together on the train, she had no doubt that her husband found her beautiful. He had told her so often enough, and she was certain he had no regrets about their marriage.

They made their way through the milling crowd and along the busy platform, their train continuing to hiss and puff steam, while porters with trolleys full of luggage rushed hither and thither and the smell of soot, smoke and oil filled the air.

It was no less hectic when they left the bustling station, and she was pleased to see a carriage bearing the Rosedale crest among the lineup of vehicles outside the station.

'Was London always this chaotic?' she said as he helped her into their carriage.

'I was just thinking the same thing,' he replied as he took his seat beside her. 'Perhaps it got busier while we were away.'

Or perhaps we have changed. Margaret certainly knew that she had, and she had her lovely husband to thank for that.

They arrived at his Mayfair townhouse and were greeted by his servants, who had readied it for their return. The last time Margaret had been in this house it had been to plead with Jacob to do something, anything, so they would not have to marry. Thank goodness he had not listened to her.

She'd hardly noticed her surroundings on that day but could see now that it was an impressive house, appropriate for a duke's London residence. Black wrought iron railings edged the steps that led to a glossy black front door, which was flanked by tall columns, giving the house an imposing façade. Inside the front door, the black-and-white tiles and marble pillars made the entranceway light and welcoming, and the area opened to a grand staircase, leading up to the next two storeys.

'Your home is magnificent,' she said, doing a small twirl to take in its grandeur.

'Our home,' he replied. 'Would you like a tour?'

Margaret nodded. He took her arm and led her to the drawing rooms and parlours, the dining room and morning rooms, then upstairs to the many bedrooms. When he showed her a small room that was obviously meant to be a nursery, a small quiver of sadness passed through her. Jacob had made love to her so many times she couldn't begin to count, but he never took the risk of getting her with child. But she did not want to think about that. She'd much rather focus on how happy he made her.

'This room might make an ideal studio,' she said, smiling and trying to forget about what else it would be ideal for.

So much had changed between them since they'd been forced to marry, and many of the terms they'd agreed on had been pushed aside in the two short months since they'd walked up the aisle. But they had never discussed children, and it was obvious that was not up for negotiation. Jacob made that apparent every time they made love. It was something she would have to accept, no matter how reluctantly.

Finally, they made it to his bedchamber, which had an adjoining door which led through to what would be the lady of the house's bedchamber.

'As we didn't get any sleep on the overnight train,' he said, 'would you like to sleep now?'

She took hold of his hand. 'I certainly want to go to bed,' she replied, causing him to laugh, as she'd hoped he would. 'But no, I'm not tired in the slightest.'

Fortunately, they did get some sleep, because the next day they had a wedding to attend.

Dressed in their finery, they took their seats in the same church where Margaret and Jacob had married just a few months ago. Henry was standing at the altar with his brother at his side as his best man. When he saw Jacob he sent him a wink, as if they were both in on a secret conspiracy.

The organ music began and the bride walked down the aisle towards Henry. She looked so sweet and innocent on her father's arm. When she reached the altar she smiled at her husband-to-be and placed her hand on her stomach. It was the same protective gesture Margaret had seen in Jacob's mother's portrait.

Her heart clenched and tears sprang to her eyes. Jacob sent her a questioning look.

'Weddings always make me a bit tearful,' she lied,

dabbing at her eyes with a lace handkerchief. She did not envy that sweet young woman being married to that callous man. In fact, she pitied her and hoped her future would not be as unhappy as Margaret suspected it might be, but there was no denying she was envious that the bride was to become a mother.

Jacob took her hand and gave it a gentle squeeze, presumably thinking she was just being sentimental. She told herself she had nothing to feel sad about. Her marriage to Jacob had worked out better than she could possibly have imagined when she'd been standing in this very church just a few months ago.

The wedding service over, they followed the bride and groom out of the stone church. As they milled around outside, Margaret noticed many of the men who had been at the Earl's weekend party were also present, along with some guests she had not expected to see, and would rather not.

'It's a delight to see you again, Jacob, Miss Whitmore,' Baroness Winterborne greeted them. 'My apologies, Miss Whitmore, I should now refer to you as Your Grace,' she said with a small laugh and a slight curtsey.

Jacob's arm slid around Margaret's waist, holding her close, and for that she was grateful. He nodded his greeting to the Baroness and her husband. 'If you'll excuse us, we need to congratulate the groom and wish the happy couple the best of luck.'

With that, he led her away from his ex-lover towards his old friend and his new wife. While Jacob shook his friend's hand and indulged in much back-slapping, Margaret kissed the bride's cheek and wished her every happiness.

She tried to smile, while battling to keep the green-eyed monster at bay, the one that had first stirred when she had realised the bride was with child and then raised its head further with the appearance of Baroness Winterborne. She tried to tell herself it mattered not. She was happy. She loved Jacob. Maybe he didn't love her or want her to be the mother of his children, but she had more than she had once thought possible. She should be content with what she had and not pine for things that were not to be hers.

It was happening already. Jacob could tell from Margaret's posture and that strained smile that she was starting to recall what the man she had married was really like. A man who'd had so many lovers it would be unlikely if they could ever attend any social event without meeting at least one of them. Including this wedding.

He should not be surprised that she was starting to withdraw from him. This was what he'd expected and it was something he would need to accept. Their time together in Northumberland had been magical, but the magic was now over and they were back in the real world, a world where he was a man who never settled with one woman for long, a man who would not be tied down.

He looked around at the other guests, at the men who were his friends, the men he had caroused with night after night for many years. That was who he was—a feckless rake, incapable of taking responsibility for anything or anyone, a man who ran roughshod over everything and everyone, including Margaret.

She was right to withdraw from him. How could she not, when reminded of his true character? For a time when they'd been alone together he had almost thought he was a different man—a good man, a man who was worthy of a woman like Margaret.

He laughed out loud at that ridiculous notion.

'What's so funny?' she asked, looking at him with those big hazel eyes he had come to adore.

'It's just funny to think that both Henry and I are now married men. Not long ago, that would have seemed to be an impossibility.'

'And both of you were forced into it.'

'Yes, I suppose that is the only way it could have happened.'

Her smile became even more strained, as he would expect, at that reminder of why she had married him in the first place—because she had no choice.

The crowd of guests thinned out and headed towards their carriages to take them to the wedding breakfast at the home of Mr and Mrs Fitzsimmons.

He helped Margaret up into the carriage and he could feel the distance growing between them. It would not be long now. Soon she would be leaving him, as she so rightly should. Then he would go back to his old life, just as they had originally agreed.

Throughout the journey she looked out of the window, lost in her own thoughts. Was this the time to have the conversation they must surely have some time soon? Jacob knew they must. It was only fair to let her know that she owed him nothing. That she was a free woman, just as he had promised she would be on their wedding day.

But he was too selfish to broach the topic now. Perhaps when they returned to their home in Mayfair. But would he be able to do it then? Or would he once again want to take her in his arms, to lose himself in her and the pleasure of their lovemaking? He knew the answer to that just as surely as he knew what a flawed man he was. He would be thinking only of himself, further proof that he was a man who should never have married, especially a woman like Margaret.

Their carriage arrived at the Fitzsimmons' Maida Vale modern terraced home. He escorted Margaret inside, where they were greeted by Gwendolen's parents and handed a much-needed glass of champagne.

He drank the bubbly liquid at a faster rate than was perhaps wise, then took another glass off the silver tray of a passing footman. Maybe a few drinks would give him the courage to speak to Margaret.

Margaret placed her untouched glass of champagne on a side table. 'If you'll excuse me for a moment,' she said, then crossed the room and exchanged a few words with one of the maids, before disappearing down the hallway.

Jacob looked around the room, at his friends who also appeared to have helped themselves to several glasses of champagne already. This was where he belonged. With other aristocratic wastrels who thought only of their own pleasure.

He took another sip of his drink and made himself a solemn promise. He would talk to Margaret before the night was over. He would set her free, just as he had promised when they'd first begun their fake engagement.

Chapter Nineteen

Margaret took a deep breath and stared at her reflection in the looking glass of the ladies' retiring room. Had something changed? Jacob was certainly acting in a strange, stilted manner that was so unlike him. Had he read her mind when she'd first realised the bride was with child? Was he aware of how much she wanted children, his children, even though that was something they had never discussed?

Maybe it was time they had that discussion. She drew in another deep breath, wondering whether she really could tell him how she had fallen so deeply in love with him and wanted them to be joined forever, not just as husband and wife but as the parents of children, and maybe one day as grandparents.

She nodded to her reflection. She needed to tell him, even if his response was to tell her that he did not want children, then at least she would have some idea of what the future held for her. She needed to know if that was the reason her outgoing and fun-loving husband suddenly looked like he was bearing the weight of the world on his shoulders.

Yes, that was the best thing to do. Ask him what had caused his sudden despondency, and then, perhaps, maybe, tell him how much she was yearning to have his child.

She frowned at herself. Or should she wait until they were back at the townhouse? That might be a better idea than having such an intimate conversation in a public place. She nodded slowly, but she still wanted to find out what was troubling Jacob. She did want to know why his manner had changed so much since they'd walked into the church. Was it seeing his old friends? Remembering his old life? Or seeing his ex-lover again? Whatever it was, she needed to talk to him. Now? Maybe. Or perhaps that too was a conversation best left till they got home.

While she continued to debate with her reflection what to do, the door opened and Baroness Winterborne entered.

Stifling a gasp, Margaret picked up a nearby comb and ran it through her ringlets as if they desperately needed rearranging. The last thing she wanted right now was to be in this small enclosed space with Jacob's former lover, and she hoped the woman was as reluctant to talk as she was.

No such luck. The Baroness's reflection loomed

beside her shoulder, looking no less elegant than she had on the night they had met at the theatre.

'We meet again, Your Grace,' she said with a small bow of her head, and Margaret wondered whether she detected a facetious note in her greeting.

'Baroness,' Margaret said, turning to face her and forcing herself to nod politely.

'I'm so pleased we have met in private,' the Baroness went on, ignoring the presence of the two maids. 'I really wanted to tell you how different you look since we met at the theatre.'

Margaret was unsure how to respond, as she wasn't entirely sure if that was a compliment or an insult.

'You're positively glowing, your eyes are sparkling and you certainly look like a satisfied woman.'

'Thank you,' Margaret said tentatively. That sounded almost like a compliment, but it came from such an unexpected source it was hard to be certain.

'And I know exactly the reason why.'

'You do?' she said, her wariness growing.

'Oh, my dear, we both know, don't we?'

'We do?'

'He does that to a woman, doesn't he?' She closed her eyes and sighed, causing Margaret's entire body to tense. There could be no doubt about who the *he* she was referring to was.

'He makes you feel adored, almost worshipped, as if you are the most beautiful woman in the world.'

The Baroness opened her eyes and leant towards Margaret as if about to make a confession. Margaret leant backwards, not wanting to hear anything this woman had to say, especially about Jacob. She should leave, but she remained where she was, as if under some strange compulsion to torture herself.

'I shouldn't really say this, but I've had one or two lovers in my time, but none came anywhere near Jacob, none made me feel the way he did.'

She actually winked at Margaret. 'The things that man can do to a woman's body...my, oh my. When I saw you walk into the church, that little smile curling the edges of your lips, with your arm through his, leaning towards him as if your body was being drawn into his orbit, I knew exactly what the two of you had been up to this morning, and I must admit I was rather jealous.'

The tension in Margaret's body intensified. 'Jealous?' What was this woman threatening?

'Oh, don't misunderstand me. As much as I'd like to have Jacob back in my bed, you're safe. Well, safe from me, that is. I'd never do anything again to endanger my marriage, and being with Jacob definitely did that. My husband had never minded me taking lovers before, but he was livid when I was with Jacob. He hated seeing me...well...looking the way you do now, and knowing that another man was causing me to behave like a cat on heat.'

Margaret's jaw clenched, her shoulders stiffened. She was certain she was not behaving in such a manner.

'That's the reason why my husband threatened divorce proceedings. He was jealous of Jacob and wanted to have his revenge. I tried throwing myself on my husband's mercy, begging him, promising to never again be unfaithful, but none of it worked.' She smiled as if this was all an amusing story. 'Do you know what made him drop the silly idea in the end?'

Margaret shook her head, unable to answer, even though she knew what had put a stop to the divorce. She had. Their fake engagement had. Jacob's plan to appear respectable had.

'I told my husband that if he put aside these foolish threats I would show him some of the tricks Jacob taught me in bed.'

The Baroness's laughter covered Margaret's shocked gasp.

'And I did,' she said. 'I now have a very, very happy husband and it's all thanks to Jacob. And while he has never reached Jacob's level of expertise, things have certainly improved for me as well, and my husband also now has a very happy mistress, thanks again to Jacob.'

She placed her hand on Margaret's arm, as if they were now the best of friends, united by their shared pleasure in Jacob's bed. 'Has he shown you how to—'

'It's lovely to see you again, Baroness,' Margaret said, finally finding her voice and cutting her off before she could say anything even more outrageous. 'But I really must be...' She was unsure what she must be doing, but she had to get away from this woman.

'Go back to your husband. Of course you must. You lucky, lucky woman. And it's not just that he's such an expert in the bedroom, he's such a wonderful man all round, isn't he?'

Despite herself, Margaret stopped. 'He is?' she asked, dreading what else the Baroness had to say, but also wanting to hear everything.

'Yes, Henry told me all about how Jacob proposed to you to save me from the divorce courts. It was so magnanimous. If we hadn't already parted, I'm sure I would have seen it as a grand romantic gesture rather than an act of kindness from a wonderful man.'

Margaret swallowed a gasp.

'I'm sorry, my dear, that's not to say your marriage is meaningless. It's just that...well, he did marry you to save me, so our time together must have meant a great deal to him, and that is something I will always treasure.'

Margaret continued to stare at her, once again lost for words.

'Oh, I didn't mean to upset you,' the Baroness continued. 'You're the one in his bed now. You're the one who is smiling like the cat who got the cream. Please don't be jealous of me. It's all over between us, I promise.'

No words could console Margaret because she was right. With all that had happened in the last few months, she had forgotten the real reason why they were together. It had been for the sake of his former lover. The Baroness had meant more to Jacob than she did, and yet he had moved on from her with hardly a backward glance. How long would it take for him to do the same to her?

And the Baroness had certainly been more rational and unsentimental about the situation than Margaret. She'd known what Jacob was like, just as Margaret had when they'd first met. The Baroness had accepted that. She had enjoyed their time together and when it was over she had accepted the situation. She hadn't been foolish like Margaret and seen it as anything more than just a pleasurable time. She hadn't been stupid enough to fall in love. Or even more foolish to think she wanted to become the mother of his children. It seemed she was still that naïve young woman who had walked up the aisle, and nothing that had happened over the last few months had changed that. If anything, she had become more gullible, more pathetic.

'As I said, if you'll excuse me, I must—'

'Yes, you must be anxious to make the most of the

time you have with him, because, unfortunately, as wonderful as it is, it won't last and it won't be long before some other pretty young thing takes his fancy, and she starts wearing that same look of delightful satisfaction. Just enjoy yourself while it lasts.'

Those terrible words ringing in her ears, Margaret fled from the ladies' retiring room. Once the door closed behind her, she stood in the hallway, her heart pounding in her chest.

She had been such a fool. A stupid, deluded fool. But no more. It was time to recapture sensible Margaret Whitmore, the woman she had been when she'd first met Jacob at the Earl's weekend party. That woman had taken no nonsense from anyone and that was what she would do now.

With more self-control than she'd thought she possessed, she pulled herself together, lifted her head high and strode into the drawing room, where the volume had risen substantially, along with the loud carousing of the Earl's friends.

Finally, Margaret had emerged from the retiring room. What ladies did in there Jacob could not imagine but, whatever it was, it always seemed to take an inordinate amount of time.

He excused himself from Rupert Penvale, who was regaling him with ribald stories of all that he had missed over the last two months, and crossed the room to join his wife.

Once again, she had adopted that disapproving look he had seen so often before they'd married, but had not seen since they had started to share a bed. His suspicions were confirmed. She was starting to remember the man he was and the reasons why she had been so reluctant to marry him.

'You were gone a long time,' he said, lightly placing his hand on her arm, hoping she would once again smile at him in that loving manner that was so precious to him, but doubting he would ever see it again.

'Yes, and I'm going to be gone for a lot longer.'

'Longer?'

'Yes, I forgot to mention earlier, but I've made arrangements to spend the evening with my friends, Primrose and Alice.'

'This evening, but...' he looked around the room at the wedding party, which had only just started '...but they are yet to serve the meal, have the toasts and so on. You must stay for that.'

'I'm sure you will hardly notice I'm gone.'

'But—'

Penvale chose that inopportune moment to stumble back towards them, and placed his arm around Jacob's shoulder as if he needed someone to hold him up.

'And no doubt your friends will be able to find

ways to keep you amused for the rest of the night once this wedding party comes to an end,' she said, sending Penvale a glacial look.

'Too right we will. After this, there's a party at—'

'What's going on?' Jacob said, cutting through Penvale's rambling and shrugging his arm off his shoulders. 'Why the sudden desire to see your friends? Can't that wait until tomorrow?'

'No time like the present,' she said with a laugh that sounded fake, then her expression became serious. 'Look, while I was in the retiring room I had a moment to think.'

'Always a danger, a woman thinking,' Penvale said, unaware that he was unwanted.

Jacob took Margaret's arm and led her to a secluded corner. 'So, what were you thinking about?' he asked quietly, fear mounting within him.

'I was thinking about the promises we made each other when we married.'

Jacob waited, suspecting that what she was about to say would have nothing to do with to love and cherish and certainly not to obey.

'We said we would allow each other to live our lives just as we had before we married, that nothing would change. Well, I think it is time we abided by that commitment. Tonight, I wish to visit my friends, and well, under the terms of our agreement, if that is what I want, you have no right to stop me.' She lifted her head in a defiant manner, as if she expected him to disagree.

Jacob attempted to mirror her stance, with his head held high, his expression impassive. 'I will not try to stop you, if that is what you wish to do.'

'Just as you have every right to go out to whatever party your friends will be heading off to after this wedding is over and—' she coughed lightly '—and behave in the manner you did before we were married, with whomever you choose.'

Had he heard correctly? Was she really giving him permission to take a lover?

'Is that what you want?' he asked, his voice calm, even though his body suddenly felt as if he'd just gone several gruelling rounds with a bare-knuckle boxer.

'It is what we both want. What we both agreed to.'

He continued to stare, trying to take in her words. It appeared he had been right. The moment she had seen him with his friends she had been reminded of the man he really was—a peacock, a man she could never respect. Their time together had not been real. It had been a delightful fantasy where two people who were never destined to be together had shared a few moments of transitory pleasure. Just as he had done with every other woman in his life.

'Right, I'll say good evening then,' she said before he could respond. 'I hope you have an enjoyable night.' With that, she turned and walked out of the room without a backward glance.

If he wasn't so painfully aware that she was right he would have chased after her, begged her not to go. But that would be the act of a selfish man, and if he'd changed in any way since he'd met Margaret, he hoped it was that he'd become a bit less selfish.

So he watched her leave, trying to ignore the way his heart was shattering inside his chest.

Chapter Twenty

It was done, Margaret told herself as she climbed into the hansom cab. She should be proud of herself for taking control of the situation. She had ended things quickly and cleanly before she lost herself even further in the illusion of a shared love between herself and Jacob.

Yes, it would hurt to hear that he had taken another lover. The stabbing sensation in the centre of her chest was sure to plunge in even deeper. But the pain would be far greater if she delayed their parting.

She had done the right thing, even if right now what she wanted more than anything else was to ignore everything she knew to be true, to run back to him and surrender herself once more to the delusion that they shared something deep and meaningful.

'Where to, miss?' the cab driver asked, alerting her to the fact that she had been sitting for some time in the stationary carriage, unsure what she was supposed to do now.

'Um...'

She hadn't thought beyond getting away from Jacob. Where to go and what she should do once she was away from him was something she had not considered. She couldn't go to her parents' house. She suspected they would send her straight back to her husband. Perhaps she'd do what she'd told Jacob she intended. Visit her friends. They were sure to give her refuge until she had time to get her thoughts straight and work out how she was to live her life. To that end, she gave the cab driver Alice's address.

The driver waited as she rushed up the path and knocked on her friend's door, only to be told by the footman that the Countess was paying a visit to her friend, Miss Primrose Fairburn.

Margaret climbed back into the cab and gave the driver instructions to take her to Primrose's Kensington home.

The closer she got to her friend's house, the more despondent she felt. Just this morning she had actually thought she was special. She had thought their lovemaking meant as much to him as it did to her, that the way they gave their bodies to each other was an expression of their love. She had convinced herself that when they made love he was showing her with his body how he felt about her, even if he hadn't said it in words. But she'd been wrong.

All she had experienced was the lovemaking of a man well versed in giving a woman pleasure, a man who'd learnt those skills by having many, many lovers before her. There was nothing special about her, and nothing special about what had happened between her and Jacob.

She was still just that wallflower Jacob had been forced to marry because she had kissed him. Their lovemaking had meant nothing. She had been the one to instigate it, and even though he had made her feel desired and beautiful, as unlike a wallflower as it was possible to feel, he did that with every woman he took to his bed.

The Baroness had opened her eyes to what deep down she'd known to be true but had been trying to deny. She meant nothing to Jacob, just as he had told the Earl after that weekend party. Or, rather, she now meant no more than any of his other lovers, possibly less than some.

She really was a delusional fool. She had tried to ignore the way he'd ensured they would never have children, but that was surely proof that he saw her as just another woman in the long line of women he had no commitment to.

And if she needed even further proof that their time together in Northumberland meant nothing to him, the way he'd changed the moment he was back with his friends had provided it. He had closed down, become withdrawn. She knew he was not a bad man, far from it, so he was probably trying to think of the kindest way of reminding her of their arrangement, so he could return to the way he preferred to live his life, unencumbered by his wife. Well, thank goodness she'd got in first and was able to retain a shred of dignity.

'Miss, we're here,' the driver said, breaking in on her thoughts.

Her mind still awhirl, she gave the man some coins, his delighted expression making it clear she had overpaid him, and walked up to Primrose's front door.

A footman opened the door, followed by her friend, so she waved the cab driver off.

'Maggie, dear, what a delightful surprise!' Primrose said.

Her friend was carrying a hedgehog wrapped in a towel. With anyone else that would raise questions, but not with Primrose.

'Do you have room for another waif and stray?' she asked, tears pricking at her eyes.

'Always. Come in, come in.'

Primrose led her down the hallway towards the drawing room, followed by the footman. 'Gloriana is unwell and off her food. That's why she's getting special attention tonight.'

Margaret nodded and was saved from having to make any comment on the state of the hedgehog's health when Alice came walking down the hallway, her arms outstretched.

'I thought I heard your voice!' she said. 'It's so lovely to see you.'

Her expression quickly changed from one of welcome to concern and she rushed towards Margaret. 'What's wrong? You look so stricken. Come in and tell us all about it.'

'He doesn't love me,' she blurted out and was instantly enfolded in her friend's arms and led into the drawing room as if she were an invalid.

'Didn't you know that when you married him?' Primrose asked, placing Gloriana into a box lined with a woollen shawl.

Alice sent a frown in Primrose's direction as they took their seats.

'Yes, I did know that,' Margaret replied, still fighting back tears. 'But I let myself forget that until tonight, when I received a painful reminder.'

Alice signalled to the footman as Primrose was still distracted by the hedgehog's needs, and asked him to bring another pot of tea and an extra cup.

'I think I might need something a bit stronger than that,' Margaret said, looking towards the sideboard, which in most houses would hold decanters of brandy, cognac and whisky. It was empty. Primrose lived on her own and presumably did not drink.

'Would you like an alcoholic drink?' Primrose asked, following Margaret's gaze. 'I believe there is some brandy somewhere in the house. I had to buy a bottle when Lady Penelope was having trouble with her nerves. Mixing some alcohol in her food was the only thing that would calm her down. Jasper, please bring the brandy and three glasses.'

Margaret did not bother to ask who Lady Penelope was, assuming she was probably a pig, a pony, a goat or some other abandoned animal Primrose had taken in.

The footman promptly returned with the bottle and three glasses and placed them in front of Primrose. She frowned at the bottle, which was almost empty. 'The servants must have been treating some of the other poor animals with the brandy. I am sure this bottle was almost full.'

Margaret and Alice exchanged looks but made no comment on how delightfully trusting their friend was.

'So, tell us what happened,' Alice said when the footman departed and Primrose had served the drinks.

'Baroness Winterborne...' she stated, barely able to say Jacob's ex-lover's name.

'I wouldn't listen to a thing that woman has to say,'

Alice said, anger rising in her voice. 'She'll just be troublemaking.'

'She actually complimented me on my appearance and said I was obviously very happy.'

Alice frowned and waited for her to explain, while Margaret took a sip of her brandy, the burning down her throat a welcome distraction from the pain in her chest.

'I assume the Baroness did more than compliment you,' Alice went on when it was clear that Margaret was struggling to explain their strange encounter.

'Yes. She told me how lucky I was to be...' Margaret paused and looked at Primrose, unsure how to phrase this.

'To be?' Alice prompted.

'To be the lover of such a talented man, who could make a woman feel things she did not know possible and make her think she is adored and beautiful,' she said, the words coming out in an embarrassed rush.

'Hmm, not exactly the most tactful thing for her to say, but hardly a reason to leave your husband.'

'She also said I should enjoy it while it lasts because it won't be long before some other young lady catches his eye.'

'Well, there you are,' Alice said, as if that settled the matter. 'She is jealous, just as I said, and a troublemaker. I wouldn't pay the slightest heed to anything she says.'

'No...yes...maybe, but she was right. When Jacob and I agreed to our fake engagement, and when we entered into this unwanted marriage, we promised we would continue to live exactly as we did before we were married and give each other complete freedom. I haven't kept my side of the bargain.'

'What do you mean? Have you stopped him from doing what he wants? Have you restricted his freedom?' Alice asked, her tone suggesting that she knew the answer to these questions would be no, which only went to show how she really did not understand.

'No, not yet. But I'm in love with him. If I stay with him, I fear that is exactly what I will try to do.' She looked at her friend in appeal, hoping she would say or do something, anything, to make the pain consuming her go away.

'Have you told him how you feel?'

'No, and I never will. We made a deal. I can't go back on it now.' How could her friend even make such a ridiculous suggestion?

'But maybe he feels the same way.'

Margaret sighed and took another sip of her brandy. 'That's the problem. I was starting to think that maybe he did. He's been so affectionate and attentive and he really did make me feel loved, as if we really were a married couple, committed to building a life together.'

'Well, there you go then,' Alice stated.

'And yes, I had been thinking I should talk to him about how I feel, but now I'm so relieved that I didn't.'

Alice lifted her hands, palm upwards, to express that she did not understand.

'Don't you see? The Baroness felt exactly the same way I did, but she was never under any delusion that she was anything but just one woman in a very long line. The only difference between the two of us is that I'm deluded.'

'You won't know that until you tell him how you feel and ask him how he feels.'

What on earth was wrong with her friend? And why was she so stuck on this idea of telling Jacob? She was being no help whatsoever.

'No, I'll never do that,' Margaret said, lifting her head and making it clear that was the end of the matter.

'Maybe it would be worth the risk to swallow your pride and be honest with him,' Alice said softly.

Margaret gave a loud sigh of frustration. That was easy for Alice to say. She had a husband who loved her deeply. She hadn't thrown herself at a rake, forcing him to become a married man against his will. Alice hadn't acted like a silly, deluded wallflower who had fallen hopelessly in love with a man because he was a wonderful lover who made her weak with desire. It was embarrassing enough to admit it to herself. She certainly wasn't going to admit it to Jacob.

'No, we made an agreement and I will stick to it, no matter how painful. And if I did declare my love for him, it would only make him feel guilty. He might even pretend to love me out of pity or something, which would be intolerable. He might be a rake, but he's still a good, kind man. What he did for Baroness Winterborne proves that. As she said, it was such a grand gesture, to marry in order to save his lover from the divorce courts.'

'I'm sure that was not the reason he married you.'

Margaret chose not to respond to that and took another sip of her drink, determined to think of the future not the past.

'I think I'll stay in London and start taking painting lessons,' she said. 'That's something I'll get out of this marriage. Now that I'm a duchess, no art teacher is likely to turn me down because I'm a woman, or expect me to paint pretty watercolours of flowers and nothing else. Or maybe I'll go to France and study under one of the new Impressionists. Yes, perhaps that's what I'll do.'

She looked from Alice to Primrose and back again. Neither of them was looking convinced by her newly formulated plan.

'If I'm away from England then I can give Jacob complete freedom,' she added.

And while she was on the Continent she would avoid all English newspapers, so she never, ever had to read about what the Duke of Rosedale was up to or who his latest lover was or think about how he'd make that woman feel as if she was the most beautiful, desirable woman in the world.

She finished her brandy and reached out to refill her glass.

'Do be careful, Maggie, dearest,' Primrose said. 'Lady Penelope developed quite a taste for the brandy even after her nerves had settled and we had to separate her from the other donkeys as her braying was keeping them up all night.'

Despite her misery, Margaret gave a small snort of laughter at her sweet, innocent friend's warning. 'I'm sure one more glass won't hurt.' She picked up the brandy bottle, then decided that perhaps her friend was correct.

'I'm sorry for braying on about Jacob.'

'No, no,' Primrose said, her face contorted with worry. 'I didn't mean that. You're nothing like Lady Penelope.'

Margaret smiled dolefully at her friend's attempt to comfort her. 'Well, I do feel like a bit of an ass.'

'Unfortunately, love can make asses of us all,' Alice said, once again rubbing her back. 'It can make even the most sensible women forget themselves and fall prey to emotions they'd thought themselves immune to.'

Margaret released a loud, sad sigh. 'That is so

true. But fortunately, Baroness Winterborne saved me from making even more of an ass of myself and made me see things clearly. I now know what I have to do. You're right, Alice, I do need to tell him how I feel.'

'Good for you, Maggie. Honesty is always the best policy.'

'I'll make it completely clear to him that from now onwards we are to live separate lives. We will both begin our new lives, or go back to our old lives, or… well, a combination of the two, or our old lives, but in a new way or something…but whatever we do, we will live apart.'

Primrose and Alice looked at her with matching expressions of concern, as if she was making as much sense as Lady Penelope after a few brandies. But it mattered not what they thought. She had made up her mind.

Chapter Twenty-One

Jacob should not be feeling surprised. It had happened sooner than he'd expected, and certainly sooner than he had hoped, but it was over. Margaret had seen him back in his old environment. She had come to her senses and realised there was no future with a man such as he. All this proved was what an intelligent, sensible woman he had married.

He looked around the room. Even at this wedding his friends' behaviour was leaning towards the riotous and he suspected it would not be long before they were encouraged to leave and continue their carousing elsewhere.

Jacob would join them. Margaret had made it clear that was what she assumed he would do, so he would not disappoint and would live up to—or should that be down to?—his deserved reputation.

He just wished he had more enthusiasm for what

was starting to seem like an empty, pointless way of filling in time.

He took another glass of champagne from the tray of a passing footman, hoping that would help him get in the mood as he watched Penvale, Fenshaw and Pettigrew begin one of their inevitable drinking games.

Fenshaw spotted him watching their antics and called out something indecipherable, which Jacob chose not to answer. But that didn't stop him from staggering across the room and slapping an arm around Jacob's shoulder.

'Now that this do is coming to an end, we're planning to go on to a party at Marlborough House. Henry can't join us tonight, obviously, the poor blighter, but now that you've got rid of the old ball and chain there's nothing to stop you.'

Fenshaw leant in closer, breathing alcohol fumes over Jacob. 'Quite a number of pretty chorus girls have been asking when Dukie Rosedale will be returning, so you can spend the night making up for lost time.'

Jacob shrugged off Fenshaw's arm and leant backwards to escape his breath. 'I'm not in the mood for partying, or for chorus girls.'

'Suit yourself, but you'll be missing out on a good time.'

Jacob expected him to depart, but he stood beside

him, swaying like a sailor who was yet to find his sea legs.

'Baroness!' Fenshaw called out, catching Helena's attention, and signalling rapidly with wildly flailing hands for her to join them.

Jacob's body tensed. He wanted the company of his ex-lover even less than that of a chorus girl. He would hate it if Margaret saw them together, in case it gave her cause to doubt his fidelity. Then reality hit him once again. She was gone. What did it matter now? He had been given permission to be as unfaithful as he wanted, even though he had no wish to be so.

'Jacob says he doesn't want to come to the Prince of Wales's party. You should be able to convince him that after being stuck out in the countryside for simply ages, what he needs is a bit of fun.'

'I believe he is having lots of fun,' Helena said. 'Now, go away and play with your friends,' she added, shooing Fenshaw with flapping hands as if he were an annoying animal which had entered the wrong garden.

Thankfully, he staggered off to join his friends, who were now under the watchful eyes of some rather tall and stern-looking footmen.

'Thank you for that, Helena.'

'You're welcome. But I'm surprised the Duchess is not at your side. I'm sure she could deal with the likes of Fenshaw.'

'Margaret has been called away.'

Helena frowned at him. 'I hope it wasn't something I said.'

'Something you said?' That seemed unlikely. Margaret had never been under any illusion about his relationship with Helena. She also knew that it was all over between them and Helena had never been a woman to indulge in dramatics or petty revenge.

'Yes, I followed her into the ladies' retiring room because I simply had to tell her how lovely she is looking.'

'Yes, she is, isn't she? But that is hardly something for you to feel apologetic about.'

'Well, I may have gone on a bit about what a wonderful time we had together in…well…in the bedchamber.'

'I see,' Jacob said, the tension in his chest and shoulders tightening up a notch.

'And well… I did remind her that you've had rather a lot of women in your life and you do tend to move on eventually.' Helena smiled apologetically. 'I should have kept my mouth shut, shouldn't I?'

Jacob released a long, slow sigh. 'No. You didn't say anything that wasn't true.'

'Sorry, Jacob, I hope I haven't ruined things for you.'

'No, unfortunately, I am more than capable of doing that myself.'

'Well, I had better join my husband, as I'm sure he will not like it if he sees me talking to you.'

Jacob watched her cross the room to join the Baron and knew he could not be annoyed with her. Helena had said nothing that wasn't true, or rather, had been true of him in the past. Right now, he could not imagine a time when he would ever want any woman other than his wife. He also had no interest in partying the night away.

Instead, he would return to his townhouse, alone. So he walked across the room to say goodbye to his friend, who he was yet to speak to since congratulating him outside the church.

'How's married life treating you?' he said to Henry with a level of bonhomie he did not feel.

'So far so good,' Henry said with a laugh, slapping Jacob on the back. 'Who would have thought that the two of us, the most unlikely men in London, would fall in love and marry?'

'Love?' That was not a word he'd expected to come out of Henry's cynical mouth.

'Yes, love. Isn't it wonderful?' Henry continued, oblivious to his friend's stunned surprise as he looked over at his bride, who was talking to her mother.

'I have to tell you, Jacob, you were right, and I was completely wrong.'

Jacob was unsure what he'd been right about, so waited for Henry to explain.

'It *is* possible to be struck by Cupid's arrow, even if in my case the little cherub's aim was slightly off when I first met the future love of my life. But on the second occasion he was right on target.' He turned to look at Jacob, wearing a decidedly infatuated expression. 'It was at the first ball of the Season. I was bored and escaping to the card room. We passed each other in the hallway when my heart was pierced.'

He paused, still grinning in that peculiar manner. 'I fell in love immediately, forgot all about the card room and became a reformed man on the spot. Love really can change a man, can't it?'

He looked at Jacob as if expecting him to agree.

'We're planning on starting a family as soon as possible,' Henry continued, once again looking towards Gwendolen. 'My lovely wife is sure there's already a little Gwendolen or Henry on the way and I do hope she's right.'

'Is that why you married in such haste?'

Henry laughed. 'It's what we told her father so he wouldn't put up any objection to us marrying immediately. As much as we enjoyed playing the game of eluding the chaperone, we wanted to start our married life and stop having to steal time alone together. But what of you?' he said, turning to Jacob. 'When are you and your lovely wife going to hear the pitter-patter of tiny feet?'

Henry looked around as if trying to find Margaret in the swirling crowd of guests.

'We have no plans to do so.' The empty space that had taken up residence inside him since Margaret's departure grew bigger and deeper.

They'd never discussed children and after his own childhood he knew he'd make a terrible father, but maybe, just maybe, with Margaret, things would be different. So much else had changed since he'd met her. But it mattered not now. She had made it clear they were to abide by their original agreement, so children were out of the question.

'Really?' Henry frowned at his friend as if his words were difficult to understand. 'Don't you feel as if you simply must be joined by children, a family of your own? Gwen and I certainly do.'

'That's because you're in love,' Jacob said, surprised to be having such a conversation with his jaded, cynical friend.

'Yes, we are,' Henry said, looking over at his bride. 'As I said, who would think the two most unlikely men in London would fall in love?'

Henry had once again adopted that smitten expression. He was certain that he never looked at Margaret in that manner. Did he?

'Just as a matter of interest,' he asked, keeping his voice as detached as possible. 'What makes you assume I am in love with Margaret?'

Henry turned his attention back to his friend. 'It's that soppy way you kept looking at her. I recognised it immediately. And when old Fenshaw joined you I could see how much you wanted to get away from him. I pointed it out to Gwendolen and she agreed. You're a reformed man. Just like me. Love has changed you. Even when you were talking to Helena, a woman reputed to be one of the most attractive in London, you looked no more distracted by her appearance than you would be if you were talking to your maiden aunt.'

Soppy? Really? Jacob doubted that, but before he could contradict his friend, Gwendolen joined them.

'I was disappointed that your wife left before I had a chance to talk to her,' she said to Jacob.

'Yes, I'm sorry. She was called away suddenly.'

'It must have been very urgent for her to leave your side,' Gwendolen said, a note of suspicion in her voice.

Hardly. She could visit her friends at any time. That wasn't the urgency. The urgency was to get away from him.

'I hope nothing is wrong,' Gwendolen continued. 'And I do hope we can all get together once my husband and I return from our honeymoon.'

She smiled at Henry, obviously enjoying referring to him as her husband. 'As I said to my husband earlier, apart from ourselves, I have never seen two people who are more in love or more right for each other than the two of you. My husband might not have noticed it at his weekend party, but the other debutantes saw it immediately. Margaret was besotted with you, just as you were with her.'

Jacob tried to make sense of her words, but it was as if she was suddenly speaking a foreign language. That was not how he remembered their time together at Henry's weekend party.

'And when we saw you swooning over each other at the church today it was obvious your time together had caused that love to grow,' Gwendolen continued.

'No, we're—'

'So, whatever little spat the two of you have had, fix it, because Henry and I want to have friends who are happily married and just as in love with each other as we are.' She looked over at the rest of Henry's friends, who were now being corralled towards the door by the footmen. 'And I think it might be a while before any of those men are struck by Cupid's arrow.'

'But—'

'And it would be a tragedy if the two of you fell out during our wedding.' She sent Henry a sly smile. 'You wouldn't want to ruin our happy day, would you?'

Jacob had no answer for that.

'So, off you go then,' Gwendolen added, making the same shooing motions Helena had done with Fenshaw. 'Go and make it up with your wife.'

It was apparent that Henry was not the only person to be changed by love, as this woman was certainly not the reserved and compliant young woman that Margaret had described.

But were they right? If someone as unlikely as Henry could be changed by love, was it also possible that he too could be? Could he become a man who Margaret could love? There was only one way to find out.

'Off you go,' Gwendolen repeated.

Following the bride's instructions, he left the room, a small spark of hope flaring inside him. He wasn't sure if he could fix things between him and Margaret, but he had to try, because if he didn't he knew he would regret it for the rest of his life.

Chapter Twenty-Two

Jacob hurried out of the house, ignoring the rowdy calls from his friends to join them, jumped into his carriage and gave the driver instructions to make haste to Margaret's parents' house.

A footman opened the door. Jacob pushed past him and entered the drawing room, not waiting to be announced.

Both parents looked up at him over half-moon glasses, the father from a newspaper, the mother from her embroidery.

'Is she here?'

The father, with frustrating slowness, removed his glasses, folded them up and placed them on a side table. 'Am I to assume you are referring to my daughter?' he asked.

'Yes, I'm referring to your daughter—my wife.'

'Have you had a little tiff?' the mother asked with

a small laugh, as if little tiffs were something rather delightful.

'Have you done something to upset my daughter?' the father asked in a completely different tone, his question coming closer to the truth.

'Yes, I have, or should I say…' He came to a halt, not wanting to waste time going into details. 'I need to talk to her. I need to explain things. I need to apologise.'

'It is a little tiff,' the mother said, clapping her hands and looking at her husband as if he too should see what a wonderful thing a tiff was.

'I think you need to explain yourself, young man,' the father said, not looking at his wife but focusing entirely on Jacob. 'Have you given my daughter reason to regret this marriage?'

To that Jacob could say a resounding yes, but he did not need the father's threats of ruination complicating matters. 'As I said, I need to talk to her so I can try and make things right.'

'She's not here,' Mrs Whitmore said, cutting off her husband before he could make any threats. 'She's probably with one of her friends.'

'Yes, that's where she said she was going, but I don't know… Can I have their—'

'I'd get there quickly if I were you,' the mother interrupted. 'Those wallflowers are likely to try and poison my daughter against you and against marriage.'

'Alice *is* married,' Mr Whitmore said, frowning at his wife.

'Yes, but to an earl, not a duke,' Mrs Whitmore said, as if that made a difference. 'She's certain to be jealous of my daughter. The whole of Society is jealous of my daughter. Why, just the other day, Lady Tilsbury tried to say that—'

'May I have the addresses of her friends?' Jacob cut her off, not wanting to be rude, but also not wanting Mrs Whitmore to start one of her monologues, especially as she had advised him to get to the friends' homes quickly before they poisoned Margaret against him.

The father rose and crossed the room to a writing desk, while Mrs Whitmore continued telling him what Lady Tilsbury had said. He scribbled something down, then handed it to Jacob, but kept hold of the piece of paper. 'Make right whatever you have done wrong, young man, or you know what I will do.'

'Believe me, sir, if Margaret does not want to reconcile with me there is nothing you can do that will cause me any greater ruin.'

With that, the father released the paper. Jacob quickly scanned the addresses, pushed the paper into his pocket and departed without saying goodbye. Again, he was showing unforgivable rudeness, but right now there was only one person whose forgiveness he wanted.

He took his carriage around to the first address on the list, but was told by the footman that neither Lady Thornwood nor the Earl were in residence, so he made haste to her other friend's address.

The footman asked for his card, making it clear that Miss Primrose was at home, so he ignored the man and entered the drawing room, where he found three women seated closely together.

All three looked up at him with wide eyes and open mouths. Jacob stood in the middle of the drawing room, suddenly unsure what on earth he was supposed to do or say.

Alice was immediately on her feet. She took Primrose's arm and, without saying a word to Jacob, left the room with what could under different circumstances be seen as unseemly haste.

Jacob stood at the door, looking unsure of himself and wearing a strange abashed expression. This was not like him. He never looked uncertain. Part of her wanted to run to him, to take him in her arms, but she stood her ground, or rather, remained seated. If she weakened now, she would be lost completely.

'What are you doing here?' she asked, pleased that her voice did not quaver.

'I...' He looked back towards the door as if trying to figure it out himself, then lifted his head and gave every appearance of puffing out his chest, exactly like the peacock she had first depicted him as.

'I've come to retrieve my wife,' he said in a decisive voice.

'Your wife?' she said, thankful that anger was rising up within her and hoping it would drive out all other confusing emotions. 'Have you now?'

'Yes, my wife—the woman who just ran out on me.'

Margaret folded her arms against her chest, covering her heart and masking all other feelings with defiance. 'Firstly, I do not appreciate being referred to as *your wife*. I am not your possession.'

'That's not what I—'

'And secondly, if you remember correctly, that was not our deal.'

'Baroness Winterborne told me what you'd discussed in the ladies' retiring room and I know that's why you suddenly fled,' he said, his words coming out in such a rush they were almost garbled.

'I did not flee,' she stated, even if she had, but she certainly was not going to admit it. 'I had simply had enough of the wedding and your friends and wanted to spend some time with my own friends.'

The confused expression remained on his face, for which she was grateful. If he had smiled at her obvious lie, she would have been even more furious at him for finding amusement in something so painful.

'I'm sorry if Baroness Winterborne upset you. She assures me it was not her intention.'

The anger bubbling inside her surged even higher. How dare he mention his ex-lover? How dare he inform her that the two of them had been discussing her? How dare he suggest that she was upset just because that woman…?

Like a deflating balloon, she collapsed back on the settee, the fight going out of her. What was the point in lying to herself any longer?

'Yes, she did upset me, but her words reminded me of our original arrangement. Something which I believe we should put into effect now.'

'Why now?'

Because if I stay with you any longer, my love for you will grow even stronger and it will be harder for me to leave. Then, when you leave me for another woman, instead of my heart being broken in two it will be shattered into a million pieces and I don't know if I'll have the strength to piece it back together.

That was what she could have said. Instead, she said, 'Now's as good a time as any. We're back in London, back among our friends, and I will hopefully soon be able to arrange some art lessons.' *Then I can bury myself away and try to heal.* 'I might even go to France and study art there.'

'France? But Margaret, I don't want us to part.'

'Not yet. But you will.'

He shook his head. 'No, never.'

'What?' she asked quietly, not sure she had heard correctly.

'I don't want us to part, ever.'

'Well, you say that now.'

He took a pace towards her. 'Margaret, I'm doing this all wrong. When I entered this room, instead of saying I've come to retrieve my wife, I should have said that I want you to be my wife.'

It appeared that he had gone mad, or had imbibed far too much at his friend's wedding.

'I am your wife. We had a wedding, remember?' *The one where we made vows that neither of us had any intention of keeping.*

'I mean I *want* you to be my wife,' he repeated. 'I *want* to marry you. I *want* us to be together till death us do part.'

Margaret's body grew rigid. Was this a trick? Was it something else he did with his lovers? If they started to stray before he was the one to move on, did he reel them back in?

As much as she would like to believe his words, this was probably all part of a well-practised approach and she was not the only woman to have been on the receiving end of his sweet words, just as she was not the only woman he had made behave *like a cat on heat*, as Baroness Winterborne had so crudely put it.

'I have Baroness Winterborne to thank for making me see that,' he added, causing Margaret to flinch inwardly at hearing him once again mention his ex-lover's name.

'It looks like we both have Baroness Winterborne to thank for making us see how things really are.'

To her chagrin, he nodded. 'Yes. She made me see that I am not the same man who left London only a few short months ago. I'm no longer the man who chased after empty pleasures in a desperate attempt to fill the void. I now know what it is like to love, what it is like to make love to the woman I adore.'

He took another step towards her. 'I don't know exactly what Baroness Winterborne said to you, but I can guarantee she never claimed I had ever been in love before.'

She continued to stare at him, not sure if this was really happening, but trying desperately to hold on to what Baroness Winterborne had said, trying to remind herself that she was nothing special, that she meant nothing to Jacob.

'But I am now. I love you, Margaret.' He took another step towards her.

'I love you,' he repeated. 'The way you make me feel is unlike anything I've felt before.' He shook his head as if hardly able to believe his words and gave a small laugh. 'Surprisingly, it was Henry and Gwendolen who pointed out how besotted I am with you.'

Margaret's heart thudded in her chest and her confusion intensified. This could not be true, but Jacob was not a cruel man, and only someone completely callous would say such a hurtful lie. Was it true? It must be true. He loved her.

His face once again became serious. 'Margaret, I love you. I want you to be my wife. I want to spend the rest of my life with you. Our wedding vows now suddenly make so much sense. I want to love and cherish you. I want to forsake all others. I want us to be together till death us do part.'

He took her hand and as if in a dream she rose to her feet.

'Margaret, all my life there has been a deep emptiness within me, one I didn't know existed because I never gave myself time to think about it. I filled up my life with constant partying so I didn't have to look into that void and see how lonely I actually was.'

He brought her hand to his mouth and gently kissed it. 'You made me realise what that void was. It was love that I was missing. You taught me what it is to love another. And, by God, I do love you, with my heart and soul.'

To her immense surprise, he dropped down on one knee, her hand still in his. 'Margaret, will you marry me? Will you let me love you? Will you give me the chance to prove how much I have changed? How much you have changed me? How much you have made me the man I want to be?'

He kissed her hand one more time. 'I want to prove to you every day the depth of my love. I want you to see that I am the right man to be the father of your children. I want us to grow old together, surrounded by our children and our grandchildren.'

Margaret gasped, warmth spreading through her body, starting at her heart and reaching her very fingertips, as a dizzying joy possessed her. She wanted to laugh, cry, sing—do something in reaction to hearing the man she loved so deeply declaring his love for her. But all she could do was stare at him, still trying to convince herself that this was real and not a fantastical dream.

'Children?' she gasped.

'Yes, children. Until I met you, I never wanted children, fearing I would not be able to love them. But you have taught me how to love and I know I will love our children.'

He smiled up at her. 'I know this has been an unusual courtship, but Margaret, will you do me the greatest honour of becoming my wife and making me the happiest man alive? If you do agree, then I promise I will do everything in my power to show you I can be the man who is deserving of such a wife. But if that is not what you wish, then yes, we will abide by our agreement, but I want you to know that I love you with my heart and soul, and even if we part I will never stop loving you.'

He continued to gaze up at her, and she could actually see tears in those blue eyes.

Tears.

If his words hadn't convinced her he really did love her, seeing tears in the eyes of the man she loved would have done so.

'So, will you marry me?'

She gave a small laugh that was punctuated with a sob as she fought back her own tears. 'Yes,' she murmured.

He was immediately on his feet and she was in his arms.

'Oh, Margaret, I love you so much,' he said when they finally parted.

'Say that again,' she said, feeling so happy she was sure it was only Jacob's arms around her keeping her tethered to the ground, otherwise she would start to float, she felt so light and buoyant. 'Tell me you love me again. I love hearing it out loud.'

'I love you. I love you. I love you,' he said, punctuating each declaration with a kiss. 'You are going to have to get used to hearing that, because you will be hearing it again and again, every day for the rest of our lives. You are going to hear it so many times you are going to get tired of hearing me telling you how much I love you.'

'Never.'

'In that case, I love you, I love you, I love you, I love—'

Margaret's lips were back on his, not because she was tired of hearing those three precious words, but because she wanted his kisses just as much. They were something else she knew she would never tire of and wanted to feel every day for the rest of her life.

Remembering where they were, they finally broke apart, but they continued to hold each other with their arms and eyes, their gazes locked together as if seeing each other for the first time, then he looked across the room and his expression became quizzical.

'Have you noticed there's a hedgehog in the corner and it's watching us?'

Margaret looked towards Gloriana, who was peeking over her box, her little black eyes fixed firmly on them.

'Maybe that is what's wrong with her,' she said with a laugh. 'She is pining for love and we've made her realise what she wants is to find her soulmate.'

'I know exactly how she feels,' he said with a laugh, before kissing her again.

Epilogue

Now that Jacob had discovered the simple truth that he was in love with his wife, he wanted to mark their union.

Their wedding had been a rushed affair, almost clandestine, and that would never do. A love as big as theirs needed to be celebrated, and to that end he enlisted the help of Margaret's two closest friends and her mother to organise an occasion that honoured them truly becoming husband and wife.

The women set to work with gusto and on the day of their proper wedding the garden of their townhouse had been transformed. Garlands of flowers were strung between the trees, creating an aisle that led up to an arch of greenery, roses and scented flowers which Margaret's mother informed him were honeysuckle and jasmine.

At the altar he waited for his bride to appear, his heart seemingly swollen in his chest with happiness.

The only sadness of the day was that his mother was not here. But he was certain that he had now grown into a man who could make her proud. After all, if a woman like Margaret was willing to marry him with no coercion, he must now be such a man.

Margaret stepped onto the carpet of petals that led to the altar on the arm of her father, looking more beautiful than he had ever seen her. She was radiant and like a nervous groom Jacob was transfixed.

She walked towards him, their eyes locked, their smiles matching, and when she joined him they took each other's hands and he lightly kissed her lips.

In front of their assembled friends and family they declared their love and commitment to each other.

'Margaret, my love, my life,' Jacob said, looking into her soft hazel eyes. 'When we married I promised to love and cherish you all the days of our lives. To abide by those vows will fill me with the greatest happiness it is possible for a man to feel. You have taught me how to love, and to be loved, and I promise I will never take that love for granted. Whatever our future holds, I am yours, wholly and forever.'

Margaret smiled up at him, tears in her eyes.

'Jacob, my love,' she said, blinking away the tears. 'When we met I did not expect to love you, but you gave me no choice.' This caused Jacob's smile to widen. 'And I never thought I would feel so loved, but that is how you make me feel. I vow to stand beside you, no matter what fate brings us, to love you fully and openly for the rest of our lives.'

'I love you,' Jacob whispered.

'And I love you,' she said, before he leant down and kissed her, while the assembled guests applauded.

Still holding her close, he whispered in her ear, 'I was going to say, '*Oh, Margaret, girl of mine, you are so fine.*'

As expected, this caused Margaret to laugh, and add, '*With hair of gold you make me bold.*'

'*Like stars in the night, your eyes are bright, Big and round and such a delight,*' they said together, then, laughing, they walked hand in hand back down the aisle.

Jacob had never intended to use his silly poem for his wedding vows, but he would love to be able to tell the lonely adolescent boy who'd penned such bad poetry that one day he would meet a woman who would take away all his pain and bring him more happiness than he could imagine.

A wedding breakfast was held in their townhouse, speeches were made, including one from Henry, who waxed not particularly lyrically about Cupid and his bow, and from her father who for once had kind words to say about Jacob.

When the speeches were over, Mrs Whitmore

approached them, a wine glass in her hand, looking even happier than she had at their official wedding. 'You two might not have known this was a love match, but I always did,' she said proudly. 'You can raise your eyebrows in disbelief as much as you like, Margaret, but I did.'

Jacob and Margaret exchanged indulgent smiles.

'Yes, all right, to begin with I just liked the idea of my darling daughter becoming a duchess, but on the night you went to the theatre I saw the way you two were looking at each other and I thought, *Those two are in love*. Even your father saw it, didn't you, dear?' she said, turning to her husband, who opened his mouth to speak but was cut off before the words could emerge.

'Why else do you think he insisted on making you marry?' she continued. 'As if Percival would make Margaret do anything that he didn't think would make her happy. He knew. I knew. We just knew that the two of you needed to discover it for yourselves. So your father insisted you head off to your estate with nothing to do except get to know each other and realise you were in love. And we were right, weren't we, dear?'

Jacob and Margaret looked at her father, who looked somewhat sheepish.

'So it would seem,' Mr Whitmore said. 'What I do know is that you *have* made my daughter very happy,' he added, shaking Jacob's hand and slapping him on the back.

'Not as happy as she has made me,' he said, smiling at his bride.

When the guests finally left, Jacob was able to present his wife with his wedding present. Two tickets to France, and a letter from a tutor at the school of fine arts, offering to provide lessons.

Margaret looked down at the tickets and the letter as if dumbfounded. 'Oh, this is wonderful,' she said, smiling up at him. Then she walked over to the sideboard and removed a small package wrapped in brown paper.

'And I have a wedding present for you as well,' she said with a laugh.

He pulled off the paper, held up the framed drawing and joined in her laughter as they both looked at the series of cartoons. The first one depicted a flower climbing up a pillar to escape a party of roosters below. In the next one a peacock appeared in the window. And the final drawing had the flower and the peacock locked in a kiss.

'That's simply wonderful, but I think it needs an additional drawing.'

'It does?'

'One where the house is full of little flowers and peacocks.'

'Oh, yes, I do look forward to drawing that one.'

He laughed and scooped up his wife into his arms. 'Then I think we'd better get started straight away.'

With that, he carried her up the stairs to begin their married life together.

* * * * *

*If you enjoyed this story,
make sure to read the previous instalment of
the Wayward Wallflowers miniseries:*

A Mistletoe Match for the Earl

And look out for the next instalment:

A Wallflower to Win the Viscount

*And why not read Eva Shepherd's
Rakes, Rebels and Rogues miniseries:*

A Wager to Win the Debutante
A Widow to Defy the Duke
A Marriage to Scandalise the Earl

MILLS & BOON®

Coming next month

ACCIDENTALLY WED TO THE PRINCE
Lucy Morris

What should I say? Magnus had made his decision in the library earlier, but now he was at a loss for words. The next sentence would seal his fate and that of his beloved Thrudheim forever.

He supposed he should just get it over with. 'Miss Mortimer, in light of our recent...accident. I think it only best that I ask for your hand in marriage.'

'What?' Miss Mortimer screamed the word so loudly that his ears rang and he winced.

She glanced up at the stagecoach, and he noticed that several people had gathered at the windows and doorway. Staring down at them expectantly like a nest of hungry chicks. Miss Mortimer scowled back at them and they hurried back into the shadows.

'Have you lost your wits?' She hissed, and then added, 'Your Serene Highness.' Belatedly and with a perplexed expression, as if she wasn't sure how she could remain polite and question his sanity at the same time.

'As we are going to be married, you may call me by my Christian name, Magnus, at least in informal settings such as this.'

She blinked with a slack expression as if she couldn't quite comprehend his words. After a moment of blankness, a strange iron-will seemed to take over her. She raised her chin and her spine stiffened, that odd conviction hardening within her eyes like granite. It was spectacular to watch, a goddess emerging from a fiery pit. 'I did not agree to your proposal!'

Continue reading

ACCIDENTALLY WED TO THE PRINCE
Lucy Morris

Available next month
millsandboon.co.uk

Copyright © 2026 Lucy Morris

COMING SOON!

We really hope you enjoyed reading this book. If you're looking for more romance be sure to head to the shops when new books are available on

Thursday 21st May

To see which titles are coming soon, please visit
millsandboon.co.uk/nextmonth

MILLS & BOON

FOUR BRAND NEW BOOKS FROM
MILLS & BOON MODERN

Indulge in desire, drama, and breathtaking romance – where passion knows no bounds!

OUT NOW

Eight Modern stories published every month, find them all at:

millsandboon.co.uk

TWO BRAND NEW BOOKS FROM
Love Always

Be prepared to be swept away to incredible worldwide destinations along with our strong, relatable heroines and intensely desirable heroes.

OUT NOW

Four Love Always stories published every month, find them all at:

millsandboon.co.uk

LET'S TALK
Romance

For exclusive extracts, competitions and special offers, find us online:

- **f** MillsandBoon
- **X** @MillsandBoon
- **O** @MillsandBoonUK
- **d** @MillsandBoonUK

Get in touch on 01413 063 232

For all the latest titles coming soon, visit
millsandboon.co.uk/nextmonth